THE COLOURS OF ASH

Blaise van Hecke

First published by Busybird Publishing 2022
Copyright © 2022 Blaise van Hecke

ISBN:
Paperback: 978-1-922691-51-4
Hardback: 978-1-922691-52-1
Ebook: 978-1-922691-53-8

This is a work of fiction. Any similarities between places and characters are a coincidence.

Cover image: Jack Howlett
Cover design: Poopy Pants
Layout and typesetting: Kev Howlett
Proofreading: Laura McCluskey

Busybird Publishing
2/118 Para Road
Montmorency, Victoria
Australia 3094
www.busybird.com.au

To Les

orange

H er face was a breath from his. 'Ash! Snap out of it.'
He blinked.

'Come dance with me.'

He shook his head, squinting through the glare.

She scowled, flashing emerald eyes.

Destiny.

She exhaled and bent at the waist, tugging a t-shirt from the washing basket – Tommie's favourite colour: orange.

Tomas sat at the table with a chubby crayon in his small hand. Purple tadpoles swam across his page. The fact that the purple oozed out of the tadpoles' pores didn't faze him.

Asher sat next to him, his long body folding on itself to fit on the child-size bench. He tried to draw something and they laughed at his funny frogs. Destiny stopped pegging a singlet and picked up an orange crayon to add something with a flourish. Her tadpoles were dangerous. Purple tadpoles crashed against orange tadpoles in the murky depths of the water where loony frogs lurked to pounce on them when they weren't looking.

'Hey, Tommie, draw me a butterfly.' Destiny flittered around the Hills hoist, her blue-black hair streaming behind her.

'Okay, Mummy. What colour?'

'Turquoise, bubba.' She continued to twirl, her bangles clacking together like off-beat horses' hooves.

Asher watched Destiny, watched her feet as they tiptoed over the cracks in the concrete.

'Come and dance with me, Ash.' Destiny swept her hand towards him and then away, teasing.

'It's too hot, D.'

'Oh come on, you party-pooper.'

He shook his head again but grinned at her.

'Okay, Tommie, you can dance with me, can't you, little tadpole?'

Tomas had his head down and was concentrating on his butterfly. Destiny stood still and frowned at them. Her eyes flashed while she reached up for the metal bar of the clothesline, suspending her body. With a shrill laugh she pushed off from the ground with her toes and started spinning in circles around the pole. The colours of her skirt and her flying hair created a dazzling rainbow. The sun glinted dangerously off her bangles, sending sparks around the backyard.

Her laughter was infectious and soon Tomas was hanging there with his mother, giggling and squealing. His little toes were spread out like propellers; his legs flew out and up as the momentum of the Hills hoist created a gust of air that made him light as a feather.

All the laughter was sucked up by the cracks in the concrete when Tomas splayed out on the ground, howling. Asher scowled at Destiny; she rushed over to Tomas to scoop him up into her arms. She held him close to her, his sweaty hair damp against his forehead, and whispered to him, cooing like a dove. Tomas was soon sobbing in great gulps. Asher breathed out slowly, unaware that he had been holding it in.

There it was, the washing, flapping about in the stiff breeze. Destiny sang nonsensical songs to Tomas who giggled at her while she lined up the red t-shirt, the purple socks and the bright yellow shorts. Maybe it was the heat that made them silly, a little mad in the head.

Destiny looked at Tomas as if a light went on in her brain and she ran over to the garden tap. 'Hey, little purple tadpole, look at me!'

Tomas turned to his mother and a blast of water in his face. Destiny gasped, ran to hide behind the wheelie bin. Tomas rubbed his hands over his face in an attempt to dry it, then opted to mop it up with his t-shirt. He spied the water pistol lying on the back step. War broke out.

Tuxedo, the cat, wasn't impressed when she got caught in the crossfire. The game stalled when she sat dejected on the steps. They stopped to stroke her until she was placated.

Dinner was fish with lemongrass cooked in foil on the barbeque. They ate it with their fingers as it steamed up their faces. The lemongrass was fragrant, the rice sticky. They gave the cat some fish as a peace offering. She forgave them.

The sun sank and they exhaled.

'Okay, kiddo, time for bed.' Asher stood over Tomas in the lounge room. Tomas ignored him, clicking two blocks to the top of his tower. He wore just pyjama shorts – spaceships and aliens. Asher admired the smooth sun-kissed skin across his shoulders.

'Tomas?'

His son pouted.

'How about a book?'

'Planets?' said Tomas, his round face inclined to his dad.

'Sure. Planets, spaceships. Whatever you like.'

Tomas headed to his room.

'Oi! What about these toys?'

Tomas sighed. Turned back.

Asher resisted a laugh at his adult-like gesture.

Together they bundled all the blocks into a basket.

'What about a kiss for Mummy?' Asher asked as they passed Destiny at the kitchen table.

Tomas wrapped his arms around Destiny's neck, kissed her lips. Destiny closed her eyes and smiled.

In Tomas' room, the nightlight shone a constellation onto the ceiling. Asher remembered working on that lampshade with Destiny for hours. Was it three attempts to get it right? Every time they'd stencilled out the stars, the calculations had been wrong. They had to account for the light travelling to the ceiling. He lay back with Tomas and together they named the stars.

'Daddy, can we put picture on the wall?'

'Sure. The butterflies?'

Tomas shook his head. 'That for Auntie Finn. This one.' He held up the crazy purple tadpoles.

'Okay, buddy, let me get something to stick it up with.'

Asher rummaged in the kitchen drawer – nothing could ever be found in there. No tape. He spotted a crumpled box of Sesame Street Band-Aids.

'Here we go, bud. You hold the paper to the wall.'

'Bert!' said Tomas, beaming.

'You betcha. He'll hold up your picture for you.'

Tomas nodded enthusiastically.

'So, what's the book tonight, Tommie?' asked Asher, tucking him into his bed.

Tomas held up two pudgy fingers.

'Okay, okay, we can do two books.'

Tomas pulled them out from under his pillow.

'Aha, you come prepared, dontcha?'

Tomas nodded and wriggled down into his bed.

Asher peered through the kitchen window that overlooked the lit-up bungalow. If he squinted, the walls of the building seemed to be straight, but it really was just a lean-to. Despite its obvious defects, or maybe because of them, the bungalow was a place that housed a world of magic. That magic was Destiny.

Destiny and her paintings.

Her exhibition was only weeks away, so she was furiously finishing off the last few pieces. She was, in fact, manic, something that Asher had gotten used to over the last few years. He also knew that in about three weeks, her mood would turn, and she would probably take to her bed.

She'd been at it for a few hours. Asher thought it was about time she had a break, so he took two Coronas from the fridge, jammed a wedge of lemon in the neck of each, and headed for the back door. He stopped abruptly and turned on his heel. He quietly peeked into Tomas' bedroom, and smiled at the sleeping face before backing out.

A snail crunched underfoot as Asher walked the path to the bungalow. *Shit!* He wouldn't have minded if he'd had shoes on, but the sharpness of the shell, followed by the soft wetness, was a sensation he would rather have done without. He stopped short of the door to listen. So far Destiny hadn't let him see any of her paintings for this exhibition.

He could hear her talking to herself, the clicking of her bracelets, and a grating sound.

He pushed the door with his free hand. 'Hey, you, fancy a breather?'

Destiny stood over a large mortar. With a hefty pestle, she was grinding away at a bright lump of cadmium, smashing it into submission. She wore an apron over her layered Indian skirt, but she need not have bothered. She had paint in her hair, up and down her arms, and her bare feet were also splattered.

'You getting any of that paint on the board?' asked Asher, grinning.

'Ha, ha, funny boy. It just so happens that I have been mixing *the* most spectacular paints ever!'

'If you say so.' Asher enjoyed goading her, loved to see the flame flare in her eyes when being teased.

'Well, see for yourself, smartarse.' She spread her arms to indicate the whole room, small as it was.

Asher stepped inside reverently. There were wood panels scattered over every inch of the floor, propped up against the walls, some balancing precariously above each other. It was an explosion of colour. Asher knew that he should not tease her because she was right: they were spectacular.

'So, what are you making there?' he said, inclining his head toward the mortar.

Her eyes glistened. 'This is *Summer Solstice*, that one, no, this one, is …'

Asher could almost hear her brain running through the possible names.

She mouthed something, then pointed at the black and announced, 'This one is *Beady Eyes*.'

'Beady eyes?' asked Asher.

Destiny nodded and smiled.

Asher held off his opinion. He picked up the nearest painting. 'Wow, D, these *are* amazing. Are you still going with the same title for your exhibition?'

Destiny frowned. 'It's too egotistical, isn't it?'

'No, I think it's great. I love the double meaning.'

'It was Rhonda's idea anyway. Too late to change now. Does kinda feel egotistical since my husband owns the gallery.'

Asher shrugged and picked up a postcard. 'Who cares? You had your following before we met. So, you've got eight weeks until opening?'

'Just under.'

'Join us for the launch of *This is Destiny*.' He swept his arm towards the walls like a game show host, spilling beer down his arm.

'One of those beers mine?' asked Destiny.

'Sorry, got carried away!' He leaned over toward her, not able to move past the boards.

The beer was cold and smooth, and Asher hoped that it would distract her from her self-doubts – at least momentarily. He licked his lips – tasted the lemon – and scanned the room, studying each image that his wife had created.

Destiny drank her beer greedily. 'That's *good*. Thanks. So …?'

Straight ahead of him was a small board, maybe forty by forty centimetres, with an image of Destiny reclining on a large rock. It sat at the top of a bare hill. She had a fishtail and seaweed tangled in her hair. Every bit of the board had minute details that could only be discovered after persistent examination.

Destiny bit her top lip. 'My inspiration comes from those stories that Dad used to tell me when I was little. I've told you some of them, haven't I? You know, those Irish myths about the goddess Áine? He used to say that I was Áine, the goddess of love, brightness, and delight. He left out the stuff about desire and fertility. I found out those things when I read up about her.'

To the left of him was Destiny leading the Midsummer Festival wearing a midnight-blue silk dress, followed by men wearing desire in their eyes.

'She's a fairy queen or sometimes a beautiful mermaid sitting on her birthing stone at Lough Gur, combing out her long hair.' Destiny wiped her hands on her apron before smoothing down her own hair. 'She lives at Cnoc Áine in a castle. She was given it … until world's end.' Destiny took another long slug of her beer.

Asher picked up a wood panel that lay near his feet. On it was Destiny, naked, her hair covering one breast, her face in ecstasy. Next to her lay a naked man, his face in shadow, his skin glistening in candlelight. Jealousy stabbed Asher. It was absurd, but he couldn't take his eyes away from Destiny's expression.

'Ash?'

'Geez, these are hot. Do I make you feel like that?' Asher couldn't help himself, knowing he'd be heading for danger. As soon as he had the words out, she bristled.

'Are you for real? This is art, for chrissake! Do you think I go fucking around just for my art?'

'I'm just teasing.'

'You can be such a dickhead sometimes.' Destiny began to tidy up her tools, storing paints that she had just made from her crushed pigments mixed with egg yolk.

'Come on, babe, I was just playing with you; you're so easy to tease, I can't help myself.'

Destiny squinted at Asher, her almond eyes gathering storm clouds. 'Glad to be so entertaining for you.' The sarcasm was sharp.

Asher put down his beer, feeling the need to get battle ready. But before he straightened his body, something hit him in the neck. It took a moment to register that Destiny had thrown an egg at him, by which time the contents had dribbled down the neck of his t-shirt and down his back.

'Aim's a bit out,' he said, before turning and bolting from the bungalow, narrowly escaping another egg that hit the wall barely a centimetre from his left ear.

'Come back here, coward!' screamed Destiny as she chased after him.

Along the dark pathway back to the house, Asher jumped out at her from the shadows. He grabbed her from behind, pinned her arms to her sides. 'Who's a coward?'

'You are,' she said, squirming.

'Who is?' said Asher, breathing softly near her ear.

'Ash the Dickhead,' she said, the venom trickling away from her, the anger vaporising as he caressed her arms.

'But you love this dickhead,' he whispered as he bent to blow on her neck.

'No. He's a pain in the arse.'

Her breathing quickened as he slipped his hand down the front of her skirt, down her belly and across her thigh. With his other hand, he moved up her belly, over her small breast, circling her already erect nipple.

She moaned softly.

'What was that?' asked Asher. His hot breath created fog in the cool night air.

Destiny moaned louder.

'I didn't quite catch that. Tell me again.' He now cupped both breasts in his hands and was rubbing against her from behind.

With a sharp intake of breath, Destiny guided one of his hands towards her crotch. With her hand still on his, she motioned him to rub. Destiny writhed against him. Asher wanted her so badly, he was ready to rip her clothes off, but he was awakened from his trance by a crack against his forehead and the feeling of liquid against his face.

'Why you little—'

Destiny giggled, ducked down and out of his arms, and ran back into her studio.

Asher was disorientated, his erection a reminder of where he thought he was going. *That little witch*, he said under his breath as he wiped at the egg that oozed through his eyebrows. 'You're gonna pay for that big time.' He had lowered his voice, trying to sound dictatorial. This only prompted more giggling from inside the studio.

'Come on, time to stop with the egg throwing, I'm going to stink for this barbeque tomorrow. You know how hard it is to get the smell of egg out of your hair?' Asher craned his neck to look through the doorway.

'No, Ash, I don't believe I've ever had egg in my hair.' Her eyes crinkled.

'You had enough fun now?'

'Don't worry, Ash, I've run out of eggs.'

Destiny was clearing away more of her tools. Asher restrained from smiling at her as her skirt was totally skewed, her apron gone. Only one button on her top remained intact.

They stood in silence.

Asher did not trust her and was on guard to run again.

A house alarm blared into the night. They paused.

'Still say you're a coward,' Destiny said with a straight face.

'If you say so,' he said.

'Yep, I say so. In fact, I'll prove it.'

She walked calmly over to him, a small bowl and paintbrush in hand. Asher looked for eggs.

Destiny dunked the paintbrush into the bowl and brought it up to his face. 'See, you even have beady eyes,' she said as she dotted his face with the brush. She stood back to survey her handiwork, nodded with approval. 'Hmm. Bit dirty there, old man,' she said as she continued to paint dots all the way up his arm.

Asher grabbed the bowl from Destiny, stuck two fingers in the black paint and wiped them across her nose. 'Could say the same for you, Miss Perfect.'

'Well … you stink, too,' said Destiny, screwing up her nose.

'No thanks to you. Now you can come wash it off me.'

'I'm not your mother. You can wash it off yourself.'

'No, I demand that you wash it off as my slave. I'm not turning up to your parents' place tomorrow stinking like this.'

'Your slave?' Destiny put the bowl of paint back on the bench and straightened a painting that lent against the wall.

Asher picked her up, her lightness making it easy for him to balance her over his shoulder. She half-heartedly kicked out her legs to unbalance him, then resigned herself to him.

'Ash?'

'What?'

'That's you in the painting, you idiot.'

He grinned, carried her down the path, stepping on yet another snail, into the sleeping house, and straight to the bathroom.

'What're you doing?' asked Destiny.

'You're going to clean me.' He placed her down on the middle of the tiled floor.

'Is that so?' She stood before him, hands on hips.

Asher struggled to contain any composure. Her small body and attitude made him want to rip her clothes off, but he resisted. Instead, he took a step closer to her and slowly unbuttoned her skirt. She stopped talking. Closed her eyes. The skirt came loose and dropped to the floor. Destiny started to lift his t-shirt but he stopped her and put a finger to his lips.

She made a zipping motion across her mouth, lips quivering with humour. It was hard for her to go slow. Asher bent down and kissed her neck. He unbuttoned the top button on her shirt, then kissed the skin on her shoulder. She moaned and reached for his t-shirt again, but he pinned her arms to her sides so that she couldn't move. He kissed her lower on the neck, then had her shirt undone. It slid to the floor.

Asher grabbed the hem of his t-shirt, shrugged it over his head, and stepped out of his shorts. 'In,' he said, pointing to the shower.

'What about these?' said Destiny, pointing to her underwear.

Asher shook his head, finger to his lips. 'In.' He turned on the shower.

Destiny stepped into the shower, picked up a large body scrubber and a bottle of shower gel from the shower floor. She turned to Asher with raised eyebrows. Asher stepped in behind her and adjusted the water temperature.

'In,' he whispered, moving her gently under the water.

She closed her eyes as water ran over her face, flattening her dark hair against her body like octopus tentacles. He gently took the scrubber and bottle from her hands and placed them on the floor outside the shower cubicle. He bent and squirted a small amount of gel, jasmine scented, onto his palm and stepped back in front of Destiny. With his right hand, Asher cupped the back of her neck and drew her closer, kissing her. Water flowed between them and into their mouths. With his left hand, Asher smoothed the gel onto her right shoulder and down over her small breast, down her side and into her underpants. He continued to kiss her gently.

He edged closer to her inner thigh. Her body squirmed, pushing towards him.

'I won't last long at this rate,' she panted.

'Shhh,' said Asher, pinning her gently to the tiled wall. 'You talk too much.' He pushed a finger inside her. She gasped. He kissed her again, pinning her left shoulder to the wall with one hand, then rubbing slowly below with the other.

'Oh, Ash, don't stop. That's sooo good.' Her head was bent back, water draining down her body. He pressed against her, rocking gently. He held her firmly as her body shuddered. Before she could recover, he lifted her, moved her underpants out of the way. Entered her. He moved in and out in slow rhythm, the water splashing against them, his feet straining for purchase on the slippery tiles.

Destiny grabbed the hair at the back of his head, moving her body in unison with his movements. Her breath was coming in staccato – as was his. He could not hold off any longer and let go with a long shudder, head bent into Destiny's neck.

He placed Destiny gently on the floor of the shower and kissed her lightly on the lips. 'Now. Clean,' he said, turning his back to her and motioning to the body scrubber. She giggled and took off her underpants and dropped them on the floor outside the shower before picking up the body scrubber.

'Yes, sir,' she said, lathering his back with foam and scrubbing at him in mock humility.

'That's, *Your Highness*, thank you,' said Asher over his shoulder.

'Oh, Your Highness, please forgive me,' she said as she rubbed foam over his hips and buttocks. 'You really are very dirty.' She turned him around and lathered his groin.

'Right, that's enough from you,' said Asher. 'You're going to the naughty corner.' He turned the taps off.

'What is it, *Your Highness*?' asked Destiny, skin glistening.

Asher grabbed a towel and wrapped it roughly around her. 'Come with me and I'll show you,' he said as he bundled her towards their bedroom.

The smell of fried chilli was sharp, catching at the back of Asher's throat. Flies congregated on his nose. He swatted furiously at them. The air seemed devoid of oxygen, shimmering before his eyes.

Mai darted around the back garden with an armload of delicious Vietnamese foods on a platter that seemed bigger than her. Asher smiled, thinking that she was indeed smaller than Destiny and he marvelled at how that was possible. Mai was a power rocket, her black hair sleek and bobbed at her shoulders, her feline eyes infinitely wicked. She was always like this, never wavered in her mood, always industrious, as if any idle moment was wasteful. Her brood of kids seemed ever-changing as she embraced any new person who seemed in need of a home – a remnant of the years she and Sean lived on a commune on the east coast.

Lemongrass and coriander teased Asher's nostrils. He hadn't had Asian food until he met Destiny, at once feeling uncultured and ignorant. It was still something he was getting accustomed to. Tomas was lucky enough to be enriched with the array of Vietnamese foods that his grandmother, and consequently Destiny, cooked. Asher's grandmother, Rebecca – his Moma – would cook him goulash and noodles, which Tomas wholeheartedly tucked into. *No fussy eater there*, Asher said to himself as he watched Tomas tackle a gigantic chilli prawn as if it were cake.

Mai held the platter up under Asher's nose. 'Here, you try prawn. Good boy.' Her black head peeked from behind the rim of the platter.

Asher had learned that refusal of food from Mai resulted in copious pouting that wasn't worth it. She measured everything in food. Your mood, the weather, her relationships.

It was okay. He liked her chilli prawns. They went very well with beer.

Casey sidled up to Asher. Destiny's youngest brother delighted in making trouble, but by now Asher was used to the triggers and no longer got caught out.

'Hey, Ash. How's it going?'

'Yeah, good, mate. You?'

'Can't complain. Been out in the bush writing some songs.'

'That's good. What's next then?'

'Recording them in Sydney next month, then gonna do a tour of the pubs. Seems country music is popular again. What's happening at your place? Destiny been behaving?'

Asher bristled. He wasn't sure why Casey asked the question. 'Not much; Tomas keeps us busy.'

'She's a handful though, ain't she.' There was no question, just statement.

Asher ignored him and offered to get Casey another beer, knowing fully that he'd barely touched the one he had in his hand.

The moods. He'd experienced them enough now to know the extent of their damage, but he wondered why Casey needed to question him about it.

Finn appeared from nowhere. Asher could never get used to it. She was so unlike her sister in every way, blonde with intense blue eyes. Her silence could be unnerving. She rarely said anything, unless she had something profound to say. Even then, what she said was often bizarre. Usually, he relied on Destiny to translate.

'Hi, Ash,' said Finn.

'How're you going?' answered Ash.

Finn smiled without answering and held up one of the drawings that Tomas had done the day before. 'These butterflies are beautiful. It's as if he's captured the very essence of their spirits. He's a true artist.' She held the paper against her chest and sighed. 'I'll treasure this always.'

The whole family was like a cosmos of its own, a strange accumulation of planets that floated and bumped into each other randomly. A group of people who seemed barely associated with each other: the union of an Irish man and a Vietnamese woman, so unlikely and yet so exotic. For an outsider, it was hard to determine who was related. None of them looked alike, and then there were the added orphans and other people's children who gravitated to their orbit – hard to tell who belonged.

Sean sat under the old apple tree, holding a coin up to Tomas' ear. Tomas drew back and looked at the coin, then at his grandfather, confusion on his face. Sean laughed and ruffled the boy's hair. Finn's eldest girl, Tyan, ran past and tagged Tomas on the shoulder. He chased her through the house and out of sight. Sean watched them go, a twinkle in his eyes.

'Some brood you're gathering here, Sean,' said Asher as he sat next to his father-in-law.

Sean nodded, his eyes moist.

'How many grandkids does that make?' Asher took a swig from his beer.

Sean shrugged. 'Who the fuck knows, mate? I've lost count of me own kids, let alone theirs.' He lent back against the tree and took a long drag on his cigarette. 'I don't even know what we're celebrating today. Do you?'

Asher searched his memory. Destiny had told him, but he was only half listening, the heat making him stupid. Birthday? New baby? Wedding? He shook his head.

'Oi, Mai!' Sean shouted to his wife.

Mai tottered over, still bearing food.

'What're we celebrating today?'

Mai scoffed at him incredulously and stormed off.

'Oops, seems I wasn't listening either, mate!' Sean tittered.

Asher caught Tyan as she chased Tomas around the tree. 'Hey, Tyan, what's the party for today?' Asher tried to act blasé about it.

Tyan looked at him, her chin down, eyes scornful. 'We do this every year; are you dumb or what?'

Asher shrugged.

'It's Summer Solstice.' The petulance was emphasised in her voice.

Sean and Asher rolled their eyes at each other. 'Summer Solstice!' they sang in unison and sat back with their beers.

'Do we even know what the fuck Summer Solstice is?' asked Sean.

'Do we know anything about what Mai does? How long you been together now?'

Sean swigged his beer and screwed up his face. 'Boy! Buggered if I know. We met in Byron Bay in the '70s. But don't tell her I don't remember. You know what they say: *If you can remember the '70s, then you weren't really there.'* They both laughed.

'Well, that's over twenty-five years. D was born in '74, yeah?'

'I guess. The commune feels like a lifetime ago,' said Sean.

'What's going on here?' said Destiny, standing over them, the apple tree framing her.

Asher and Sean squinted up at her and shrugged.

Destiny stretched up her arms and yawned. 'This weather makes me so sleepy. You two have the right idea.' As she stretched, she knocked a branch of the gnarled old tree and an apple thudded to the ground. 'Hmm, must be meant for me,' she said as she scooped it up and bit into it with relish.

'Hey!' said Sean. 'You can't do that!'

'What?' said Destiny, her mouth full.

'You can't eat an apple without polishing it first. It's bad luck.'

Destiny stopped chewing. 'Why?' she said, blanching.

'It's a challenge to Satan if you don't polish it first,' said Sean.

'It's only a challenge if you believe in Satan,' she said defiantly.

'If you say so.'

'Yeah, I do,' said Destiny but she turned the apple in her hand and threw the rest of it towards the chooks. 'It tastes bitter anyway.' She stomped away towards the food table.

'How you two going then?' asked Sean.

Asher reflected on the night before. *Damn good*, he thought. 'Yeah, all good, I reckon.'

'She's a handful, I know, mate, but she's got the biggest heart. And so much fun. She was always hot and cold as a kid. Zero to a hundred in seconds. It was exhausting but luckily Mai is up for that kind of challenge. Kinda fits with the whole Irish thing too.'

Asher nodded. The shower flashed into his mind again and he felt his dick stir. 'Oh yeah, she's a handful alright.'

'What about Sam? He giving you any grief about it all?'

Asher flinched. He wasn't used to these kinds of questions from Sean. Sam. Was Sam giving him grief? They didn't see him much. Always traveling. And Tomas was three now. Hadn't enough time passed that Sam would be over it?

'Nope. Don't see him much these days.'

'Really? But you two got that gallery together. Doesn't he need to be around for that?'

'No. It pretty much runs itself. Rhonda, our manager, and Max are both there to cover opening hours and hanging shows and things like that. Sam and me, well, we do more of the networking and take care of the background stuff. Only really need to be there if we need to cover holidays or there's an opening or something like that.'

Sean took another swig. 'Cool. So Destiny got a show coming up?'

'Yeah, work is almost ready. They're pretty good. She finally let me see them yesterday.' A flash of her in the garden at night came to him.

'Ha. What would happen if they weren't good?'

'Now you and me know that isn't possible.' Asher took a swig from his beer.

Sean nodded. 'Yeah, she has talent. Hope she keeps at it. People with talent can go off the rails sometimes ...'

Asher didn't know where this conversation was headed.

'Anyway, mate, can't wait to see the show. When is it?'

'Daddy?' Tomas stood in front of Asher and Sean. Sweat pasted his hair flat to his head.

'Hey, Tommie. What's up, matey?' Asher sat up and leaned towards his son.

'Granma Mai yelled at me,' he sniffled and rubbed at his face that was smeared with sweat and dirt.

'Oh. What did you do?'

'I-I-I was trying to catch a chicken and ... and I ... and I chased it all the way round the garden and I ...'

'Poor lamb is exhausted,' said Sean, placing a hand on Tomas' shoulder. 'Might want to get him down for a nap, mate. All this running around in the heat with the cousins is making them all batty.'

Asher nodded. He stood and bent down to pick up Tomas who was now blubbering incoherently.

'D?' he called to her across the yard.

Destiny turned to them. She had been deep in conversation with Finn.

Asher mouthed, *Let's get going?*

'What's up, babe?' Destiny walked over to them and rubbed Tomas on the back.

'I think we should go. This boy is tired.'

'What about the bonfire later?' Destiny was like a child herself being told she couldn't have an ice cream.

'Really, D. He's three. There's no way he'll last till dark. Look at him. He's almost comatose.'

Destiny sighed. 'Okay, okay. Let's go. But next year, we're staying for the bonfire.'

'Yeah, whatever. There'll be others.' Asher hoisted Tomas higher onto his shoulder.

'Hey, everyone! We're gonna get going. Tommie is done. It's too hot.'

Mai came bursting through the back door of the house. 'You can't go now. What about the bonfire later? Tommie youngest. He get to light it.' Her whole body quivered.

'Sorry, Mum, he's totally done!' Destiny smoothed the back of his head.

Mai pouted. It was comical but Asher held back on laughter. The heat was getting to them all.

The summer heat was oppressive inside the red Honda – and rising – as the car barrelled along a country road on its way home. The afternoon sun slanted through the trees, stabbing bright light at the windows.

Asher gripped the steering wheel and squirmed. Sweat rolled down his neck in steady rivulets. He thought about the questions that Sean had been asking. What were they about? Should he be worried about Sam? Maybe Sean was just making conversation. He was like that. An Irish man can never shut up. Must always be talking.

Besides, Sam was away a lot. He was really the person who went out and networked with galleries and artists all around the world. Asher could hardly keep up with where he was at any particular time. Where was he now? New York? Maybe he was back in Melbourne? Asher shook his head. It was nothing. Sean was just asking dumb questions.

Asher frowned at the dashboard. 'You'd think that an expensive hunk of metal like this would have a decent air con, wouldn't you?' He spoke directly at the car.

The chink of bracelets distracted him, but Destiny was facing the other way. She tucked an errant lock of hair behind her ear and stared dreamily out the window. 'That was a great get-together, wasn't it, babe?'

Asher continued to jab at the buttons, muttering under his breath.

Destiny pulled off her sandals and put her feet on the dashboard; her crimson toenails glistened under the glass of the windscreen.

'Do you think Ma is getting frail?'

'Come on, D, do you have to do that?' He was arching his brows at her feet as she rolled her eyes. She moved her feet to the left. Asher sighed. He tried not to count her toes.

'Your mother is no more frail than I am. Sometimes I wonder if she takes speed. Damn this thing, come on!'

'Hey, Daddy, there's a big cow,' Tomas crooned from the back seat, pointing out the window. He'd slept for fifteen minutes and was refreshed.

'Yeah, mate, that's great.' Asher frowned at the dashboard, trying not to look at Destiny's toes.

'Look, Daddy! That horsey is huge! Daddy, look!'

'Damn this bloody thing!' said Asher.

'Mmm ...' said Destiny.

Asher scowled. 'Damn it's hot!'

'Have some of my juice, Daddy.'

'Fuck this,' said Asher, punching at buttons.

'Uh, oh, Mummy, Daddy said a bad worrrd.'

'It's okay, Tommie, Daddy's just a little bit hot.'

'Silly Daddy.' Tomas giggled.

'Gee, you two jabber on ...'

'Don't worry about it, Ash.'

'Don't worry about it?'

'Yeah, it's not that big a deal.'

'Do you remember how much this shit heap cost, D?'

'You're only making yourself hotter.' She gazed at him, emerald eyes shining.

'What would you know, D?'

She put her hand on his forearm. 'Did you know that what the world spends on weapons in one week could feed the whole world for a year?'

'Jesus, where do you get this shit from?'

'It's true. And just imagine what people must put up with in Africa without air con or even water?' Her eyes misted.

Asher bit his lip, looked at her toes. *How does she fit them in shoes?*

'Ash! Watch out!' Destiny lurched towards the steering wheel just as Asher realised that a truck was on their side of the road.

There was a flash of light when metal hit metal and the weight of Destiny shunted into him.

black

I open my eyes.

It's quiet except for a slow creaking sound and something hissing behind me. Long shadows fall across my body. My left ear rests on warm concrete. I lift myself onto my elbow. Pain bursts from my ribs. I gasp, drop down, clutching at my chest.

With shallow breaths, I ease upright into a half-sitting position. My legs are deadweights. My arms shake. In front of me is a car door, the window shattered, the metal reshaped into a modern sculpture. It would make a good piece in the gallery. At my right is a car seat that has been lifted straight out of a car and placed nonchalantly in the middle of the road.

Road.

Why am I in the middle of the road? The bitumen is warm, almost sticky, and liquid trickles from the wreckage.

Wreckage.

I scan the landscape before me. *Wreckage.* My synapses flare. Wreckage!

'Destiny? Tomas?' I try to gather my body together to stand up but one leg is numb. I look down at my legs and recoil. My right thigh has a gash in it; skin, muscle, tendon is oozing out.

'Tomas!' I try to breathe. *Calm down.*

There he is, sleeping in his booster seat, in the middle of the road. My breath catches. *Thank you*, I mouth, skyward.

I shuffle over to him, commando style, and pull him into my arms. He is angelic and pure in sleep, exactly as he was when I checked on him last night in his bed. I'm glad that he's asleep and can't see my leg. That would give him nightmares for a month. Tomas is strangely still considering the accident has hardly touched him; there is no mark on his body, but he is limp.

Lifeless.

I smooth back his hair, which is matted and sweaty, evidence of a day of playing with his bigger cousins. I rock him in my arms. 'Aunty Finn loves that drawing of the butterfly, Tommie. Can you do one for me later?' I stroke his hair and face, trace the outline of his lips – they are a perfect bow.

A deep, guttural sound fills the air. Destiny is upside down in what is left of the car. There is steam or smoke billowing around her. I gently lay Tomas on the ground, not wanting to wake him. I should move with more urgency, but I'm fighting against an unseen current.

I grit my teeth and stand. The pain threatens to unbalance me, but I breathe through it and shuffle towards Destiny. It isn't clear where the remains of the Honda or the remains of the truck are. Destiny groans.

She's bound up with debris that is grotesque. I try to clear away metal in order to get a better idea of the situation.

I stop.

'Destiny?'

For a split second I think it isn't her, but logic tells me it must be. I try to adjust to the vision. Her hair is covering most of her face. Blood! There's so much blood.

'Destiny!'

I scour my brain for first aid procedure. DR ABC. Yes! Danger. Is there danger? I scramble through my brain. There's fuel everywhere and we're strewn all over a fucking road. *Fuck!*

I check my pockets for my phone. It's gone. I scan frantically, but everything is mangled, unrecognisable.

'Destiny? Can you hear me, babe? I'll get help – we're gonna be okay.' My voice cracks. *Wake up Ash, this is a nightmare …*

'Ash?' Destiny's voice is garbled, like something obstructs her throat. 'Ash! Where am I? Tomas?' She thrashes within her confines. 'Ash!'

I lean into her. 'It's okay, babe. We were in a car accident, but you're okay.' I stop. Should I tell her that, about the accident?

'Ash!' Destiny thrashes again and I try to reach in to touch her. She stops, goes limp.

I look wildly around me, up and down the road, willing someone to come and help. I see something in the distance, a shimmering shape that becomes solid within seconds. The blaring red lights are a relief and I stand as tall as I can, waving my arms above my head as if any idiot wouldn't guess we were here.

The ambulance stops several metres away. The paramedics emerge from the vehicle with steady purpose, giving me confidence that they can fix everything. *Thank you.*

'Hey, mate,' says a short balding man. 'Someone called triple zero – they had to drive up the road a bit to get reception …'

I have trouble focusing on his words. I point to Tomas, waving my arms. 'You're just in time … my boy … he needs something, quick. One of those heart-starter things.'

The paramedic looks at Tomas, then at his partner, before squatting down beside Tomas to check his pulse.

I blink at them. 'No, he just needs a jolt.' The panic rises in my throat, wrapping itself around my larynx and constricting it like a python to the point that I can't speak.

'Mate, it's okay, we'll take care of him, calm down.' The man holds my eyes and places a hand on my arm.

I clutch at my neck with both hands, shaking my head from side to side.

'Is there anyone else here?'

I freeze. Contemplate the question. The words go into my ears and whiz around my brain, trying to find their target. *Anyone else?* Yes! 'Yes, my wife, Destiny.' The words are strangulated, barely audible. 'She's under here.' I kneel carefully beside the car.

The man bends and waves his partner over. 'Quick, Stan, there's a lot of blood loss. Gotta work fast!'

I sink to the ground, the gash in my leg sending shards of pain through my body. I watch the two men work on my wife's body and hear another siren. A wave of nausea pounds me.

I lift my head slowly as a young woman bends close to my face, her mouth moving in silent shapes. I frown at her, trying to read her lips.

My eyes flutter, bringing me in and out of light until, eventually, nothing.

35

There is a constant beeping to my left. I wrestle against drowsiness, pull myself to the surface. Open my eyes. Everything is white, unfamiliar. I try to pull myself upright but my body feels anchored to the bed. My right leg throbs so I reach down under the sheets. There are mountains of wrappings over my thigh. *The accident …* Flashes of memory come to me: Tomas in his booster seat, Destiny upside-down.

I look out the window to get my bearings but there's only concrete and a slit of light from the sky above.

'Hello?' I don't know who I'm calling but I figure there's got to be someone nearby.

The curtain opens from the other side of the bed. 'Well, hello, sleepyhead.' A nurse smiles at me. I don't know what is more dazzling – her smile or her red hair.

'Where's my wife?'

She smiles again but I know she's stalling.

I try to sit up and break out into a sweat, pausing at a half-sit. 'Stop smiling at me and tell me what the fuck is going on!'

She frowns but I can tell she's used to belligerent people. 'Your wife, Mr Anderson, is on the fourth floor. Intensive care.'

Somebody steps out from behind the nurse.

'Sam?'

My brother shuffles closer as the nurse disappears behind the curtain. He plunges his hands into his pockets. 'How you feeling?' His voice is raspy.

My stomach spasms. 'What's wrong? Is D gonna be okay?'

'She's had extensive surgery. She's in a coma.'

My stupid brain tries to compute it. She's alive. But Tomas? I don't think I want to know the answer, but I whisper, my throat catching, 'Tommie?'

Sam sucks in air and looks down at me but not in the eyes; he shifts his weight from one leg to another.

'Sam?'

He brushes his hair with his hand, eyes welling with tears. 'He's …'

'Gone?'

He nods. Blinks. Faces the ceiling.

'No! Not Tomas!' My voice fills the room as I thrash in my bed. The nurse rushes in and leans over me, a syringe ready for my arm.

'Shh … It's going to be okay … The angels are taken from us too soon …'

Waking is like deep diving and that slow ascent to the surface, lungs bursting with the need for oxygen, your body desperate to live. When I finally smash through, I'm on another planet, an alien left behind from a discovery mission.

I spend these waking moments trying to relearn who I am, where I am, and why I'm here. Once I've done that, the enormity of all that knowledge pounds at me and the physical pain crowds in.

Doctor Ryan, the surgeon, stands by my bed, waiting for me to wake. I've only seen him once on one of his rounds, but I was pretty groggy. I can't remember anything he told me except that Destiny needs a skin graft on her arm. And that I was lucky not to need more surgery because my leg was healing well.

Lucky me.

'There he is. It's hard to catch you awake, young man,' says Doctor Ryan.

I find this a weird comment. He can't be much older than me.

I try to pull myself upright. I hate these contraptions that are meant to help you haul yourself up; they're wobbly and hard to manoeuvre. I give up halfway to sitting and fall back in the bed. At least the nurse has elevated the end of the bed so I'm half-sitting anyway.

'Hey, doc.' It's an effort to open my mouth.

'Leg is going well,' he says as he scans the clipboard in his hands. 'You should be able to start bearing weight in a week or so.'

'Destiny?' I ask.

'The skin graft went well. Took some skin from under her upper arm. She hasn't woken at all though.' He scribbles notes. 'Oh, and I'm very sorry about the baby.'

'Thanks, doc. He wasn't a baby anymore, will … would be four in a few months.'

'No. I mean the baby.' He's still scribbling notes.

'What do you mean, what baby?' I'm wide awake now.

He peers over his glasses at me. 'Did your wife know she was pregnant? We guess about seven, maybe eight weeks. You weren't told that it didn't survive?' He is irate, but I can tell he's trying to cover it. Someone will be in trouble now.

'We didn't know she was pregnant.' I'm still trying to process this. I'm not liking how he calls the baby 'it'.

'It was early days. Your wife may not have known yet. It's no surprise that such an horrific accident caused her to lose it. We only know she was pregnant because of routine blood tests.'

Questions scramble around my head. Did Destiny know? We were going to have another baby? A brother or sister for Tomas. Eight weeks? That would mean … due September?

'How big is a baby at eight weeks?' I ask.

'Not big. Maybe this.' He holds up his fingers to indicate a size, maybe one-and-a-half centimetres. 'I'm not an obstetrician, though, so don't quote me on that.' He attempts a crooked smile.

'So you wouldn't be able to tell the sex?'

He shakes his head and places a hand on my forearm. 'You'll be able to have more children, Mr Anderson. You and your wife will recover from this and in a year or so will be able to remember it as a bad chapter in your life, but you will move on.'

Really? What shit do they tell these doctors to spout? I can't formulate an answer, so I nod dumbly. He turns and leaves. He must be satisfied that he handled me well.

'Excuse me, sir …'

There's a weight on my arm. I open my eyes to a young woman with large green eyes.

'I'm sorry to disturb you …' She glances quickly at her clipboard. 'Um, Mr Anderson, but I need to talk to you about your son …'

I sit upright. 'Tomas?'

She nods, the corners of her mouth downturned. 'I know this is difficult … with your wife …' She nods at Destiny and then at a sleeping form huddled in a chair beside her bed.

I remember where I am and twist to ease the pain in my ribs. I spend more time here in this crappy vinyl armchair than my own room on the sixth floor.

'Do we have to do this now?'

The woman whispers, 'Yes.'

'They give you the great jobs, huh?'

'These things have to be done, sir.'

'Call me Ash, please.'

'Okay, Ash. I need to find out what you wish to do with the body.'

My breath snags. *The body?* I look over at Destiny. The sleeping form next to her sits up. 'Hi, Moma,' I say gently.

Moma smiles weakly.

A stone lodges at the top of my oesophagus. I swallow to try to dislodge it. It shreds my throat. I'm hoarse.

'I have no idea.'

The woman shuffles papers on her clipboard. 'Will you have a burial or cremation?' she asks gently, hands shaking.

'Um …' I turn to Moma for an answer, but she's turned towards the window, eyes welling with tears.

'If you don't have specific religious beliefs, maybe cremation would be best?' The woman's pen hovers over her form.

'I guess … but when can we have a funeral?' My mind struggles to focus.

'Your wife has extensive injuries. I was told that she may need more than one lot of surgery once they bring her out of the induced coma.'

I swallow again. 'But she won't see him.'

'It may be weeks before she is able to leave the hospital. We suggest that you don't delay this … um …'

'Asher, my darling.' Moma is at my side, squeezing my arm. 'No matter what you do, it will be hard to accept. Let us have funeral soon. When Destiny ready, we do something special with her and the ashes of our baby boy.'

I hold her hand and nod, my throat impassable.

I wake with a start.

'Sorry, mate, can't drive this damn thing.' Sean is sheepish from behind a wheelchair.

I haul myself into a sitting position, the bedsprings whining with every movement.

'Need some oil, old man,' says Sean, grinning stupidly.

'Need more than that,' I say, wincing. I feel faint, my body peppered with pain. 'What's going on?'

Sean fiddles with the chair. 'I have to take you somewhere …'

'Where?'

Sean exhales slowly. 'It's gotta be done.'

'Jesus, Sean, just get to the point!'

'Okay. We gotta go shopping. For a coffin.'

Blood rushes from my face. 'Shit! I can't do it. Just get the funeral people to choose one for me. Nothing fancy, simple. Fuck no …' I slump down into the pillows. *You can't fucking make me do it.*

'Look, Ash. It's no picnic for me either. It's gotta be done. We'll do it together. This is … was … your son. My grandson.' He chokes on the last word.

'Fuck it. I can't. I can't, won't say goodbye to him.'

Sean's voice wobbles. 'Ash, you gotta do it. Life gives us curly ones. You have to send him off properly.' He sits awkwardly in the chair nearby. Grief has shrunken him.

I bring my fist down heavily on the bed. 'Why? Why Tomas? He's a baby, for chrissake!'

Sean rubs his face with a gnarled hand. 'Who knows how God works, son? He has a plan for all of us.'

'God? Since when do you believe in God?'

He laughs softly. 'Can't erase a childhood of God-fearing, Catholic priest sermons, mate. I don't know what I believe in anymore.'

I shake my head.

'C'mon, Ash. Let's go do this. For your son.'

Sean wheels me into the funeral parlour on the ground floor of the hospital. This is not the kind of shopping I ever thought I'd have to do. A woman emerges from a side door and smiles at us.

'Good morning!' She's too chirpy.

I cross my arms over my chest.

'Mr Anderson?' she asks, extending her hand to me.

I'm the one in a wheelchair, so good guess, lady ... I keep my hands wedged under my armpits.

Sean shoots his hand out to her. 'Hi, I'm Sean. Father-in-law.'

She smiles that fake smile and I want to slap the stupid bitch. 'Hello, Sean, my name is Helen. Welcome to Serenity Funerals.'

Sean nods with a stupid puppy face.

'How are we today?' she asks, tilting her head sideways.

Fucking great. Two kids dead, wife almost dead ... How about you don't ask any more dumb questions and get on with this?

'How do you think, Helen? I'm here to buy a coffin for my son.'

Her smile disappears. 'I'm so sorry. That was a really insensitive question.' She leans down and touches me on the shoulder. 'This is never an easy situation.'

Her honesty pricks me, and I feel guilty for my petulance, but her pain isn't anywhere near mine. 'Let's get this over with.'

Sean rubs my shoulder and I relax – a little. We follow Helen through the door and down a short corridor that opens into a large showroom. Full of coffins. *Shit!*

Helen turns and smiles brightly again, sales hat back on. She sweeps her hand in an arch. 'Any of these can be made to order in the appropriate size.'

This woman really has a shitty job.

'Did you have something in mind?'

Did I? As if this has ever been on my mind, present or past tense. I shake my head. My hands are clammy. I wipe them on my track pants.

'May I make some suggestions?'

I shrug.

'For children under five we suggest a white coffin. These three styles work well in a small size. What do you think of this one?'

They are all the same to me. Sean is struggling too. It never occurred to me that this is his first time also. What if he knew there were two gone?

I point to the coffin furthest from us. It has softer angles than the other two.

Helen nods. 'Let's go into the office and talk about the service.'

We file after her and I study the coffin as we pass, trying to imagine it the size of Tomas. I am outside of my body, disconnected from everything. Sean and Helen talk about details that I can't relate to and my brain shifts within my head.

'Mr Anderson?'

I open my eyes. Always fucking dozing. *I'm still in this shitty place?* Her badge says 'Nurse Wilkins'. I think I've seen her before.

'Yeah?'

'We're going to bring your wife out of her coma in about an hour. Do you want to be there?'

I sit up. 'Yes! Will she still be in intensive care?'

The nurse nods. 'I can take you up in your wheelchair.'

'I don't need that thing anymore.'

'It's regulations. It's easier for me if you're in a wheelchair. We'll get you some crutches later.'

I can't be bothered arguing.

'Do you need help dressing?'

I wave her away. I'm already halfway out of bed but I pause; pain snatches my breath away. I look out of the window into the street below. I envy those people going about their day. A mother and child skip along the footpath, the small boy clutching his lunchbox. I glance up at the clock – time for kinder.

Wait. It's nearly the end of the year. No kinder. Maybe childcare.

Did I miss Christmas?

Intensive care is another world compared to the floor I'm on. Nurse Wilkins pushes me along the dark corridors in hushed silence. The only sounds are the wheels of the chair against polished lino and beeping machines.

Destiny's room is at the far end, and I wish this chair would move quicker. We turn into it, and I crane my neck to get a better view of her.

'If she's out of a coma today, does that mean she'll be able to go to the funeral?' My voice is amplified in the quiet room.

'I wouldn't get my hopes up. Even when we wake her, it will take some time for her to come out of it fully. When is the funeral?'

'Tomorrow.'

She shakes her head. 'Let's take this one step at a time. Why don't you get comfortable while we sort things out to wake your wife. I'm sure you'd love to talk to her?'

I nod automatically but I'm not so sure. What am I going to say to her? I sit back into the chair beside the bed and watch absently as Nurse Wilkins gets busy with wires and buttons.

Hi, Destiny ... D ... Hey, babe ... how you feeling?

Fuck! Maybe I should've stayed in bed until this was all over. Let one of them tell her about Tomas ...

'Mr Anderson?'

I flinch.

'She's coming to. But she'll be very groggy, probably incoherent. Just stay close to her and let her know that you're here.'

'Will she know me? I mean, her memory will be all there?'

'Oh yes, she might just take a day or so to readjust and work out where she is. She's been out for a while and is well dosed up on painkillers.'

I drag the chair closer to the bed and lean in. It's hard to really see her past the tubes and bandages. She's so tiny in the bed and I want to hold her, protect her, but it's too late.

I haven't done that. She's going to hate me just as much as I hate myself.

Her head moves to the right and her lips part to let out a tiny groan.

'Destiny?'

Her brows knot and she turns towards me.

'Destiny, babe, it's me, Ash.'

She groans again and screws her face up. She's fighting her way from her deep sleep. Her eyes open and she looks directly at me.

'D, you're in the hospital. It's me, Ash.' I squeeze her hand and kiss her on the forehead. Relief washes over me.

Destiny frowns and scans the room. Her brain must be trying to compute everything. I think she recognises me.

'Tomas?'

I freeze. I'm not ready for this question so soon. I smile and lean in to kiss her again, stalling for time.

Her gaze is unnerving. 'Tomas?'

'He's … we were … there was an accident. A truck ran into us.'

She frowns again. 'Tomas?'

Fuck. I'm in a sweat now. 'He's gone, babe. He didn't make it.'

She turns her head to the wall, closes her eyes.

'Destiny?' I want to ask her about the other baby. Did she know? Why didn't she tell me?

'Mr Anderson?'

I jump. Was the nurse behind me all this time?

'You'll find that she's very groggy. I think we should let her sleep.'

'Can I sit with her a while?'

'Of course.' She bustles on the other side of the bed, leaves the room.

I squeeze Destiny's hand, stroke her fingers. 'Did you hear me, babe? He's gone, our baby's gone … We didn't know how long you'd be out so we organised the funeral. It's tomorrow. It would be good for you to be there. To say goodbye.'

Now I'm wondering if we should include this other baby in the funeral? I don't know if anyone else knows. Do you even consider it a baby when it was so tiny, not even yet a boy or girl?

I'm crying. I need her to wake up. I can't do this on my own. I don't want to say goodbye.

I hold Destiny's hand with both of mine. I inhale deeply and hold my breath, willing her to wake up, until I can't hold my breath any longer and the exhalation thrusts out of my body in a mixture of frustration and grief.

I rest my head on the bed, still holding her hand, and close my eyes. My breathing soon takes on the rhythm of the machines.

I wait.

T he coffin is simple. Small and white.
  So small.

Casey and Sean carry it awkwardly down the aisle of the church, squirming in too-tight suits. I sit in a wheelchair – useless – my bandaged leg throbbing with pain.

There are faces in front of me, twisted in anguish. My brother, Sam, cradles our mother's head on his shoulder and grips the hand of our grandmother, Moma.

Finn sits up front embracing her harp. She played that harp when Destiny and I got married, as we walked up the aisle. She's strumming it gently and swaying alongside the strings, almost in a trance. It's a haunting sound that makes my skin prickle. She sings a beautiful Celtic lullaby that floats around the room with eerie reverence. I can't make out the words. As the music fades, Mai starts wailing softly. Keening. It sets everybody off. Except me. I'm too dazed to feel anything.

I can't work out where my body is, wound up tight. I don't want to say goodbye to my son. If I don't do it, he'll stay here forever. I turn my head to the right. There's my older brother. *Arnold the rock.* He's big-bodied and big-hearted. He places his palm on my shoulder and smiles. He knows the correct measure of a smile – not too large for this solemn occasion but enough to give me comfort. He nods and squeezes my shoulder. I try to remember when I last saw my big brother. Is it five years? Surely not. Some family reunion this is. If he didn't live so far away, I'd have visited him more often. He's the nearest I have to a dad, but I don't think he could deal with our mother anymore. I know how he feels, but somehow he always got the worst of her, as if he were Dad.

Some New Year this is. We should be breaking New Year resolutions now. Not saying goodbye to anyone. Not Tomas.

Now all I can think about is the fact that Tomas is sleeping inside that coffin. I should've gotten a better one. Vibrant. It should be more damn brilliant. Destiny would have painted it in spectacular colours. Rainbows. Yes, he deserves rainbows. I need to stand up and tell people to stop while I go get another one but my brother's hand is on my shoulder, pinning me to the chair.

I want to join Tomas in there for an eternal sleep. Oh, yes, a long sleep is what I need. I'm so, so tired.

I watch the chaplain standing at the podium, dais, whatever it's called. *Does he know why this happened? I don't know this man. He doesn't know me, or Tomas.* Words float up and out from the man's mouth. Meaningless. *God's plan? This is God's will? A will to rip my heart straight out of my chest? What did I do to deserve this shit?*

The man waits, clasping a heavy bound book against his chest, and bows his head. Is it my turn to speak? Arnold pushes the wheelchair to the front and squats behind me, leaving his thickset hand on my shoulder. The weight is good, but I can't bring myself to look up at the sea of faces in front of me. I don't want to see the blame in their faces, the accusations that I killed my boy.

With a shaking hand, I dig into my jacket pocket for the folded paper. This morning I tried to write something fitting for my son. I know the words on this piece of paper fail. I unfold it, willing my hands to be still. As I do so, there is a flurry of movement to my left. Hundreds of butterflies take to the air from a cage held by Finn. She returns my gaze with a long, slow nod and smiles. I wonder if she knows about the baby? Then I wonder about having butterflies in a church. Is that a good idea?

I see all the faces of my family, my whole body numb. I start to speak but no sound comes. I pause. Try again. There are no words. I screw up the paper into a tight ball. I can't even do this right. First, I kill my son, now I can't give him a decent send off.

Fuck!

The priest comes over to me and places a hand on my head and nods to the organist, making the sign of the Holy Ghost with his spare hand. As the lament of the organ fills the church, I realise that the coffin is being taken away.

There is my mother.

I hope that she might save me from the horror of saying goodbye. Tears stream down her face. She shakes her head with despair.

Mai wails louder.

red

I jerk awake. As I sit up, I can feel Destiny's eyes on me. I struggle to clear my mind. *How long have I been asleep?* I stand to move closer to her, but I can't read her face. She's staring straight at me but there is nothing of my beautiful wife.

'Hey, D, how're you doing?'

The words are lame. She continues to stare at me steadily. I have to turn away, the intensity too much. I'm thankful for the bandages secured around her head, but shudder when I look at her, remembering the blood and gore on *that* day.

I'm swaying. It's stupid to be lost for words with the love of my life. I swivel on my good leg to sit on the edge of the bed, wary of sitting on her. She doesn't move. I take hold of her hand.

'We're going to be okay, babe, just you see.' My voice is broken, rasping, my words falling into a chasm.

Something dark flits across her eyes, almost imperceptible. I don't know how to read her, so I continue to prattle on about the hospital. Meaningless small talk.

'Where's Tomas?' asks Destiny.

I recoil as if she's cracked a whip across my back. 'D, babe, you know where he is.'

'I want my baby.' Her voice is low.

Now I don't know if she's talking about Tomas or the lost baby.

'But, D, we lost him.' I break into a sweat; my scalp prickles.

'Well, find him now,' Destiny growls. Her voice isn't connected to her.

'D, I think you need more rest. I'll get the doc to come and help you. Okay, babe?'

Destiny looks at me, that unknown darkness lingering, and turns her head away.

I shuffle from the room, not knowing what to do. I can't lose both of them.

I limp to the nurse's station, searching for a doctor. They never seem to be around, only turning up at the important times.

'Ah, nurse, I really need to talk with the doc about Destiny.' I peer over the bench at her as she scribbles notes. The ward is dark, the lights turned low.

'What's the problem?' the nurse asks.

'I'm not really sure. She seems to have forgotten that Tomas is dead. She's asking me to find him …'

She nods and puts down her chart, pushes her glasses back up her nose. 'This is very normal, dear. She thinks if she doesn't acknowledge it, it won't be real.'

I have trouble concentrating on her words; my bottom lip is raw. Have I been chewing on it? 'So, when will she know it's real? Should I be doing something? And what about the baby she lost? Should we tell her?'

'It's a lot to process. She may not have known she was pregnant. I suggest you wait until you feel she's strong enough.'

It's good to have someone tell me what to do. I'm anchored. 'Okay.'

'Don't worry. You'll know when she's processed it. Just be patient. In the meantime, I'll get a counsellor to come in and have a chat with her.' She places a hand on my shoulder. 'Don't worry, love, you'll get there.'

I relax a little and give her my best smile, but it feels crooked, and must be grotesque.

I turn back towards Destiny's room. Fear holds me. I can't face her. How do we get through this? I don't know what to do with myself. I shuffle back to her room and watch her from the doorway. She doesn't move, her head facing the wall. I can't tell if she's sleeping or not. I plunge my hands into my pockets and turn away.

I turn into my room and Mum is waiting in the vinyl armchair next to my bed. A nurse has remade the bed and lunch sits waiting – coagulating – on a tray.

As soon as she locks eyes with me, she starts crying. 'How is she?'

'In denial.' I draw in breath, my ribs straining in my chest.

'Oh, Ash. If only you'd been able to swerve …' She dabs her cheeks with a tissue.

I let out the breath. The last thing I need right now is my mother. I don't want to hear about 'what ifs'. I do not have the energy to answer her. It was not a question anyway, so I sit on my bed and swing my legs up onto it. The pain is vast.

'I can't bear this, Ash. The loss is much too great.' Mum sits in the armchair and lets out a long, overdone sigh.

'What do you want me to say to that, Mum?' I try to keep out my anger but it's pushing at me. It edges into my voice.

'Oh, darling. I know it's hard for you. No parent wants to outlive a child, but a grandchild!'

'Get out.' I keep my voice low, try not to lose my shit.

'Why? I'm your mother! I want to help you get through this.' Her eyes widen.

'You know what? You're *not* helping. I'd really like you to leave.'

'But Ash …' She's dabbing at her eyes now.

I press the button for the nurse.

'Everything okay here?' The nurse is harassed. They're a team member down today.

'Can you please ask my mother to leave me alone?' I lay back on the pillows and close my eyes.

'Come, Mrs Anderson. Ash is in a great deal of pain. Let's give him some time to rest.' She takes Mum by the elbow.

Mum shrugs out of her grasp. 'No need for rough handling. I'll see myself out.' I hear her stomp out the door and along the corridor.

I reach for some painkillers, swallow them with metallic water. I lie back. Wait for them to take me away.

y bag is packed. I don't think I can wait for Sean to pick me up and take me home. It's only a ten-minute taxi ride. I pick up the phone in the hospital foyer and dial his work. The secretary says he's out back with a client and she'll give him the message when he comes in.

As the taxi pulls out into traffic my stomach churns. The smell of traffic fumes burns my nostrils and I see a flash of metal. I close my eyes to the memory and try to regulate my breathing. Try to think of home. What is home?

I jam the key into the front door and push at the handle. It sticks a little before opening to the silent house. I brace myself and step over the threshold.

A thought comes to me. Maybe the last weeks have been a dream, no, a nightmare, and Tomas is asleep in his bed right now.

I shamble towards my boy's bedroom, a smile ready on my lips as I burst through the door. But all that welcomes me is a darkening room. A beach ball sits on the rug beside the bed and two slippers are side-by-side on the floor, one a little skewed next to the other. The bed is made; no little body creates bulges under the covers, no night-light shines up towards the ceiling. No dark-haired boy lies sleeping in his dreams.

I frown at this scene, certain that I am about to wake. My breathing shortens and I sit heavily at the end of the bed, wrap my arms around my torso – holding my body together. I'm sure it will unravel at any moment; the skin will shred away and my pulsing veins will be exposed. I shiver but it must be at least twenty-eight degrees in here. Maybe the little bugger is hiding from me. I hear him giggle.

No! Ash, you fuckwit, he's not here.

I trace the spaceship on the bed cover with my finger. He is, *was*, so obsessed with space. Planets. He knew all the planets. I smile. I see him, head bent over his favourite book. Where is it? I search the room and spy it on the bookshelf: *Encyclopaedia of Space*. I smile and I'm safe. Yes, he's here.

I'm so tired. Smoothing the bed, I lie down, my big stupid head engulfing the child-size pillow. I push my nose into it, inhale, then gasp with pain as my ribs strain against my bruised chest. I kick off my shoes, aware that this place is sacred now. Turning onto my back, I try to imagine what this was like for my little man. It feels safe and happy. I study the ceiling where normally the night-light would shine, creating a halo above the bed, a myriad of stars.

Daddy is so sorry for not looking after you. Daddy was hot and grumpy on that day, and I promise never to be grumpy ever again.

I'm aware that you should never promise such a thing to a child because they always call you out on it when you don't keep a promise. But now I don't care what is right or wrong, I just want my son. I will make bargains, even with the devil, if it means having my boy back.

I hear sobbing. It is forlorn and wanton. Big gulping glugs of pain that fill the room to the ceiling. I sit up to search for the source, my chest heaving, sucking in air, realising that the sound is coming from me and yet feeling separate from it. Haven't I cried enough?

Heaviness descends on me in this wonderful place that smells of my lost boy. I allow my body to sink into the mattress and close my eyes.

A noise jolts me awake. I open my eyes to darkness without moving my body. 'Destiny? Tomas?'

I'm in the kitchen without realising I've moved, my ribs scraping within my chest. 'Hello? Destiny, is that you?' The mournful house remains silent except for the old whirring fridge that pops and wheezes.

I head straight for my armchair in the living room. The house is too quiet. There are no footsteps on the wooden floors as Tomas chases his big beach ball down the hall or the sound of Destiny chasing him. Squeals and laughter no longer fill every corner of the house. All I can hear is my own breathing, a labouring that isn't respectful.

I sit in my big old armchair, unable to get up again to find the remote to turn on the TV – I need to drown out the silence. I remember the cat but have no energy to get up and find her.

The night is growing old. I struggle to get comfortable, my ribs aching, my leg a dull throb. *How much out of ten?* the nurse would be asking me. I would shrug dumbly. My body shimmers and pulses. I can't pinpoint any sensation. It's all pain, but numbness at the same time.

The phone rings.

I've dozed off and it's a new day, the sun peeking through the closed curtains. My head is drunk heavy. I slept like a drunkard, too.

I push myself up from the chair, wincing, and shuffle to the kitchen. 'Hullo.' I struggle to make myself sound awake.

'Ah, Asher, my darling, it is you grandmother. I ring to see how our darling Destiny is.'

'Hi, Moma. What time is it?' I rub the back of my neck, stiff from sleeping upright.

'It is seven o'clock.'

'I was at the hospital yesterday, and Destiny was doing okay. But she doesn't believe that Tomas is … gone.'

The word *dead* can't be said out loud.

'Oh yes, I know how it is. The poor darling not want to think about her baby dead.'

I shudder and wonder how she can use the word so freely. 'What am I going to do, Moma?'

'You do nothing. She need time. You just need to look after her and make her well again. Time will come when she can pretend no more.'

'You always know what to say, Moma.'

'I have much experience with pain, my boy. You say hello to Destiny for me.' The phone clicks.

I sit back in my armchair and think about Destiny with the bandages wrapped around her head. I wonder what they're doing now, at the hospital. Is she having breakfast? Or is she still lying there facing the wall, waiting for Tomas to come in and show her his latest drawing?

My thoughts are interrupted when my eyes fall on a small box on the mantelpiece. I squint at the blue object, trying to read the silver script on the side. *Tomas Sean Anderson.* So small … I stand up and go over to the mantelpiece, finger the box. Without my glasses I can't read the inscription, but I assume it is the name of the funeral parlour. I have a flash of Tomas lying on the road. He is so peaceful. Not dead, just sleeping. I shudder, willing the image away.

I pick up the box and weigh it in my hands. Who put it here? Has Sean been here to check on the cat? *This is all that's left.* I sit heavily on the couch holding the box aloft, not wanting to disturb it. I close my eyes, remembering the size of the white coffin, a vision of Tomas sleeping peacefully inside. Something solid rises in my chest and settles in my throat. *Why! Why us?* I ease the lid from the box and stare at the plastic packaging. I can't stop my hands from trembling. I try to swallow the wedge in my throat that's firmly stuck there. I place the box gently on my lap and peel the plastic away from the contents. The ball dislodges from my throat and shunts from my mouth. *Tomas!* I sense the ghosts of my ancestors gather beside me, nodding. *Yes, that is all that is left. All the colours! You expected pure white ash, didn't you?* I dip my head and finger the contents with shaky fingers.

I stare at the ashes for a long time, unable to connect them with anything. I frown at the texture, touch a white particle. I recoil in horror. Bone! It's a fragment of bone! My fingers tingle as if burned. I squeeze my trembling lips together and hastily rewrap the plastic covering. The lid glides on with a sucking motion.

There's a sound in the hallway. My nerves are so ragged I no longer know if I'm imagining things. 'Tomas? Is that you?' I sit forward on the couch and cock my head to the side. There's a swishing sound brushing against the wall.

'Tomas?' I say as I heave myself up and slowly make my way to the mantelpiece. I return the box carefully to its place and walk to the door to the hallway. I can't move swiftly. Everything is in slow motion, my body not connected to me.

I pause, hear another sound, something scraping against the floorboards. I step out into the hallway.

'Who … who's there?' I expect to see Tomas facing me with his new beach ball wrapped up in his arms. But there's the damn cat. She saunters up to me and wraps herself around my ankles, meowing hello. There's a mixture of relief and disappointment at seeing her, then I remember that Tomas would never again be looking up at his daddy with his beach ball in his arms. I pick up the cat. She protests, then purrs. Her fur against my face smells clean and familiar.

I put her down and follow her to the kitchen and rummage in the cupboard beside the fridge for her food. I stop to stare at the bottles of liquor. I need something to calm me down, something to help me forget. I fill a glass to three quarters, then go back to my armchair. I sit down and flick on the TV. Taking a large swig, I grimace. Tuxedo meows loudly. Fuck, I forgot to feed her.

I go back into the kitchen. I poke around the freezer and throw a handful of ice cubes into my drink, take another swig, this time grimacing slightly less. This is not enjoyable. It doesn't take anything away. I hold the glass up to the light, hoping that the deep caramel liquid will provide some semblance of rescue. I take a long drink this time and cough, my chest burning. Warmth surges through my body. I close my eyes, willing the fluid to work a little faster, taking another swig, then another in rapid succession. The glass is empty. I refill it. I'm a little calmer. I scan the room. What was I doing? The cat waits patiently, tail swishing across the lino floor. She is regal. I scrape the cat food into her bowl and she sniffs at it distastefully, almost sighing as she tentatively pecks at it.

I go back to the TV and sit heavily in the chair. Air escapes the seat with a whoosh and immediately the cat jumps up in my lap and purrs. *Did I feed her?* I flick from channel to channel. It's all white noise. I turn it off, sit back in the chair. The cat sways a little in half sleep; her purring fills the room. I absently brush her coat. She purrs louder. I take another swig and grimace again. I put my head back and close my eyes.

The doorbell chimes. A glass falls from the arm of the chair as I sit up. I am confused, but I think it's empty.

'Destiny? Tomas?' I get up from the chair, the cat landing silently on her feet. I walk as quickly as possible down the hall to the front door, almost tripping on my boots. The doorbell chimes again. 'Yes, yes.' I say, opening the door. 'Destiny, you're home?'

A woman stands at the door with a baking dish in her hands. She is bewildered. 'Ash, no, it's, it's me. Finn. Isn't Destiny still in the hospital?'

I brush my hair out of my face, look at Finn, then past her, searching for Destiny. She should be back with Tomas now, shouldn't she? Is playgroup over yet? I try to focus. Finn's face comes into view. She's concerned and I can't figure why.

'Oh, hi, Finn, sorry, I was sort of nodding off. Lost track of time … Destiny should be back soon.'

Finn squints at me and sniffs. 'It's only ten in the morning, Ash. Are you okay?' She steps closer, ready to move into the house but I'm waiting for Destiny. Where the fuck is she? She always takes forever to get back.

'Yeah, sure, I'm fine, why?' I crane my neck to see over her but there's no sign of them. Now I can't remember what time playgroup finishes. Maybe it's too early.

'Hey, Ash, I've got a casserole here for you, I'm sure that cooking is the last thing that you want to think about.'

She makes a vague attempt to smile. I bring her into focus again. What the fuck is she talking about? *This sister of yours is loopy, Destiny.*

My breath hitches. Shit! Destiny is in the hospital. Tomas is … Fuck! I'm going mad. *Get your shit together, Ash.*

'Yeah, thanks, Finn.' I try to sound sane, but I'm sure she thinks I'm losing it. I blink, trying to think of something to say. But what do you say? *Hi, nice day, isn't it? Wife in hospital, son de—*

'Well, are you going to let me in? Ash, can I come in?' Finn steps towards the door. I step aside but she has to push past me to get inside the house. She's small, like her sister, and I breathe in a strong waft of jasmine from her hair.

Finn heads straight for the kitchen and puts the dish on the bench. She takes off her poncho, throwing it over a chair. 'Ash, I think we need a good strong cuppa. What do you think? Have you had breakfast?' She doesn't wait for me to answer, just continues to talk, puts on the kettle, opens the fridge, scans the contents. 'What have you eaten the last few days?' She begins throwing things straight from the fridge into the garbage bin.

Finn peers at me over the fridge door. I'm standing in the doorway, lost in my own house in my own body in my own life. I'm staring at the floor, studying the lino squares with careful consideration. The lines seem to suddenly be non-symmetrical.

'Ash?' Finn stands upright and closes the fridge door.

'I killed them, Finn,' I say, my body moving towards the floor. Something is pressing down on me from above, compressing me. I can't stand. Somehow, I'm on the floor, on my knees, my hands held up before me. Desperation envelops me. I want to die, want out of here now. I cannot and will not stay here another minute. 'I killed them; I killed my boy. How can I live now that they're gone?'

Finn runs over to me and kneels on the floor. She's close to me, the smell of jasmine warm and heady. Her small arms gather me to her and she pulls my head into her neck.

'No, Ash, no, it's not your fault. You can't blame yourself. The truck was on the wrong side of the road. Destiny is going to be okay.'

I'm sobbing now. Big wells of pain bubble up from my stomach and burst through my mouth. I'm ambushed from all sides. I can no longer hold it at bay. I unleash my pain into the kitchen in shudders and cries that could wake the whole city.

I'm at the hospital again. Same time as yesterday. This is my routine now. It's the only way to move through the day – watch the clock.

Tick.

This way, I don't need to think about anything.

Tock.

I can move one foot in front of the other, on auto.

Tick.

Destiny and I occupy the same space every day but we're mostly silent. What the fuck is there to talk about?

Tock.

One week, two, three. I'm losing count as each one merges into the next. The only difference being that Destiny's hair is growing, millimetre by millimetre. In fact, I think I can hear it growing. Yes, there, can you hear it? It's like a tiny little bug wriggling along her skin, blue-black against the scalp.

Most of the time, there's only about a metre of space between us but it may as well be the Gulf of Carpentaria or the Grand Canyon. If I touch her, she flinches. If I say, *I love you*, she just nods.

Just about the only thing of interest is the movement of bodies in and out of the room. Some stay one night, some two. The longest since Destiny's been here was two weeks. He had a burst appendix and oozed a vile green liquid for at least a week.

It's feeling like autumn now – her favourite time of year. When I leave at night there's a gentle balminess to the day that softens my seared edges. Summer has left me bereft in more ways than one.

And so, the time has crept forward, just like that bug that crawls across Destiny's head. The bandages are off now, so she is less like a mummified child. The scar on her face still makes me wince, though I try to hide my reaction. It runs the full length of her head from the top left temple, snaking its way all the way along her jaw, then stopping at her chin. It's pink and raw and reminds me of an earthworm.

And so.

My wife has become riddled with bugs and snakes and worms. But she is very much alive, and she hates me.

While Destiny's scar has changed its own landscape, my breathing has improved, and my ribs are almost mended. A four out of ten by now, I'd say. Tomas is not spoken of. We hover, suspended. Waiting for some defining moment. *What would this be?* I wonder. *How long can she play this game? Is it possible for her to stay locked inside that place forever?* I tremble at this thought. I've lost Tomas but at least I still have Destiny, but do I?

Every day, I enter her room hoping for that twinkle in her eye to let me know that she is back. Anything different to this slow, dripping, torture.

I sit in the visitor's chair beside her bed like some idiot interloper. I silently try to burrow into her brain, her soul, trying to find her buried beneath the bandages and painkillers that I think must be holding her captive. I'll slump back in the chair, defeated. But still, I'll call her in my head. *Destiny, where are you? Come back to me*, as if I'm searching for her in our backyard. I'll lean forward and grope for her hand, squeeze it gently. She'll turn to me and smile a stranger's courteous smile. It's far worse than no smile at all.

At home, I sit in her studio amongst her portraits to meditate. I foolishly hope that by chanting her name she'll come back to me. I need some proof that it's her in that body and not some imposter put there by some cruel god.

And so, this is the ritual continued every night after visiting the hospital. I plan to do this until she comes home to me. Be damned if I'm going to lose all three of them. I've added Tomas' name to the chanting even though I know that he won't come back. But we sit together chanting Destiny's name, willing her to come back to us.

What would we have called the next baby? I imagine a girl. I've searched the house for any evidence that Destiny knew she was pregnant but there's nothing. No pregnancy test, no GP visits. It's as if this baby never existed.

Nothing changes. I'll find Destiny just as I left her yesterday, her small body hardly disturbing the expertly made bed while she stares vacantly out at the changing leaves. Her favourite time of year.

'Destiny?' I nudge her shoulder.

'Hmm ...' She turns, groggy with sleep.

'It's time to get ready for the opening.'

She frowns.

'Remember? Your exhibition?'

She nods slowly, moves gingerly.

'You sure you want to do this? People would understand if you weren't there. Dr Michael isn't so keen for you to go.' I help her to sit up.

'No. I'm okay. Can't let Rhonda down. It's only for a couple hours.' Her eyes are lost to pain, fatigue, heavy drugs.

'I brought your blue dress. This the one you wanted?' I hold it up to her.

'Yeah. That's fine. What shoes did you bring?'

'Shit! I'll get Finn to pick them up on her way.'

Destiny shakes her head. 'Don't worry. I'll wear my slippers. They match. Kinda. I'm going to be in that stupid wheelchair anyway.' She sits on the edge of the bed, feet dangling, her small body enveloped by white. White hospital gown, white bandages, white sheets.

'Why do you have those on?' I point at the bandages on her head.

She deciphers my words.

'The bandages. I didn't think you needed them anymore.'

She nods, the words landing in the right place. 'I don't. But I don't want to freak everyone out tonight.'

'Okay, but we'll have to take them off to shower.' I help her to her feet, and we shuffle towards the bathroom.

Destiny sits on a moulded plastic chair, fingering the bandages. She unclips the end. Unravels them. The white cloth coils into her lap and I see her face more clearly.

'Is it really bad?' she asks.

I open my mouth, but nothing comes out. She sighs, touches the side of her face with a flat palm.

'Can you get me a mirror?'

I shrug.

'Ash?'

I want to tell her how beautiful she is, but I know she won't believe me. But she is beautiful, and that ugly scar hasn't taken anything away. It just takes a bit of getting used to.

'It'll get better, D. It's still healing.'

She spies the mirror over the sink and shuffles over to it. She peers into the small square. The bathroom is badly lit so I'm sure she sees something more grotesque than it is.

She touches the scar with the tips of her fingers, traces the ropey-ness like she's reading braille. She turns away, unreadable, and starts to undress.

'Ahh, who knew a shower could be so good?' says Destiny, eyes closed.

I smile at her. 'The simple things, huh?'

'Are there many people coming tonight?' Her face is tight.

'Pretty good turnout, I'd say. You have a good reputation.'

Destiny puts her hands on her hips. 'They probably want to gawk at the accident victim.'

'Come on, D, people like your work.' *But yeah, they probably do want to come and gawk at you, see how you're handling losing a kid …*

'We'll see. Not sure how Rhonda managed to make something out of those paintings. I wasn't finished.'

'She's done a great job. I was there this morning. She only left out two pieces. Here, let me help you with that.' I guide her dress over her head, avoiding her face as much as possible.

'I'm a ghoul!' says Destiny, standing timidly in her blue dress, the bandages freshly wrapped. 'I must have been crazy to let you talk me into this.'

'Me? It was Rhonda if I remember rightly. I didn't think you were ready.'

'Don't avoid the obvious. I may as well have come straight out of an Egyptian pyramid.'

'Maybe this might help?' I hold up a blue silk scarf.

'Ash, you're a genius!' She grabs the scarf and begins wrapping it around the bandages, straightening it while squinting at the mirror.

'I can't really take the credit for that. Finn's idea.' But secretly I lodge this small score into the bank. The first deposit.

Destiny nods. 'She knows me. How's this?'

'Beautiful, of course.' I stroke her arm. She flinches and I recoil as if burned, the account overdrawn again.

'Let's get you into that wheelchair. We've really gotta get going.'

'I feel like I'm going to a stupid wedding or something. They can all wait.'

She slumps into the wheelchair. At least no one will see how much weight she has lost sitting in the chair.

'Here's your slippers,' I say, sliding them onto her feet. I'm distracted by her toes; I count them. Still twelve. Would our daughter have had twelve toes like her mother? I want to ask her about the baby but now isn't the time.

'Told you they match,' says Destiny.

'So they do. Ready?'

She shrugs.

A yellow taxi pulls up to the front of the hospital. 'You take a wheelchair?' I ask.

'No problem, man.' The cabbie tries hard with the vernacular, his thick accent making it comical.

'Where's our car?' asks Destiny.

I'm thrown off course. 'It got totalled in the acc—'

Destiny stops me, her palm facing me like a traffic cop. She leans out of the wheelchair and fumbles into the back of the taxi, her face tight. As soon as the taxi moves out into the traffic, she squeezes her eyes shut and grips the edge of the seat, knuckles white.

The gallery is teeming with people by the time we arrive, half an hour late.

'Destiny!' Rhonda runs up to her, arms extended. She bends to hug her then, confused, air kisses her on either side of the head. 'You look amazing.'

Destiny scoffs. 'Hi, Rhonda.'

Rhonda kisses me. 'Amazing turn out, boss.'

'You've done a great job. Well done.'

'You ready, D?'

Destiny exhales. 'I guess so.'

The three of us enter the main gallery. There is barely space for the wheelchair but the crowd parts as soon as they realise who we are.

Someone close by starts clapping. Another person joins in. Soon the whole room is a thunder of applause. I raise my eyebrows at Destiny. *Told you*, I mouth. But I'm such a liar, I could never anticipate this reception.

Destiny is bewildered as a balding man in a too-tight suit approaches her. He bends down to kiss her on the cheek, 'Destiny, these paintings are spectacular! I've bought *Summer Solstice*. It's hot in so many ways!' He gives her a wink.

Destiny sits mute, her lips mouthing words that don't form.

A woman pushes the first man away. 'My turn, darling. You can't hog her all night. Destiny! What can I say? I bought *Twins*. Can't wait to have them in my lounge. You've outdone yourself.' She air-kisses Destiny on both cheeks and swans away.

Destiny doesn't have time to respond to any of the stream of people who line up to congratulate her. She sits and nods, face upturned. The only words forming are *yes* and *thank you*. I can see her neck getting sore from peering up.

'Hey, Rhonda, I'm worried Destiny will get tired. Can we give her a break?' I ask.

'Shit! How stupid of me. Let's get the official stuff started. That'll give her a break from the adoring fans. Can you believe this turn out? Almost half of the paintings are already sold!'

'Really! That's fantastic. That'll give Destiny a boost. C'mon, let's get this crowd organised.'

Rhonda shouts into the microphone, 'Whoohoo! Hello! Everyone, can I ask you to make your way down the front?'

The room is so packed that nobody needs to move, they just turn to face the podium. A hushed silence descends as they wait.

'Thank you, all, for making your way out tonight to help us launch this spectacular collection, *This is Destiny*,' says Rhonda.

The crowd erupts with whooping and wolf-whistles.

'I'm not going to bother explaining this exhibition because I think you all get it! More than half is already sold.'

The room explodes in clapping and more whistles.

Rhonda holds up her hands to quieten the room. 'I'd like to invite our special guest to open the exhibition, Mirka Mora.' Rhonda extends her arm to her left as Mirka ascends the three steps up to the podium.

The crowd goes nuts. Destiny is wide-eyed at seeing her idol in front of her. It's hard to hear Mirka over the crowd and before we realise it, she's leaving the stage.

Destiny holds her head.

'Hey, babe, how you doing?' I squat awkwardly beside the wheelchair.

'Not sure how much longer I can last.'

'Okay. The official stuff is over. Want me to make excuses?'

Destiny holds her head in her hands, her face contorted with pain. 'Yes.'

'Excuse me everyone! As you know, Destiny has been in hospital. She's a little worn out …'

People nod in sympathy and murmur in understanding.

We push through the crowd again, the paintings watching us, red stickers on just about every one of them. I lift Destiny into the car, her body light as a child and trembling. I wish I could take her home.

'You're a hit, D!' I say, buckling my seatbelt.

Destiny stares out the window. 'I don't even recognise those paintings. That's not me anymore …'

We sit in silence the whole way back to the hospital.

The nurse, Sheila, gets busy as soon as we wheel into the ward, seeing Destiny white and haggard. She *tuts*, tucking her into her bed and giving her a dose of morphine to send her off into Neverland.

I leave her there in her white bed, facing the wall, to go back to the silent house.

I check Tomas' bedroom. The bed is made, and everything is in place. I resist the temptation to park the slippers neatly side by side. It's almost twelve weeks now. Twelve slow, tortuous weeks. I can finally bring Destiny home. It's been lonely here without her. Without both of them. Although I talk to Tomas all the time.

Shit, I'm nervous. I don't know why. The house couldn't be any more ready for her. I should check Tomas' room again.

It's fine. I'm pretty sure that it's the same as it was the day before he left. Although I've been in here every day, been on the bed. I've probably used up his scent and there's nothing left for Destiny. I feel like a goddamn teenager. Hands are shaking, heart racing. I'm full of clichés. Get it together, Ash. This is a happy day. This is the first day of our new life.

Destiny is sitting on the chair next to her bed, the nurse having already made the bed up for a new patient. She is wearing her black leggings and a long black jumper. She is so small, fragile. Her hair is short now because it was shaved on one side to deal with those ghastly wounds. My stomach turns at the memory of them. She is elfin with this hair. I want to gather her into my arms to protect her.

I won't touch her, though – been stung too many times. I know she still hates me. I hate myself. I plan on spending the rest of my life making it up to her.

I step into the room, not knowing if she's aware that I'm here. She turns towards me. She's staring right through me. She's stuck somewhere, unreachable.

'Hey, babe, you ready?' I force words out.

She stands and walks over to her bags. I beat her to them. There's a slight burn in my damaged leg at the sudden movement.

'D, you can't be lifting anything heavy, your arm still isn't right.'

She stands upright, winces.

I study her more closely. She won't look at me. I step closer to her in an attempt to connect with her, but she steps back the tiniest bit. Or is it a flinch? Annoyance rises in my gut. Why is she pushing me away? But I *do* know. I haven't protected my family. I deserve it. Telling myself this doesn't seem to lessen the frustration, though. I don't know what to do with this knot that keeps binding up my insides. Who can I direct this irritation towards? Destiny for not reaching out to me? The truck driver for being a bloody idiot? I know it was my fault for being a grumpy shit that day but *Jesus* it was hot and that damn air con just wouldn't get going. Maybe if I'd been more attentive I could've avoided the truck, seen it earlier?

I'm shunted out of my thoughts by a sniff. I'm pretty sure Destiny is crying.

'Hey, shh babe, it's gonna be okay.' I try to be convincing, but I know I'd never make an actor. I step towards her again but what I want doesn't happen, no melting of her small body into my waiting arms. I sigh and hoist her bag from the ground. 'Well, we may as well get home. Don't know about you but I'm sick of the sight of this place.'

Destiny's head bobs. I take it for a yes and we leave the room. It's a long walk with my bad leg and her slow shuffle. I imagine we look like extras from a Michael Jackson video. An old guy watches us in the corridors. I scowl at him.

The quietness of the house is profoundly amplified when I push open the front door with the weight of Destiny's bag. I can hear the pounding of my heart as if through a loudspeaker.

I take the bag through to our bedroom at the end of the hallway. I drop the bag and retrace my steps.

'D, you okay?'

She is poised at the doorway to our son's bedroom, her body up against the closed door.

'Want to go in?' I ask.

Destiny drops her head and leans in against the blue door. The little wooden sign that says 'Tomas' drops sideways. She shudders and squeezes her eyes shut. I go to her as quickly as my stupid legs allow and envelope her shoulders with my arms.

'It's okay, D; we can get through this together.'

I turn the doorknob and push the door away from us. Destiny shrinks, not moving.

I've just realised, with relief, that she hasn't rejected my physical touch. This is going well; yes, we can get through this together, can't we? I guide her towards the bed, and she sits tentatively on the end of it. I see our son's room through her eyes as her head moves in a circular motion: the wall of books to her left, the giant teddy from the local school fete last year, the paintings from playgroup on the wall in front of her, the little table with some pieces of Lego scattered across it, and then to her right, as her head moves towards the other end of the bed, there is the drawing from the day before. The day before *it* happened when we were out the back drawing loony tadpoles. She freezes, stares at the picture. I recall vivid details of Tomas and me sticking it to the wall. I'm surprised that Bert is still holding on.

'D, shall I put the kettle on?'

I'm lost. A cuppa fixes everything, doesn't it?

She doesn't answer.

Instead, she kicks off her slippers and slowly moves up the bed to lie down. I can understand that. I've done the same over and over. She's going through the motions that I went through but she's a couple of months behind. Let's hope she catches up so we don't spend the rest of our life out of sync. I need to tell her that I've done this, too. That each day gets just a tiny bit easier. But I don't think she's ready to hear it. I'm not sure that I really believe it myself.

Her eyes are closed, her elfin head dark against the pillow. She is a better fit than me. She curls herself into a small ball, wraps her arms around her torso. I wish that I could curl up with her, then all three of us would be together, but I know that she needs to be alone with him. The bed is too small anyway.

I leave the room, closing the door behind me.

The sounds of Destiny washing herself in the bath make me tingle as if it is my own skin receiving treatment. I close my eyes and follow the contours of her naked body with my fingers. I feel every goosebump. The small mole under her left breast helps me navigate her form as my memory of each landmark brings me to her stomach, then her thighs. Finally my hand rests on my own thigh and then my erection.

All desire vanishes when I remember Destiny's face the last time I had an erection in front of her. She didn't say anything, but I inferred it to mean, *How can you want sex when our baby is dead?*

I've watched her scars turn from angry, livid pink to ragged silver, and I still wait for her to forgive me. I'm ready to start living again but all she can manage is to sigh. If she would just come back to me from her faraway place, I could start to make it up to her. We can be happy again. But when can we start?

I lie on the bed, propped up on an elbow, and watch Destiny through the half-open door of the bathroom. I watch her as she emerges from the bath, her skin glistening from the heat of the water. Her smallness still awes me, even after so many years, and the memory of her being pregnant with Tomas makes me smile. I fall back on the bed contemplating the ornate cornices of the bedroom ceiling. How many arguments did we have about the colours to paint this damn room? I shake my head. It'd be good to have something like that to fight about now.

I inhale deeply and get up. I'm restless. Sex would help but I know that isn't going to happen. And I don't have the energy to take care of myself. It's getting late but not late enough for sleep. God knows that sleep comes to neither of us these days. I make my way down the hallway, past Tomas' untouched bedroom and out onto the back deck. Winter is pretty much settled in now, everything dormant, quiet. I cross my arms over my chest, the muscles flexing against themselves. Can we ever be normal again? Is this how it will be forever? I guess I deserve a lifetime of punishment.

In the next street, a dog barks at something. I close my eyes and see Tomas playing out here. Sadness wells up inside me, but I've cried so many tears. I think they're all used up. I try to squeeze some out. It would be a good release.

Daddy loves you, little tadpole. Daddy loves you.

I remember holding my son in my arms at the car wreck and shudder. No man should outlive his child. *Children.*

I turn to walk back into the house, walk from room to room until I come to his room. I sit on the bed. I can't say it's untouched anymore, but it's the same as the day he left it. Our sanctuary. I search the room, surprised how it has not changed at all. 'Hey, Destiny, when did you last go into Tommie's room?' I strain to hear her answer, unsure if she can hear me.

'I come in here every day.' She stands in the doorway. 'I haven't touched anything, except the bed. I lie in there to talk to him, then I remake it.' She thinks it a reasonable activity, this talking to the dead. It is. I've been doing it longer than her.

'Does he talk back to you?'

Destiny's face tightens. 'Is that a joke?'

'No, D, it's a serious question. I talk to Tomas, too, but he doesn't talk back to me.'

'Well, no, he doesn't talk to me either. I just hope that one day …' She hugs herself.

Her clothes are dishevelled. She isn't wearing any bangles, no coloured things in her hair. She hardly brushes her hair these days.

'Hey, D, have you done any painting lately?' I dive right in. Fearless. No, foolish.

Destiny stiffens. She shakes her head and tucks some hair behind her ear as she so often does absentmindedly. Only it's not long enough yet to warrant it. 'I don't have any projects at the moment, so I haven't bothered to get out my paints.'

'You never needed a project before.' I know I'm pushing into dangerous territory now, but I want something to goddamn happen. I no longer care about being sensitive.

'There's nothing I want to paint.' Her tone is flat.

'If Tomas were here, you'd be painting with him.' I hold my breath, waiting for the tirade. Hoping for it.

There is that familiar dark flash in her eyes. I almost smile. Aha! I chew on my bottom lip, try to keep it under control.

'He isn't here though, is he?'

Heat flows from her. Pure anger. Yes! She turns her body towards me flat out and leans into the room, her arms rigid at her sides.

'And he will never be here, so why should I bother painting ever again?' She rises onto her toes in an attempt to tower over me. It's almost comical.

'No, he isn't fucking here. Does that mean we just curl up and die ourselves?' I know this is risky, but she can't hate me any more than she already does.

She starts to say something, then closes her mouth. Her face crumples. I want to take it all back.

'Yes, I want to be dead, I want to be with my baby. I want to be with him right now!' She turns on her heels and runs. I jump up from the bed and follow her. She's crying now, running from room to room, hunting for a way out. I catch up with her at the front door and grab her around the waist before she can open the door and run out into the night. She struggles, screaming. Flailing. She ducks down out of my arms, but I manage to grab her, hold her firmly. I hold her as close as I possibly can. She is soon weary.

'I just want my baby back,' she whimpers. She melts into me as I rub her back.

'I know, I know, I want him back, too.' My voice croaks.

Destiny pulls away from me, walks down the hall. 'I'm tired. Going to bed.'

I stay where I am, standing at the front door, my arms loosely by my sides. A deep sadness washes over me. How will we ever get past this?

M oma sets the teapot in front of me. 'Can you pour this for me, Asher dear? My wrist plays up today.'

I lift the pot and inhale the rich aroma. It's one of those smells that always reminds me of her. She is very frail today, which frightens me. I need her badly now.

She shuffles from the kitchen with a plate of biscuits. She smiles knowingly as she places them in front of me. Do I imagine a twinkle in her eye? She eases herself into her big armchair, expelling air as she does so.

'Ah, dear Asher, your old moma isn't as lively as she once was.'

'You're doing very well, Moma, considering what your life has been.'

'Ha. All my troubles a very long time ago.'

'Well, how has your week been?'

'Ah, so you change the subject on your old Moma, is that how it goes?'

'I don't want to bring back bad memories for you.'

'You think I ever forget?'

'I'm sure you don't. I don't even know how you went on living after it.'

'Ah, mysteries. You live in spite of atrocities. Or you live to spite the people that wronged you. Who knows, Asher?'

'There are times when I don't have a reason to live.'

'What! What you tell me, Asher?'

'Tomas is gone, and Destiny is living but gone.' Should I mention the lost baby?

'And you would give up that easily?'

'I don't know what to do.'

Her brows furrow. She is silent, fingering a loose thread on the arm of her chair. 'You are the only one who means everything to me,' she says quietly.

'You still have Mum, Arnold, and Sam.' I'm ashamed. What a spoiled brat I am.

'You mother and I was never close, and you know how I think of Samuel. Arnold lives too far away. He is stranger.'

I am sad she and Sam haven't been able to patch things up. But I say nothing. Sam isn't one who needs defending. 'I don't know what to say. I don't know how to deal with this shit.'

Moma frowns. 'You think you are the only one in the world to go through this, how you say, *sheet*?'

Heat flushes my cheeks. 'She blames me, Moma, for Tomas. And I blame myself. I'm an idiot. I don't deserve to have Destiny or Tomas.'

'It was accident. If blame is made, it is at truck driver!' She is animated now and cursing under her breath in Polish.

'You don't know how I feel, how I lie in bed at night, not sleeping, listening to her sigh beside me.' Anger rises at the unfairness of life.

'I don't know how you feel?' She stands in front of me now, both fists clenched at her sides. Instantly she is ten years younger.

Fuck! How could I be such a fool? The ghosts of those lost and forgotten press in around the room to rise up behind Moma, glaring at me.

'I know how you feel, Asher. I spend fifty-five years not sleeping. I had to choose between my brother and my mother. I could not choose, so I chose myself, thinking that I was smart. Well, some smart alec I was. They laugh at me, take them both away. I never see them again!' Her shoulders slump and she's suddenly old again.

I stand to embrace her, tears brimming. She's howling now, beating at my chest with her fists. I pull her down to the couch while still enveloping her with my arms, holding her tightly, rocking gently, kissing her forehead. 'Shhh, it's okay, Moma. I'm so, so sorry.'

It's getting dark. I pull away from her. We're both exhausted. We sit on the couch in silence, the sounds of peak hour traffic increasing outside.

'I have idea, which might help.'

'I'm sorry for being such a spoilt brat.'

'You are not spoilt brat. You hurt. I know how it is to hurt. Destiny, too.'

'I wish I could take away your hurt.'

'That can never happen. Let us not worry about the past. We must find a way to go on. I miss my little Tomas, as well.' She heaves a sigh that brings her upright.

'What's your idea?'

She hesitates, starts to speak, then stops and looks out the window. She pushes herself from the couch and walks around the table to switch on the lamp. I sit forward on the edge of the couch in anticipation.

'There is somewhere that you and Destiny can go to get away from the city. Somewhere that Tomas is not reminder.'

'What do you mean?'

'I still have house in country. No one live in it for long time. You and Destiny should go there for holiday.'

I try to make sense of her words. Country? Then I remember the old farm. Sam and I went there for the summer holidays for years.

'I thought you sold it years ago.'

'You grandfather and I buy it long time ago. We wanted to live there and make a life where we could grow our own food to be preparing for anything. But the land in this country is very harsh. It is hard to grow things. It was hard to be away from other people.'

'It's been years since I was there. I can't remember how far it is.'

'Not far. Maybe one hour.'

'Why don't you talk about this place?'

'You been there many, many times when little boy. You and Samuel would come to stay with us to give you mother a holiday from being with you both.'

I nod, flashes of memory coming to me. I can understand the need for a break. Sam and I were a handful. 'Did Arnold come, too?'

'No, he would stay at home to help you mother. It was the only time for him to get her attention.'

I rummage around in my memory. I have vague images of the farm, but it could be anywhere, even from a television show. 'But when did you leave there?

'I not remember. Many, many years.'

'Why'd you leave?'

'It make you grandfather crazy. I not want him to go there anymore.'

'Is it haunted or something?'

'No, it just you grandfather. He go strange there. I think it from the war.'

'Maybe I could go and see it?'

'Yah, that be good. You go before you talk to Destiny.'

I pull up to the wire gate, tyres crunching on the dirt road, grab the scrap of paper that Moma gave me and check the number. 'Lot 26' is painted roughly on a piece of scrap wood nailed to the fence post, so I guess this is it. I tentatively open the cattle gate and limp along the road, feeling like an intruder. Nothing is familiar. I count backwards. How many years would it be? Fifteen? Twenty?

The liquid calls of a bellbird make me smile. I pause to follow their progress amongst the trees, but they are elusive. A clearing appears ahead and there stands the farmhouse, quiet and lonely. I hesitate at the front of the house and lean against a tree, watching it. Vague memories come to me but nothing solid. Despite having permission to be here, I don't want to go inside. Instead, I wander around the perimeter of the house, look at the veggie-patch choked with weeds, peer into the water tank that backs onto the house. My skin prickles with anticipation, I guess I want this to be our solution, but it's not clicking for me.

I stand next to an old tree, withered and gnarly. I think it's an apple tree. The bark rough against my palm. I swear it whispers something to me. *Hello?* I must be hearing things or maybe it is just the way the breeze travels through the bush. A hushing sound that is soothing. I stroke the tree: *Hello back.*

There's an overgrown track that goes downhill from the back of the house to the swimming hole. That's something I do remember, so I stride along the track with purpose.

There's the river. I always thought it was a long way from the house but it's only, maybe, two hundred metres. Standing at the edge, I suck in air. A breeze skips across the water, rippling the surface and fluttering amongst the gum trees. The pool is not as I remember it. Years of flooding have changed the contours of the river, but it's familiar.

The smooth stones gleam under the surface of the river. I imagine myself here with Destiny and a brood of children eating watermelon. They're over there on that fallen log, juice dribbling down their chins, cackling with glee, dodging each other's pips as they fly through the air. I watch myself grab a big fat rope and go hurtling into the pool like Tarzan.

A skink rustles through the bushes. The hairs on my neck bristle and I scoff at myself, remembering that I'm alone, there's no one here to see my skittishness. The temptation of the river is too much to ignore. I look around the bank and back up the track for any signs of life. It's foolish to be modest. I shrug off my t-shirt and jeans. It's not especially warm. The midday sun is weak through the trees, spring barely arrived. Discarding all my clothes onto the rocks, I hold up my arms as if in battle and run headlong into the water.

I am hit by an electric shock. The icy water slices pain right through my body. I resurface with a gasp that is a mixture of pain and exhilaration. *Arrggh!* My body erupts in goosebumps, and an uncontrollable shivering takes over.

Soon I've adjusted to the temperature, though I have no feeling in my fingers and toes. I get a good idea of what it must be like to die of hypothermia, and this water isn't nearly that cold. The river is crystal clear, not like the river in Melbourne that is like a dirty soup. My naked body is morphed below the surface. Little fish swim around my legs. They are probably harmless, but are there eels here? Or maybe other fish that we can catch and eat? I've never been fishing, so that's something I should try one day.

I emerge to sit on the fallen log, the bark rough against my butt. I'll have to drip dry. I wish the sun was stronger but I feel alive, invigorated. I think even my leg is a little better? Probably just gone numb! It's impossible *not* to respond to this place. The tall silent river gums sway in the breeze, whispering to me. I nod. The stream babbles as it flows busily over the rocks in the shallows. It dances in little rapids and swirls, impossibly clear and pure, the sunlight shooting rainbow colours into the sway. All this exists here while the rest of the world toils away. I am full of joy and belonging. My chest might burst open and spill it all out and be lost.

Yes! This is what we need. This is where we can find each other again, find some way to move forward. Staying where we are is only going to keep us in a holding pattern. How long can we sustain that?

I dress quickly; need to get her here now. My damp feet won't allow my socks to go on easily – coarse grains of sand are stuck between my toes – so I brush my feet and jam them into my shoes. I'm halfway up the track, still buckling my belt, the trees urging me on.

I glance at the house in passing. Is it smiling? I stop, put my hands on my hips. I move on. *I'll be back. See you soon.* There is a rustling through the old fruit orchard. Am I'm being waved at?

Back in the car, reality hits me. *Will Destiny go for this? Am I mad?* She'll like the river and the veggie-patch will be a challenge. There's nothing to lose. No more than we already have.

The long winding drive home gives me plenty of time to rehearse my words, but also plenty of time for my anxiety to increase. As I pull up to our little house. I look at it as if it's a stranger.

I grab the front doorknob; my heart is stuttering. I don't know what I'll do if Destiny isn't into the idea. We need this.

I throw my keys down on the hall table. 'D?' I call.

'I'm just here,' says Destiny from the stove.

'Oh, hi, babe.'

'What've you been up to?' she says over her shoulder.

'Hey, you wouldn't believe where I just went.'

'Hmm …'

'Destiny, I want you to think about something for me. This is a big idea, but I have a really good feeling about this.'

She pulls herself up; I'm deflated. She says nothing but continues to nudge at some onions frying in the pan.

I shut my mouth, fearful that my babbling will put her off. She continues to push the onions around the pan aimlessly. She shifts her weight onto the other hip. All I can hear is the ticking of the kitchen clock and the sizzling of the pan.

'Moma has a farmhouse in the country. She says that we can stay there for a while, have a little holiday there. We can stay as long as we like.'

'Since when does Moma have a house in the country?'

'She's had it for a while. She lived there with Zeke when they first came to Australia.'

'Is that where you used to go for your summer holidays?'

'Yep.'

'I thought they sold it years ago.'

'I thought so, too, but Popa wouldn't let it go.'

'What's it like?'

'It needs a bit of work, but the land is beautiful, untouched. And there's a river.' The river will be the sweetener.

'Well, Ash, you do have some pretty wild ideas,' she says.

My body slumps. I flop onto the nearest kitchen chair and watch her back in despair, scrambling around in my brain for a good argument.

'But I'm into seeing it.' She turns to me, brandishing her wooden spoon like a schoolteacher.

'What did you say?'

'Let's give it a try.' She is passionless, so I'm not sure if I heard right.

'You mean you *are* willing to leave here for a while?' I say hesitantly.

'I hate this house,' says Destiny.

I'm shocked. *Really? Why?* But I'm too focused on the positive outcome to go there.

'How would we earn a living though, Mister Genius?' says Destiny matter-of-factly.

I laugh at this. She's always the one with the harebrained ideas. I study my wife closely. We really are strangers.

'Oh, I haven't thought about that just yet. I wasn't sure that you'd be into it. Your exhibition did very well, so that'll keep us going for months.'

I resist the urge to grab her around the waist and kiss the life out of her.

'Destiny?'

'Yeah?'

'I love you.'

'I know.'

'This is going to be a great thing for us.'

Her face clouds over momentarily but then she smiles weakly. 'Yes … we need something.'

W e drive up to the house and stop under the gnarled old apple tree. Destiny stands in front of the house, hands on hips. *Is she talking to it, too?* She stomps up the three steps to the veranda and plunges the key into the lock. The door opens with a loud creak.

'Needs oil.'

She doesn't stop, just pushes on, inspecting each room. I follow, taking in small details, the layers of dust over everything. The inspection doesn't take long because there are only four rooms. Destiny opens doors and cupboards, making a list in her head, I guess.

At the back door, she cranes her neck to scan the yard. 'Where's the river?'

I point to the path, and she heads straight for it. I catch up to her at the pool, her small back squaring me off. Her eyes are closed, face turned up to the trees. Is she sniffing, or breathing in the clean air? Quietly, she peels off her layers of clothes, walks straight to the edge and plunges in. She breaks the surface with a yelp.

'Fuck, this is cold!'

I grin.

She swims up and down the river, every now and again duck-diving to the depths of the pool. Finally, she emerges dripping and pink and falls onto her back on the sand, her naked body spread out under the trees in submission. I follow suit but find it hard to stand the icy water for long, my toes curling up in protest.

We lay beside each other, shivering in the cool breeze, the sun peeking through the leaves. The cold has numbed me but my skin is invigorated. I want to know what she's thinking but I'm too scared to break the silence. I turn my head. With her eyes closed, she is peaceful, and I can't help but stare at her nipples that stand to attention. My dick stirs. It brings back a distant memory of a beach on the east coast where we nuzzled amongst the sand dunes.

'I'm starving!' says Destiny, pulling on her singlet. Her nipples poke through the fabric. I groan inwardly.

'Hot drink would be good,' I say as I pull on my jeans over my erection.

'Let's sleep here tonight,' says Destiny.

'Really? We didn't bring bedding or much food.'

'There's enough bedding here and we have the esky with our picnic stuff. We won't starve. Just one night.' Destiny marches up the path towards the house.

The taps in the kitchen splutter rusty water from the tank that soon clears. We go out to the tank but can't see into it.

'How are you meant to know how much water's in there?' I ask.

Destiny's eyes twinkle with amusement. 'Easy, you duffer. You just go tap it up and down until the sound changes.' She goes up to the tank and bangs on it with her fist. 'It's almost full,' she says with pleasure. 'That means I can boil up some water, clean this place out, and maybe even have a bath.'

'Ah, but there isn't a bath around here anywhere, there isn't even a bathroom. Is that a toilet house over there?' I point at the tiny building with its door tilting awkwardly on its hinges.

'It's called an outhouse … Anyway, I'll figure something out for a bath.' She starts collecting wood in her arms.

'What're you doing, D?'

'Time to see if that old potbelly works and make you that hot drink. The electricity isn't on, so we need fire to boil the water. Come on, lazy bones, you're the one who wanted a tree change. It'll be hard work to get this place going.' She trots off, bending to pick up twigs as she goes.

She lights the fire in the potbelly. Soon enough there's a fire roaring in it and a pot of water boiling away on top of it. This first cup of tea is the best I've ever had, and I can't take my eyes off her as she bustles around the house.

An hour, maybe two, passes. There's washing hanging out under the eucalypts. All the furniture is heaped out the front of the house and the floor is mopped. I've watched Destiny with delight. I follow her, accepting her orders to carry this bucket and move that chair. After eight or nine months of sighing, this is a small relief. I'm hoping this will last longer than just this day. She isn't smiling, exactly, but she is determined and busy. A sense of purpose surrounds her.

We're carrying the kitchen table back inside, trying to manoeuvre the legs through the door. An old ute pulls up beside our car and stops. A man heaves himself out of the driver's door, his big-booted feet creating puffs of dust as they hit the ground.

Destiny and I stop, the table held between us.

'Gidday! Saw smoke comin' out the chimney. Place's been empty for a long time, so thought I better check it wasn't on fire.' His voice matches him – big and cumbersome. 'The name's Bruce.'

I put down my side of the table so that Destiny has to follow. I smack my hands on my clothes to rid them of dust and walk over to the man to shake his hand.

'Um, hi, how are ya, mate?' I say.

'And your name'd be …?' says Bruce with a grin.

'Oh, sorry, Bruce, my name's Ash and this is Destiny.' I turn to face Destiny with raised brows.

'Wow, them's funny names, ain't they? Where you folks from?'

I don't really like how familiar the man is and want to wind up the conversation quickly. 'We're staying here for a while; my grandmother owns the place.'

'Oh, yeah, Rebecca, eh? Haven't seen her an' Zeke out here for years. How the hell are they?' Bruce screws up his face as he grinds a fingernail into his earhole.

'Rebecca is okay, but Zeke died about two years ago.' I wince – two years.

'Oh, sorry, mate. Didn't know. That Zeke was a real good bloke.'

'And how do you know them?' I'm getting annoyed with this visitor; he's too familiar with my family.

'I live next door at the Patterson farm. It was me dad's, you see, and when he kicked the bucket, I took it over.' He shuffles a toe at the powdery soil. 'I was pretty young when your grandparents lived here, but. Don't know why they didn't come here no more. When I was about twelve, I'd hang around after milking time with that Zeke, and he'd tell me stories about Poland. Some of 'em made me skin crawl but I think he needed to tell someone. Now I think they probably weren't stories for a twelve-year-old but, hey, they lived those horrible things, ya know?' Bruce continues to scuff at the ground absentmindedly.

It's odd talking to a stranger about my grandfather. I turn back to Destiny, but she's gone into the house.

'Mate, it's been good to meet you. We've gotta get this stuff sorted but once we're settled in, maybe we could get together. Have a beer or something?'

'Oh, yeah, that'd be great, mate,' the older man says passionately. 'I could tell you lotsa stories about your old man, too. I helped him build that bunker, ya know.'

I overlook the fact that Zeke isn't my old man. 'Did you say bunker?'

'Don't you know? It's bin a few years, can't rightly remember where it is neither, but, that old Zeke, he got it in his head to build this bunker, right, in case of a war. It's not far from the house neither. Probably overgrown with weeds an' stuff. Mighta fallen down even ...'

I search my memory for a bunker but find nothing. I'm wondering what to do with this man when Destiny comes out laden with a tray of cups.

'Well, the missus knows what to do, eh?' Bruce chuckles.

'Thought we could have a cuppa since we've been working so hard.' Destiny puts the tray on the kitchen table.

'Too right, ah, Destiny, cuppa'd go down a treat.' Bruce walks up the steps to the veranda, helps himself to a mug, then heaps it with three teaspoons of sugar.

'I don't remember you when I came to visit as a kid,' I say.

'Yeah, probably around the time I went off to uni. Did animal studies. Then I met Mary and we travelled a bit.'

'Makes sense.' I pick up my mug. 'Hey, D, Bruce reckons my grandfather built a bunker here.'

I roll my eyes at Destiny. She frowns.

'Yeah, it were built into a rock face an' I remember there was a tree real close, so it were well hidden. That Zeke had it real well organised. Spent a lot of time in there. He liked to scribble in a little book. Said he was writing his life story. Sometimes he'd cry though, an' talk in his foreign dago language. He was good to me, though – would let me hang out with him an' teach me stuff. It were him that taught me to tie a good strong knot in a rope.' Bruce stops talking, drops his head in embarrassment.

'Do you reckon you could help me find this bunker?' I ask.

'Could give it a try. It weren't far from the house.' Bruce raises a hand to his hat, lifts it and scratches his head with his other hand. He turns his head to scan the yard, squinting in each direction, scratches his head again and replaces his hat.

'Hey, you two, maybe we could hunt for secret bunkers later, when we have this house sorted?' Destiny stands with both hands on her hips and bobs her head at the furniture that litters the yard.

'Yeah, righto, how's about I give youse a hand here?' Bruce downs his tea and wipes his mouth with his sleeve.

He helps me carry the table back into the kitchen. The rest of the sparse furniture is soon back in the house and Destiny brings in the washing from the line. She makes up the bed on its wrought iron base, using hospital corners like she learnt from Moma.

Bruce lingers on the veranda when we've finished, peering out at the trees in concentration. 'Hey, um, Ash mate, I can't see where that bunker might be. It's getting late now, but maybe tomorrow, after I've done the cows, I could come help ya find it?'

I lean on the doorframe, observing the trees. 'Yeah, okay. No hurry, mate, we've got plenty to do around here anyway.'

'You should really think about clearing this place out too, 'cos its coming up to bushfire season, ya know?' Bruce is serious.

'What do you mean – clear it out?'

'Ya need to make a clearing 'round the house. Get rid of all the dead wood an' stuff. Otherwise, youse giving a fire plenty of dinner to feast on.'

'Oh, okay, I'll think about that.'

'Now don't go being a slack bastard, mate, bushfires is serious business. I'll get some of me mates over an' we'll give youse a hand.'

I envision a mob of Bruces descending on the house and shudder. 'Don't worry 'bout it, mate. We'll work it out.'

Bruce shakes his head. 'Just give us a hoy when you need some help. Country folks is always ready to help. This place is well stocked up to feed a fire, hasn't been cleared out for years.' He adjusts his hat.

'Okay, thanks, Bruce, for helping with the furniture.' I hold out my hand.

'No worries. We's neighbours now, so just give a yell if youse need anything. Tell Destiny I'll see her later, eh?' Bruce gets in his car and reverses away from the house, dust billowing in his wake.

We eat as darkness descends quickly over the little house. I light some candles Destiny found under the sink and sit amongst the flickering lights. It's very romantic and all I want is to draw her to me, breathe her in, smell the river water and fresh air.

We're exhausted. We slide into the freshly made bed and lie there, listening to the creaking stumps of the house. A light breeze rustles in the trees outside the window, everything unfamiliar.

There's a tapping against the iron roofing above us that's soothing as it increases in depth and time. It's raining. The pitter patter is hypnotic, and we sink into the pillows surrounded by the bush. The smell of rain permeates the room.

'Nothing like fresh sheets, eh?' I balance on one elbow searching for Destiny's outline in the dark.

'Yeah. If I was rich I'd get someone to change the sheets every day.'

'Did you bring this bedding?' I ask.

'Mmm? They were in a metal trunk at the end of the bed. I think they're linen. They're soft from being washed so many times. Can you believe how white they are? There's even hand-embroidered initials on them.'

'Is that what all that washing was?'

'Yeah. It's been packed away so long, smelled of moth balls …'

'What are the initials?'

'Umm, RF.'

'I think they must be Moma's.'

'Mmm …'

I let Destiny sink into sleep. I'm happy to have her warm, naked body against me. My brain fires up. I'm thinking about the baby. I don't think Destiny knew she was pregnant. What would be the use of talking about it, only to make her upset if she didn't know? Wouldn't it just compound the pain of losing Tomas? I resolve to leave it alone. What she doesn't know won't hurt her. At eight weeks, could you say it was actually a baby anyway? It's good to be able to put this to rest, stop thinking about it. We need to try to get back to some kind of normal life, maybe even think of having another baby.

What a fantastic day this has been. It's a small step away from the limbo we've been in. I'm so grateful to Moma for suggesting we come here. Even this one day has been great medicine.

And what about this guy, Bruce? Real salt of the earth, he seems to be. I get the feeling you can't do much without the neighbours knowing about it. I'm interested to hear more about Popa from him.

I thought I knew my grandfather, but I guess there's more to him. I try to imagine them here, in this bed. I can't see it. Moma's words come back to me. *Funny in the head.* What did she mean?

They are different people through the eyes of Bruce. I guess this is normal from family. You only see one side. I'm the grandson. I know them as doting old people, but they lived a lifetime before I really knew them. I'll ask Bruce questions tomorrow about what they did here.

And the bunker.

Exhaustion steals over me. The house whispers, laughs, and I fall asleep, smiling.

I wake before light. It's colder than I expect. I dress, wishing I had my Ugg boots. 'I'll make tea,' I say to Destiny.

She is croaky with sleep. 'Okay. No hurry though. My eyes are glued shut ...'

I smile. This will be a good day. I know it already. This is it.

I add kindling to the sleeping embers in the potbelly, coax it back to life and put the old cast iron kettle on to boil. It's going to take a while.

I step out onto the front veranda and breathe in the new day. Everything is damp from rain and smells robust. The wattle flower scent is syrupy, eucalyptus stringent. Birds are chattering; sunlight is creeping through everything. This is nothing like being in the city. Our house would be all traffic, people yelling at each other, the garbage truck whirring and clanging. I survey the land around the house. I can't see any sign of a building of any kind. I guess it's fallen down by now. I can't imagine Popa being that good a builder.

Bruce is right about the need for a clean-up. There are fallen branches, piles of debris everywhere and parts of the fences have fallen over. It's just occurred to me that there is an orchard right in front of me. It's not obvious at first because the trees aren't in straight lines. They seem to form a circle. But they are laden with fruit. There must be bucketloads of them. Below the trees are layers of old fallen fruit from years gone by.

At least we won't need to worry about firewood for a while. I walk towards the orchard. I thought this orchard was just apples but there are a few different types of trees with only lemons and mandarins in fruit. I pick two mandarins for Destiny.

The nearest tree is old. Its trunk is twisted and gnarled; the bark silvery grey. I touch it with the palm of my hand. It bows to me. *Sorry. Hope I didn't startle you.*

A sparrow lands on a branch above, its beady eyes following me. 'Go on! Shoo! Shoo!' I wave my arms at it and it flutters away, only to land on the next tree over.

I move further into the circle of trees, checking out the fruit. It looks good, but this city boy has no idea. The sparrow is watching me, the interloper come to steal *his* fruit. It flitters from tree to tree, chirping to others in the area. He must be a bit of a leader.

It rests on some vines. I can't work out what the vines are growing over. Something winks as the sun hits it. I figure the bird is collecting trinkets for its nest. But I can't leave it. I'm curious. Isn't it magpies that collect things? I walk over to the vines. The bird chirps to its mates. There's something else under the vines. It's a door! It's painted green and brown, army fatigue-like, and has a recessed handle that can only be seen up close. I push on the door, but it barely moves. The sparrow is frantic now and I realise I've mistaken it for a male because it's guarding chicks. I can hear them squeaking for their mother.

I push at the door again. It's stuck fast. I yank at the handle, and it gives. I charge at it with all my weight. It opens with an almighty grunt, the vines rustling, sending the birds into a frenzy.

The room bleeds into view as the door groans on its hinges, the light spilling across the ground. My eyes try desperately to adjust to the darkness. The air is tight, and my throat constricts. The space inside seems to moan in greeting. I stand rigid, all senses alight.

I open the door as wide as possible, letting in more light. As I turn around, hunting for something to prop the door ajar, I see a light switch on the wall.

I whistle in surprise and flick the switch, forgetting that the power isn't on but a crackling buzzes somewhere in the room; a dim yellow light spreads around the walls. Rows of metal shelves line one wall. They'd probably wink in the light if it weren't for the layer of dust. *The bunker.*

I take a breath to steady myself and step into the room. There're enough supplies here to last a family months: tinned peaches, tinned beans, jars of coffee, jars of sugar, boxes of matches, boxes of candles, batteries (now oozing fluids), rolls of twine, cooking oil, salt, pepper. There's a small table near the open door with a reading light, a jar of pens and pencils – their ends chewed – and a glass of brown water. A spider has made its home on the lamp, its silky thread cascading from the lamp head to the base making a silvery skirt. A row of books is along the back; some I've read: *To Kill a Mockingbird, Pride and Prejudice, War and Peace* – a decent library to fill many hours.

Wedged into the end of these books is a thick orange notebook warped from age and use, the corners dog-eared. I tug at it and hold it up to the light. *Memories of Yesterday* is scrawled across the front, the ink faded. The pages within the covers are filled with the same cursive script, some in English, but most in an unfamiliar language. My skin tingles. *Popa.* The book is alive to me, and I know that what I hold in my hands is important to me and probably to Moma. I open it. At the top of the first page it reads *Zeke Solomon.*

'Popa, it's you,' I whisper.

I close the book, hold it to my chest and sense the presence of my grandfather and all his ghosts in this room. They gather around me, wanting to tell me what they know, crowding me, but I don't want to listen. I swat at the air around me to ward them off, turn around and bolt from the bunker.

As I approach the house, I remember the power. There shouldn't be any. I turn back to the bunker and realise I left the light on. I go back, flick the switch off and close the door more respectfully.

I walk the perimeter of the house to see if there's a power box and sure enough there's one at the back not far from the back door. We assumed that we needed to connect power so didn't even check. I unclip the latch on the cover of the box and open it carefully. There are spiderwebs all over the joint, so I'm apprehensive about what I'm going to find. I step back in disgust but can't see any spiders. Picking up a stick, I roughly clear away most of the web to see the fuses.

There are a couple of switches here, main switch and an isolator. I flick that down and a loud *thunk* sounds from inside the house. Is that power? I wait and turn my head to listen but there are just the usual sounds of the bush around me.

'Ash?' calls Destiny. 'What're you doing out there? The lights just came on!'

I sprint into the house to find Destiny standing at the bedroom door, naked, squinting into the bright light of the main room.

'Seems like the power is on,' I say, scratching my head.

'You mean we could have had lights on last night?' says Destiny.

'Yeah, but the candles were good, don't you think?'

'Yeah. It's a bit chilly. Where's that drink you were bringing me?' She's shrugging on a jumper, smoothing down her hair.

'You'll be warmer with bottoms on too,' I say, pointing at her naked lower half.

'Ha, ha. Such a comedian,' she says, hunting for socks and pants.

Yes. This is going to be a good day …

'Are you gonna stare at me all day or make me tea? Don't be an ape standing there.' She's balancing on one leg, pulling on a bright pink sock.

'Yes! Tea for my princess is coming!' I move over to the stove where the water is boiling and half-evaporated.

'What've you been doing out there?' asks Destiny, shuffling over to the kitchen bench, now fully dressed, albeit haphazardly.

'Just getting an idea of what's here. It's been so many years. I found the bunker and these.' I hold out two mandarins to her.

'Nice. That's our breakfast. What's the book?'

'Not sure. Might be a diary, but most of it isn't in English. Might be my grandfather's.'

'Oh wow, these mandarins are so sweet,' says Destiny, mouth full. 'The cover of the diary is the same colour. Maybe Moma can translate it?'

'Maybe.' I shove it into a drawer and take a wedge of fruit from Destiny. 'Oh yeah, that's good.'

'What's the plan, genius? If we're staying here a while, how's it going to work?'

'You mean you want to stay?' I ask.

'Sure. In fact, I'm happy to not even go back to the city from this very second.'

'Really?'

Destiny nods.

'I guess I can go back, get a few supplies and we can take it day by day? I better bring the cat here, too!'

'Sounds good. I'll make a list.' Destiny rummages in her handbag and gets out a pad of paper. 'First thing we need is a bath.'

green

We're settling in well here. I'm still adjusting to the fact that the kettle takes a long time to boil – I must get an electric one – and the birds wake me far too early, but there's no hurry for anything. Spring progresses rapidly and it seems like all of us have new life unfolding. Sounds a bit new-agey, I know, but being here kinda brings that out in me.

The quietness of Destiny is now a solitude that I no longer try to puncture. I'm happy that she at least lets me touch her. There's promise in that. It makes the suspension of time bearable; time seems to have less meaning here.

I'm starting to be real, not ghostly in her unseeing eyes. The weight of her sorrow is enough to keep us both shackled to the pain. It's something so palpable that I wish I could burn it in the potbelly when I light it each day.

It's early evening. I sit reading on the front veranda, Tuxedo sprawled at my feet. The warm spring sunshine has hypnotised us all. I can hear Destiny out the back of the house somewhere, probably pottering amongst her tomatoes, fussing over them like some protective mother. I wince at that unbidden thought – *mother* – and turn to Moma, as if she might have read my mind. She's come to stay for the weekend and dozes quietly in the overstuffed armchair. I wonder if she's ever gotten used to the Australian weather.

I spread my book face down on my lap and try to follow Destiny's movements. She's energetic. I rest my head back against the couch and close my eyes, following her in my mind.

A small breeze kicks up from the south, bringing a freshness from the river, and carried on it are the low murmurings of a tune that Destiny is singing. I lift my head and grin. I almost hear the clicking of the rusty key as it wrestles with our shackles. It's as musical as Destiny's melody. *How many months?* I try to add them up. A jolt of guilt. How could I not know how many months it is since he left us? What is it? Ten months, eleven?

It's been that long since I last saw Sam, too. I wish he'd get in touch. It would be good to have him to talk to. He disappeared quickly after the funeral. The only thing I get is the occasional postcard or a fax through the studio.

Snippets of Destiny's song reach me again. I frown; is that a lullaby? No, it's a folk song. I grin again and turn to Moma. Her eyes twinkle with delight.

'She comes back, my darling.'

'Yes, she does.' I sit up on the couch, invigorated by the breeze and the song. A song that's building in volume.

'Hey, you two lazy bones, what's going on?' says Destiny, hands on hips. 'Isn't it about dinnertime? I'm starving.'

'Mmm, I suppose it is, but let me just recover for a sec. Did you hear that singing on the radio? Whoever it was really can't hold a tune …'

Destiny frowns. 'What radio?' she asks.

Moma stifles a giggle.

I silently count the seconds as I watch the realisation dawn on Destiny's face.

'Why, you smartarse!' says Destiny, her lips quivering. 'Should I stop singing?'

'Oh no, just sing a little quieter so you don't scare the kookaburras away. It'll be dusk soon; see they're waiting over there to begin their own chorus.'

Moma giggles and I rejoice at the childlike quality of it.

Are my girls coming back to me?

Destiny has worked hard to rebuild the garden bed next to the water tank. I've left her to it since I'm clueless about what to do. She spends hours out there with her arms in the soil up to her elbows, handpicking seeds and pushing them into the ground with her thumb. At the end of the day, she comes in with soil on her face, her hair askew under her big straw hat which engulfs her tiny head. She doesn't laugh like she once did, but she sighs less. That's something, isn't it?

Within a month or so, we'd settled into this little farmhouse and we're getting used to the simple pleasures of a quiet home. Bruce visits every other day to say hello. We've gotten used to him, too. Sometimes he'll bring fresh milk, still warm, from his cows, and Destiny will drink it straight from the metal bucket, the frothy whiteness leaving a moustache on her upper lip. He also brings cow manure for *her garden*, which she treats like gold, grabbing the bags from his ute and taking them straight out the back. Bruce laughs at her determination but is a little wary of her whimsical nature. He always brings her some offering from his farm, from his missus.

'Don't worry, Ash,' Destiny says. 'When my garden gets going, I'll make them something with my tomatoes.'

I look out over the veggie patch. It is promising, but I can't imagine what she could possibly give them. I'll get something from the city the next time I need to go to the gallery.

What a mind reader! There's Bruce pulling up beside the old gnarly tree. He gets out of the car and rummages around in the back of his ute. Whatever he has must be delicate. He is a giant trying to carry a precious artefact. Mary must've been baking again. I secretly hope it's her sour cherry pie. I salivate at the thought of it.

I meet him at the front door. 'Morning, Bruce. You got something from the missus?'

Bruce grins. 'You could say that. Where's Destiny?'

'Out back – where else?'

'Reckon she might like this little bundle.'

I reach out to receive the bundle but recoil. It's alive! 'Ah, mate, what's this?' Before Bruce can answer, a wet nose pokes out of the blanket and nips me on the wrist. 'Why, you little devil!'

Bruce laughs and crosses his arms over his chest.

'What's going on out here?' says Destiny, brushing soil from her arms.

Bruce is suddenly shy. 'Hey, Destiny. This little cheeky thing is the last of Daisy's litter. He's the runt. No one wants him for a working dog. I'd keep him but we're keeping his brother, Browny, and we've got three dogs ...'

I pass Destiny the squirming bundle. 'Wow, he's a beauty. What kinda dog is it?'

'Red heeler. You want him?'

Destiny's eyes are soft.

'Um, geez, I'm not sure our house in the city is good for a dog. Too small. How much you want for him?'

Bruce steps back, embarrassed. 'No, I'm not tryna sell him. I want you to give him a good home. They're real easy to train.' He scuffs the floor with his boot.

Destiny holds the dog close to her face.

'What you think, D?' I ask.

Destiny hugs the puppy into the hollow of her neck. 'He's adorable!'

'Bruce, mate, I'm not sure. We don't know how long we'll be here …'

'He's beautiful. When we go back, I'll walk him on the beach every day. It'll be fine.'

'Hmm, what about Tuxedo? She might not like a new family member.'

'She'll get over it.' Destiny rubs her face on the puppy's head.

'Well … I guess it's a deal. Is he old enough to leave his mother? He's tiny.'

Bruce's face splits with joy. 'Oh yeah, he's nine weeks now. As I said, he's the runt. The other puppies would steal his turn at Daisy's teats. I've been giving him cows' milk to try 'n fatten him up.'

The puppy is now licking Destiny's face; she giggles. She jumps down the two steps to hug Bruce. 'Oh Bruce, thank you so much. He's a keeper. Does he have a name?'

Bruce's face is bright red. He shakes his head. 'Nah, we never name an animal until we know it's gonna live and stay on the property. You can name him.'

'What ya think?' asks Destiny.

I shrug. 'Red?'

'Oh that's really original!' Destiny screws up her face at me.

Bruce chuckles. 'He's a chocolate colour but their coat changes around two years old and becomes a more … rusty kinda colour. Every second red heeler is called Red, but.'

'How about Rusty?' I say.

Destiny shakes her head and holds the puppy aloft. 'He's too precious to have a name like that. He's like a … nugget of gold!'

'Goldie?' I offer.

Destiny frowns. 'Nugget.'

Bruce chuckles again.

'What's wrong with that?' asks Destiny.

'Ah, nuthin. Just made me think of boot polish.' He reaches out and takes the puppy from her and starts to polish his big boots with it. The puppy chews on his bootlaces and we fall back with laughter.

As we sit down on the veranda with the obligatory cup of tea, Sean pulls up in his old truck. It's all happening here today. There's something big wrapped up on the back of his truck.

'It's here!' squeals Destiny.

She skips down the steps to her dad. Sean envelopes her in his arms.

'What's going on, you two?' I ask, leaning on the veranda railing.

Destiny is ready to pop with excitement. 'It's Ma's old tipi. We had it on the commune a million years ago.'

'And what are we going to do with a tipi?'

'This is going to be my bathroom!'

'Of course. Why didn't I think of that?' I turn to Bruce and he laughs.

Destiny is oblivious to my sarcasm, tugging at the bundle on the truck. 'Well, genius, you gonna help set it up?' She stops to put her hands on her hips.

'Sure, but shouldn't we entertain our visitors first?' I fan my hands out to indicate Sean and Bruce, the puppy bundled up in Bruce's lap.

'Maybe everyone could help?' She puts on her best princess pout.

We lug the bundle towards the river and I realise Destiny has already prepared a site for it. It's not easy setting up a tipi, even with four people, but we get it done and leave the front flap open towards the river.

'If this is going to be your bathroom, D, where's the bath and how will you heat the water?'

'I'll find a bath. Might check out the tip tomorrow or go into town to the building wreckers. Wouldn't it be awesome to find a clawfoot bath?'

Bruce straightens up. 'Hey, love, we got an old clawfoot bath over at the farm. It's out in the paddock. Been turned upside down; might be okay inside?'

Destiny smiles. 'You just happen to have a clawfoot bath hanging around?'

Bruce reddens. 'It came out of the old bathroom when Mum renovated a few years back. She wanted something modern.'

Destiny leaps up and hugs Bruce around the neck. 'You are the best!' She turns to Sean. 'Dad, can we go get it now, while you have the truck here?'

Sean nods.

I stand at the back door, stretching my arms above my head. I resist the temptation to crawl back into our warm bed, especially now that I've looked out at the valley shrouded in mist. But Destiny is up and I want to know why.

Where are my damn Ugg boots? There's Destiny out at the veggie patch; she is busy. I grab my duffle coat from the peg near the back door and struggle into it.

Nugget is following Destiny around the garden in haphazard lines, sniffing every nook and cranny, while Tuxedo sits on the garden edging, watching his every move. Destiny bends and whispers to her precious plants. Her hair is almost grown out now, becoming a bob, like her mother's. It's dishevelled and she's wearing her old woollen coat and moccasins; her legs are bare. Ha! I think she's naked underneath. Every movement from her makes me ache. She fingers the lavender spears; I wish she'd do that to me. I'd give anything to have her in my arms, have that same attention.

Destiny squats next to a tomato plant. The sun bursts through the mist and creates a halo around the garden. Mornings are like that here. Magical. She caresses a tomato and plucks it gently from the bush. Holding it above her, she turns the fruit in her hand, and brings the tomato to her lips reverently, tracing the skin. She opens her mouth, sinks her teeth into the tender skin, through the flesh – pale red liquid dribbles down her chin – and murmurs.

My blood is hot, surging through me, just as the sun bleeds over the hills and through the trees. I walk slowly towards Destiny, afraid of breaking the spell.

'Hey, D, gorgeous morning ...' I stop, waiting for her reaction.

'Oh, mmm ...' She nods, her mouth full, her lips glistening with tomato juice. 'You've got to taste these tomatoes.' Her face is screwed up with the motion of chewing. 'It's really early for them to ripen but we've had so much sunshine ...'

I'm more confident now and keep moving to her. 'Well, you know I don't like tomatoes, but I'll give it a go.'

I reach out to take the fruit from her but she snatches her hand away, implying that she's going to feed me. I step closer to her. She holds the tomato to my lips and I bite into the sweet thing, warm and alive.

The juice dribbles down my chin and Destiny giggles. This is so bizarre. I laugh at the absurdity of eating a tomato at daybreak. She wipes my chin with the sleeve of her coat, her own tongue mimicking the action.

I clutch the front of her coat and pull her closer to me. Her coat falls open and I pull her naked body closer still. She doesn't resist. *Thank you, God!* So here we are, in the garden, the birds twittering around us, the sun steadily rising above the trees. I breathe in her hair, the heat from her naked body. Then Destiny stuffs the rest of the tomato into her mouth, squirting juice onto my face.

'Watch out, young lady. There are repercussions for such misdemeanours.' I try hard to sound serious.

'Oh, really?' says Destiny pawing at my face with both hands. 'What repercussions might they be?'

'Well, severe physical punishment, then time in community service.'

'Is that right?' She narrows her eyes. 'Well, then, I plead guilty to all charges.' She holds her arms above her head in surrender, her small body open to me.

I hold her head in my hands and kiss the ragged scar along the outline of her jaw, then wrap my arms around her. I need her as close as possible. She clasps her hands behind my neck, a wickedness in her eyes, and lifts herself, wrapping her legs around my thighs.

I carry her back into the house.

It's getting late and Destiny is still pottering around in her tipi. I have no idea how it will become a bathroom, but she's been working on it for days.

I trundle down the path towards the river where we set the tipi up. The sun is just hovering above the horizon and a kookaburra goes off above me. This tells me there's about ten minutes left of daylight. The chill of a spring evening is descending.

'D, you down here?' I ask, peering into the doorway.

There are lit candles all around the perimeter of the room and the clawfoot bath sits off-centre with a little potbelly – fire burning brightly – next to it, the chimney going up through the centrepiece of the tipi. Destiny lies in the bath, water up around her ears, eyes closed. There must be oils in the bath, something sweet like orange, and maybe lavender?

'Earth to Destiny,' I say through a funnelled hand.

Destiny opens her eyes and smiles sleepily. 'Oh, hi, Ash. Must have dozed off. Want to get in?'

This is one time she doesn't need to twist my arm. I'm out of my clothes and lowering my body into the hot water just as the darkness closes in outside. I can no longer see the river through the doorway.

'How?' I ask.

'Huh?' She's half asleep.

'How'd you get the water down here and heat it?'

The candles splutter around us, creating a warm glow. I now see they are all handmade of various colours, which makes the room a kaleidoscope.

'Oh, easy. We're downhill from the tank, which means I can syphon water through a hose and that little baby,' she indicates the potbelly, 'can heat the water as it goes through it. This is how we did it on the commune.'

Here I am in a bath, on a river, surrounded by candlelight with my beautiful wife. This has to be the most incredible moment of my life. 'This is amazing, D.' It's just about the lamest thing to say, but I'm choked up.

'I did tell you,' she says, eyes closed again.

'Yes. Yes, you did,' I answer as I play with her toes.

Destiny opens her eyes again. Her eyes sparkle in the candlelight.

'You are very dirty. What have you been doing?' She attempts to sound stern.

'Sorry, D. This farm work is dirty work; what can I do about it?'

Destiny reaches over the edge of the bath to where a stool sits with various items on it such as a hairbrush, face cloth, towels, and essential oils. She grabs a long-handled scrubbing brush and brandishes it at me.

'Here, scrub yourself with this,' she says, grinning.

'I'd rather you did it.' I splash her.

'I'm not your mother.' She throws the brush towards me.

'Then maybe I'll scrub you?'

'I'm not dirty. Thanks, anyway.'

'Want me to make you dirty?' I ask, trying not to laugh at the cheesiness of the conversation.

Destiny nods, biting her lip.

I drop the brush and move towards her, careful not to spill too much water over the edge of the bath.

I check my watch. They'll be descending on us in about forty minutes and Destiny is off somewhere.

'Hey! D, where are you?' I poke my head out the back door and frown. 'There you are!' I say, pushing branches from my face along the path. 'What're you doing? Everyone's gonna be here soon.'

Destiny has her back to me, her little butt perched on the fallen tree. She doesn't move. The river shimmers before her, waiting.

'D? Did you hear me?'

'Yes. I heard you.'

I grunt, put my hands on my hips. 'Come on then, let's sort out the table. We've still gotta set it up under the apple tree.'

Silence.

'Geez, would you talk to me?'

Destiny shakes her head, hunches forward.

I stride towards her. 'This isn't the time to go off daydreaming.' She lifts her face to me. She's been crying. *Fuck!*

I squat in front of her. 'Hey, babe, what's going on?'

'I'm …' she mumbles.

'What?'

She shakes her head again, hugging herself.

I put my hands on her knees. 'C'mon, D, tell me. There's nothing you can't tell me.'

Her eyes well with tears and she covers her mouth with her left hand. She shakes her head again and shudders.

I wrap my arms around her. It must be the anniversary tomorrow. I'm dreading it, too. 'Shh. Shh.' I rock her gently.

'Ash?'

'Yeah?'

'I can't do it.'

'It's gonna be okay. All your family will be here soon. They understand. It's hard for them, too.'

'No. It's not that.'

'What, then?'

'I'm … I'm pregnant.'

I pull back, not sure I've heard her properly. 'What do you mean?'

'What do you think, doofus? We. Are. Going. To. Have. A. Baby.'

A baby. My synapses buzz. I purse my lips. *Why is this bad?* It isn't. It's fantastic. I smile. 'But that's great!'

Destiny tenses. 'No, it isn't! I can't do it. I don't want a baby!' She's on her feet, body rigid.

'Wait! Don't I get a say in this?' I try to keep my voice down but anger is building. *You can't take this away from me …*

'NO!' Destiny is on her toes, eyes flaring.

'Woohoo, hello, where is everyone?' Mai's voice trails from the house.

Destiny's eyes widen. 'Shit! They're here already.'

'Your family is always early.' I stand up, plunge my hands into my pockets.

'There you two are!' Mai waddles towards us grinning, arms outstretched. 'Happy Summer Solstice!'

Destiny remains facing me, away from her mother, eyes squeezed shut. I'm paralysed.

'Hello? What's going on, you two? That puppy is shredding cushions up there …'

'Hello, Mai,' I say, my voice catching.

Mai stops. 'You two fighting?'

'You could say that.'

'This is happy day. No fighting allowed.'

'Well, talk to your daughter about it.' I scowl.

Destiny tightens her lips, as if to say, *Don't you dare.*

'Destiny? What is this?' Mai tugs at her shoulder, forcing her to turn around.

Destiny grimaces. 'It's nothing, Ma.'

Mai examines both of us. 'No. This is not good. You tell me now.'

'It's none of your fucking business!'

Mai bristles and slaps her daughter. 'How dare you! Nothing can be so bad.'

'Oh, yeah? Tell her, Ash.'

I mumble.

'Don't be a coward now! Tell her!'

'She's pregnant.'

Mai's face brightens. 'Baby? How that bad news?'

Destiny turns away.

I rub my eyes with the palms of my hands. 'Destiny doesn't want to keep it.'

'Wha—'

I nod, emboldened by Mai's reaction.

'Hey, you lot. What's going on? That puppy is causing havoc up there.' Sean stops to scan each of our faces.

Mai swivels to Sean. 'YOUR daughter want to kill her baby daughter!'

'What daughter?'

'She pregnant. But she want to kill it!'

'How d'ya know it's a girl?' I ask.

Mai shrugs. 'I know. Sean! You talk to her. I go do food.'

Mai tramps back towards the house, fists clenched, swearing to herself in Vietnamese.

Sean inclines his head slightly, raising his eyebrows. I take this to mean I should make myself scarce so I follow Mai, keeping my distance.

I can hear Destiny snivelling behind me, then Sean's gentle voice as he takes her by the shoulders, leading her further away from the house.

The house is chaos.

Nugget has dissected a cushion on the front veranda, leaving feathers scattered everywhere. It's like a roost of chickens has been slaughtered. Kids are running circles around the house, using the front and back doors as entry points, and Mai is in the kitchen barking orders.

'Whoa, big fella!' says Bruce as he and his wife step up to the front veranda, almost bowled over by a small child. Bruce grins up at me.

'You'll need danger money today, mate,' I say, extending my hand to Bruce, then Mary. Mary giggles and straightens the dish in her hand.

'I've made a trifle, love. Shall I take it through?' she asks.

'Yeah, thanks, that's great. My mother-in-law has taken charge.' I step aside to let Mary into the house.

'So, big mob comin' today?' asks Bruce.

'Yeah, I think so. Not sure who's coming, actually.'

'How 'bout we get something organised here? I reckon we've got enough to make a cricket team.' Bruce nods at me.

My mind is clouded. 'Um, I guess. I don't have any gear, though.'

'No worries, mate. Always have it in the back of the truck. The farm boys use it at smoko time. I'm usually umpire.'

Within minutes, a game is going in the front driveway, calming the place down. I listen out for Destiny and Sean. *This baby. It's a good thing, yeah? I like the idea. No, I love it. But what if Destiny doesn't? What if Sean can't bring her 'round? A girl. How can Mai know it's a girl?*

'OUT!' shouts Toby, holding the ball aloft triumphantly.

'Okay, Josh, it's Billy's turn to bat,' says Casey from the veranda. I look up. I hadn't realised my brother-in-law was here. I nod at him as he gives me a thumbs-up.

As Billy takes the bat from his cousin, I swat at flies, straining to hear Destiny's voice. *A baby girl …* I study Casey's youngest, Skye, imagining a Destiny-like version. They'd be similar. Dark hair. Big eyes. Petite face. *C'mon, Sean, talk sense into that woman.*

'Okay, everyone. Food time!' Mai waves her arms from the front door.

'Aww, one more bowl? I just got in!' says Billy petulantly.

'Don't worry, mate, we'll pick up after tea.' Bruce winks at him.

The table is set up under the apple tree, groaning from an eclectic mix of food that includes Mai's chilli prawns and Mary's trifle. The children, hungry from the game, load up their plates and take off to the orchard – setting up a picnic in the centre of the trees – leaving the adults in peace.

'I'm starved!' says Sean, patting his stomach.

My head snaps up. He gives nothing away. Where is Destiny?

She stands near the veggie-patch, hugging herself. I resist the urge to stride over there and demand that she keep the baby.

Standing close to Sean, I ask, 'So?'

Sean smiles. 'I reckon you're having a baby, Ash. But she'll need time to get used to the idea; she's scared. Maybe give her some space, eh? You know how she gets if you crowd her.'

I nod, relief flooding me, and put my hand on Sean's shoulder.

'So, big brother, how's it hanging?'

I turn around to face my brother. 'Sam! I didn't know you were coming. I've been trying to track you down.' We throw our arms around each other.

'Yeah, sorry 'bout that. Been O.S. Got back last week and Mum told me this was on. We came together.' He inclines his head towards our mother, who is talking with Moma.

'That's great. What you been up to?'

'Been in New York talking to some agents. Having an exhibition over there next year.'

'Cool. So you've been taking photos?'

'Not much. This might be a bit of a retrospective. "The best of Samuel Anderson".' He trails his hand in an arc as if his name were up in lights, then rolls his eyes.

'And Kelly?'

Sam's eyes darken. 'Nah, that's over. Crashed and burned!'

'Really? What happened? You two seemed really tight. How long's it been – eighteen months?'

Sam shakes his head. 'Don't worry about it, Ash.' He crosses his arms over his chest.

'C'mon, tell me.'

Sam holds back. I know he wants to tell me. Was he really in love with Kelly? He seems to be truly hurting.

Sam gives me a bear hug. 'Forget about Kelly, Ash. There's someone else out there for me.'

I hold him at arm's length and look him in the eye. 'Sam, seriously. You seem cut up about this. Talk to me.'

Sam sighs. 'Shit, Ash!'

I laugh. 'You can't get anything past me.'

'Alright, but you might not like it.'

I hold up both hands as if to say, *Bring it on*.

Sam hesitates again, sizing me up.

I nod.

'Okay then. Kelly says we can't be together because I'm not over Destiny.' He steps back slightly, anticipating my reaction.

A knot bunches in my stomach. 'Are you?'

'Of course! We were over years ago. How long you two been together now? Six years?'

I nod.

'Anyway. What difference does it make, Ash? Kelly doesn't want me. Even if I haven't gotten over Destiny, which I *have*, she's with you now and you two seem happy.'

'I guess.'

'Now, tell me what you two have been up to out here. Never figured you as a country bumpkin.' He puts me in a headlock, ruffling my hair.

I groan and roll my eyes. 'Geez, Sam, you're twenty-seven years old. When will you stop that?'

'Never!' says Sam, tackling me to the ground.

'Hey, you two. Eat some food!' It's Mai, shoving a platter of chilli prawns under our noses.

'Mai! You're looking good!' says Sam, me pinned under his knee.

'Hello, Sam. We not see you for long time. Not since funeral.' She says what we all think.

Sam stands and brushes off his clothes. 'Yeah, I know. I've been in New York.'

'Ash tell you news?'

Sam turns to me. 'News?'

I shake my head at Mai, but I know I can't stop her.

'Destiny have baby gir—' She takes off to rescue the barbeque meat from Nugget.

'You had a baby girl! When did this happen?'

'No. Destiny hasn't *had* a baby. She's only just pregnant and Mai thinks it's a girl.'

'Wow! That's good news … isn't it?'

'Yeah. I think it is, but I'm not sure Destiny does.'

Sam scans the yard and stops when he sees Destiny sitting next to the veggie-patch. 'Yeah, she doesn't seem too excited.'

'She's scared. Me, too.'

'Want me to talk to her?'

'Don't know what you can say. You know how she is when she decides something.'

Sam snorts. 'Do I ever!'

'You know what? Let's just enjoy the party. Give her time to think about it. Hopefully she'll come around.'

'Sure. I might go catch up with a few of these loonies. That okay?'

'Yeah.'

Sam pats me on the shoulder, then heads towards Sean.

I desperately want to talk to Destiny, but what do I say? I don't want to undo any good that Sean has done. I watch her huddled on a seat beside the tomatoes, lost in thought until Nugget comes bounding over to her. She smiles and scratches him behind the ears.

I take advantage of this and wander over to her. 'Hey, babe, wanna beer?' I hold out a bottle of Corona to her.

Her face is puffy from crying. 'If I'm gonna have this baby, then no.'

Shit! Dumb move. 'Sorry. So … you are gonna have it?'

'Don't have much choice, do I?' She fidgets with one of Nugget's ears.

'Well, you do. It won't be that bad, will it?'

'There's no way I can feel the same about this one … after To—' She covers her mouth, stifling her voice.

I move closer to her. 'Shhh, it'll be okay. We've got months to get used to it. I think you might be surprised. Just think, a little girl …'

Destiny sinks into my chest. Nugget yaps about our feet, battling for attention.

'Did you know that Sam's here?' I ask.

Destiny tenses in my arms and sits upright. 'No. Why's he here?'

'He's my brother and this is a family get-together.' I'm surprised by her reaction. 'You have a problem with him?'

She smiles feebly at me. 'Of course not. We just haven't seen him for a long time … When did we last see him?'

'He was at the funeral, and he came to the hospital quite a bit when you were out of it.'

Destiny squints, trying to order the information into her memory. 'Okay, but that's a while ago now. Where's he been since?'

'He's been in New York, planning some retrospective.'

'Is Kelly here, too?'

'Dumped him.'

'Really? They seemed tight.' Destiny scans the yard and settles on Sam.

'I thought so, too. She broke up with him because she thinks he isn't over you.' I study her reaction.

Destiny leans her head on my shoulder. 'That's dumb. It's been years now. The break-up was mutual.'

She stands up, straightening her blouse.

I pick up Nugget who proceeds to lick my face clean. 'Why don't you go say hi?'

Destiny shakes her head. 'There's plenty of time. Where's he staying?'

'I don't know. I guess at Mum's. You want some food? Your mum's prawns are as good as ever.'

Destiny has a faraway look in her eyes. 'Yeah, I probably should. Haven't eaten all day. Not sure prawns are a good idea …' She rubs her stomach with a flat palm.

I lean into Destiny and kiss her in the hollow of her neck. 'I love you, D.'

She closes her eyes and nods.

'Let's go find some food.' I reach for her hand.

As the sun descends into the valley, Mai rallies everyone into making the bonfire.

Bruce is concerned. 'Have you checked the fire authority, luv? It's fire season, ya know?'

Mai waves his questions away as if swatting flies. 'It okay, Mr Bruce, we do it here in clearing and we have water tank just there.' She waves at the water tank to prove it.

Mary smiles and pats his arm. 'It'll be okay. It's a big clearing here.'

The idea of a bonfire makes the children industrious, and before long they have a mound of kindling towering before them.

'I guess it's a good way of clearing all that rubbish up around the place,' says Bruce, hands on hips. He scans the orchard and spots a dead branch under a tree. 'Hey, Ash, you haven't really done much of a clean-up around here. Remember the fire season is here?'

'I know. Tell the truth, not sure what I'm doing.'

Bruce tuts. 'City slickers …' he says knowingly to Mary.

Mai whistles. 'Okay everyone, it nearly time to start.' She holds her arm high, pointing at her watch. 'Where Skye?'

'Here!' Skye steps forward, anticipation jiggling every ounce of her little body.

'Skye! This year you're first year to light the fire. You youngest.'

Skye's face splits with joy. If Tomas were here, he'd be the one to light it.

Mai hesitates as realisation passes over her. She glances at Destiny, then Sean, and throws her arms in the air. 'Okay, it time. Here, Skye, you light the fire.'

The children move in closer, the idea of fire intoxicating. Mai lights a rod with cloth wrapped around one end, then hands it to the girl.

Skye moves in closer to the pyramid, touches the wood with her torch, but only smoke rises from it.

The children encourage her with instructions on how to light it and she shoves it in more confidently. Small flames rise, then larger, licking at the dry tinder hungrily.

Within minutes the bonfire is raging and the crowd claps with joy.

We eat and drink well into the night, enjoying Mai's usual solstice ceremony at 10.22pm.

'Okay, everyone, it time!' Mai's shrill voice shoots skyward.

Someone groans.

'Who that!' asks Mai, her head darting around the crowd.

Sam elbows Billy, who rolls his eyes.

'Now, everyone. Big circle.' Mai waves her arms around.

Feet shuffle into position and sweaty hands clasp each other.

'Good, good. You know what to do!' Mai clasps her hands together, delighted.

Nugget wanders into the middle of the circle, nose down, tail up, zigzagging across the space.

'Watch out, Nugget, Nanna Mai might sacrifice you!' Toby yells.

Laughter rings around the yard. Mai looks sideways at him in mock anger. 'You be careful, boy. Maybe I sacrifice you!'

Little Skye breaks rank and runs in to scoop up the puppy, then re-joins the circle with a wriggling Nugget.

'Okay, enough silly business. It almost time. Are we ready?'

No one is game to do anything but nod, the flames of the bonfires flickering yellow lights on upturned faces.

'Now. Close eyes,' says Mai.

Everyone bows their heads and closes their eyes, the crackle of the flames and buzzing crickets now the only sound in the bush.

'We thank you for the sun!' says Mai. 'We honour you, oh sun goddess, for the life you give!'

My thoughts drift off. *A baby girl? Is it really a girl? Is this good? Yes, at least a girl won't remind us as much of Tomas.* My face is hot from the fire, and I can hear Mai's high-pitched voice but can't focus on words.

The crowd disperses once Mai has dismissed them. Some of the younger children are packed off into tents out in the orchard. The older children start up new games, taking off into the darkness.

Destiny gravitates back to her veggie-patch. The tomatoes glisten in the moonlight, plump and red. She touches one and it falls into her hand, an offering. She smiles.

I watch her from the kitchen window, imagining a small girl child hovering at her feet. I hope Mai is right.

As I turn from the window, I see Sam walking towards Destiny.

He says something I can't hear, stands at a distance.

Destiny turns to him, face in shadow.

He waves feebly, says something.

She answers by wrapping her arms around her body.

Sam watches the sky and digs his hands into the back pockets of his jeans.

Destiny asks him something.

Sam shrugs.

There's tension between them, but maybe it's me. I try to read their faces, but they are eclipsed in the moonlight.

Sam moves a little closer, but I can't hear what he says, music drowning everything out. Casey is showcasing his new songs.

As the conversation wears on, Sam's body becomes more stooped and he walks away, defeated.

Sam and Mum have had an argument; they never seem to be able to go longer than three days. So, he's here now at the farm, camping out amidst the apple trees. I love my brother, but his presence changes the whole vibe of the place.

Maybe it isn't over between Sam and Destiny. Not properly, anyway. Or maybe I'm just reading more into things than I need to.

Since Sam told me what Kelly said, I'm preoccupied with it. Before that, I'd never thought about him and Destiny together. I thought they'd crashed and burned, too, like so many of Sam's past relationships. But maybe I'm wrong. Now I find I'm watching every interaction between them. At times they seem fine, at others they're deep in conversation, exchanges that are tense or heated.

'Cooee!' I call as I approach his old sagging army tent.

'Is that you, Ash?' asks Sam, his voice muffled.

'Yeah, can I come in?'

'Sure.'

'What you up to?' I ask, ducking my head to enter the tent.

'Not much. Bit of reading. Bit of thinking.' He is gaunt.

'Everything okay?'

'Yeah. What's up?'

'Nothing really. Was gonna head into Melbourne for a few hours. Check on the gallery. You wanna come for a ride? Rhonda would love to see you … and I reckon it's good for you to show your face around there occasionally.'

Sam scratches his head. 'Nah, the place runs perfectly without me around; Rhonda does a great job. You think?'

I nod. 'I couldn't have done without her over the past year.'

'You've kept it solid though. I'm happy to be more the silent partner. Business is obviously good?'

'Yeah. People are buying art. Not worried about the prices we put on pieces. Destiny's exhibition sold out in a week. We've been living off that.'

'That's great. You should see what sort of dollars you get in New York. It's almost embarrassing the prices they're putting on my new exhibition.'

'That's great, Sam. Maybe you can bring that exhibition to Sasher Studio?'

'Sure, why not? It's going to San Fran first, though.'

'Gee, you've conquered the US!'

He snorts. 'Hardly. I've just been schmoozing a lot. And I mean a *real* lot. Besides, Aussies are the flavour of the month over there. I'm just cashing in on it.'

'Haven't Aussies always been flavour of the month over there?'

Sam laughs. 'Probably.'

I laugh, too. 'Okay, I'm off. Sure you don't wanna hang out?'

'I'm good, thanks,' says Sam, squinting at the book in his hand.

'Okay, I'll see you tonight, for dinner. Might pick up some fish or something.' I back out of the tent and head towards the car.

'Wait!' says Sam, poking his head from the tent. 'I'm almost out of ciggies. Can you get me some?'

'When you gonna give up those cancer sticks?'

Sam chuckles. 'I'm here for a good time, not a long time, Ashie.'

I love this drive to the city. It allows me to clear my head.

It's been a while since I showed my face at the gallery. Rhonda, God love her, has just signed up Jeanne Jeanne. That's going to be a huge exhibition. I squint, trying to remember the dates for it. Is it August?

I can't help but smile when I walk into the gallery. It never gets old. I remember the day we opened back in '93. Sam and Destiny were just together then; we were all so young.

'Ash!' Rhonda rushes at me, throws her arms around me. 'I didn't know you were coming in today. How are you?'

I stand back, overwhelmed by the welcome. 'I'm okay. Thought it was about time I came in to check up on you.'

Rhonda smacks me on the shoulder. 'As if I need checking up on! It's quiet in here at the moment. People must still be in holiday mode.'

'So, Jeanne Jeanne …'

Rhonda squeals. 'I know! I'm so excited. Can you believe it?'

'How'd you pull that off?'

'I didn't. It was your brother. He's so well connected. I didn't realise till I talked to Jeanne.'

'Really? But how?'

'Something to do with New York. Some guy he knows over there. Jeanne was very impressed. He connected us!'

'Wow!' I rub my chin. I really do underestimate my brother sometimes. *Most* times. 'So when is the exhibition?'

'Late November. Just managed to rearrange the schedule and get everything sorted for the annual calendar. I can't wait, Ash!' She shivers and hugs herself.

'Well done, Rhonda. I hope you know how much I appreciate you running things down here.'

Rhonda nudges my shoulder with a fist. 'Don't worry 'bout it. I love this place. Might need a bit of a break sometime soon though. Gotta get my energy up for Jeanne.' She grins stupidly.

'My God, Rhonda, I never knew you were such a groupie!'

Rhonda giggles.

'But of course, we'll work out a holiday. Just let me know when you want to go.'

'How's Destiny?' Rhonda asks seriously.

'She's doing okay. A lot better actually. The puppy helps …'

'And …?'

I wonder how much to tell her. It's been a week; maybe Destiny will keep it. 'Actually … she's pregnant.'

Rhonda gasps. 'That's great! It *is* good, isn't it?'

'I think it is. Destiny needs convincing.'

'She's not getting rid of it, is she?' Rhonda covers her mouth.

'No. But she wanted to.'

Rhonda lets out a long breath. 'Thank God for that! Take it from someone who'll never get to have kids: it's a gift!'

'I know that. And I'm sure that she knows that. She's just scared.' My stomach drops, pity for Rhonda pooling in my belly.

Rhonda rubs my arm. 'I'm sure she is. Oh, Ash, a baby. This is so exciting. It's gonna be a huge year!' She reaches her arms above her head and arches them around her body.

I grin, my body relaxed. 'Thanks, Rhonda. It's so good to be able to talk to someone outside the family.'

'Ha. Don't worry 'bout it. We're buddies. I'm so happy for you.'

'Thanks. So enough about me. How's Rhonda's love life?'

Rhonda's eyes sparkle. 'Well … actually … I met someone …'

'You've been holding out on me!'

'I was getting to it. There's lots to catch up on. How 'bout we sit down and have a coffee rather than stand here like two scarecrows?'

'That coffee machine is good,' I say, breathing in the aroma from my cup.

'You paid for it, boss. Hey, has Destiny been painting? With the success of her last exhibition, she really should try to follow it up. It'd be good therapy for her, too.'

'I was thinking that. Her stuff is out at the farm but she's reluctant to get it out. It's tainted or something.'

'Why don't you get her some new supplies? A different medium. You know how much she loves a new thing. She won't be able to resist.'

'Brilliant! Have I ever told you how amazing you are, Rhonda?'

Rhonda beams. 'Well, not for at least half an hour …'

I chuckle. 'How is it that you're so wise?'

'I am a qualified art therapist, don't forget, not just a brilliant curator.'

'Okay, so what sort of supplies should I get?'

'I've got a whole kit out back. It's for watercolour. You can take that if you like; should be enough paint to get her going. Might just need to go to Eckersley's and get some nice paper.'

'Thanks. But you know what? You've been avoiding telling me about your new man …'

I drop in to Moma's place on my way home. I try to visit her at least once a week, but we talk on the phone every day. I like to check on her. Make sure she's okay. I have a dread every time I visit that I'll find her on the floor, no one being able to help her for days.

I press the front doorbell and hear it peal inside. There's no sound. I press it again. I turn my head towards the door to listen and then I hear a tiny shuffle deep in the hall. It gets louder and I breathe out in relief.

'Hello, Moma!' I say as she opens the door.

'My sweet boy,' she says. She gives me her left cheek to kiss, then right, then left. Then she turns – slowly – to shuffle back down the hall.

'What have you been up to, Moma?' I ask, watching her tiny frame in the darkness ahead.

'Oh, this and that. I just make apple cake.' She smiles knowingly.

'How did you know that I like apple cake?' I tease.

'A little bird told me,' she says, tapping the side of her head.

'Well, you better give me a big slice!' I pour the tea.

'How is Destiny?' asks Moma.

'Not bad,' I say, stuffing my mouth with cake. She's put extra cinnamon in this one and it's got a crisp, sugary top to it.

'The baby?'

'Lots of morning sickness, but everything is on track.'

'That good.' She nods into her teacup.

'What else you been doing, Moma?' I ask.

'I do some knitting for the baby. I not go out too much. My friend, Margaret, she die.'

'Really? When'd that happen?' I know they were friends for years.

'It happen yesterday. The funeral on Friday.'

'Want me to take you?'

'Oh, yes, that be good. Thank you, Asher, darling.' She smiles at me, but I feel loneliness seeping into her. I think Margaret might be the last of her real friends. It must be hard to get old and lose people around you.

'I'll come on Friday morning, and I'll stay with you at the funeral if you like?'

Moma smiles weakly at me. 'You such a good boy to you grandmother.'

'You need to tell me about these things, Moma. I'm always available if you need me, okay?' I put my hand on her arm to push my point. Her skin is cool and papery.

She nods again.

'Now that we have our city house rented out, and the gallery pretty much takes care of itself, I have plenty of time, Moma. This is thanks to you letting us stay at the farmhouse. I'd love for you to come and stay with us.'

'Maybe I will.' She isn't convinced.

'I don't think it's haunted. I think what happened to Popa is more about the war.'

'Yah. Maybe you right.' She places another slice of cake on my plate.

'You are going to make me fat!' I say as I stuff my face again.

Moma giggles.

I love this trip back to the farmhouse. It's long enough to feel like you're going somewhere. After talking to Rhonda, I'm invigorated. I really hope this new guy, John, is the one for her; she deserves to be happy.

I'm grinning stupidly as I make my way down the last road towards home. I can't wait to give Destiny the goodies from Rhonda. To see Destiny paint would mean that she really is coming back to me.

There's the house. I swear it's smiling at me. Is that Destiny rushing from the orchard? Of course it's her. She's agitated. My belly twists. Instinctively I know that there's something going on, a secret being kept from me. My hands shake.

I imagine the two of them in the tent, bodies twined together, Destiny's face in ecstasy. Like the painting. Maybe that's Sam in the painting? I shake my head to clear it of these pictures but they persist. Sam's lips on her lips. Sam's lips on her shoulder. Sam tracing the line of her scar.

I park the car and wait a few minutes. My pulse is out of control, my breathing shallow. *Get yourself together, Ash. You're imagining this shit.*

'Whoohoo!' I sing as I enter the house, arms laden with art supplies.

'I'm in here!' calls Destiny from the couch, her voice quivering.

'Hey, babe, I had the best time in the city. You should've come with me.' I force out a ridiculous upbeat persona.

'You been spending all our millions?'

'Ha! No, most of this is from Rhonda. She was … cleaning out her studio … and wondered if you might like to try these watercolours. She reckons there should be enough to get you going. I got some paper on the way home.'

'I'm not dumb, Ash.'

'Whaddya mean!'

'I know you two are cooking up a scheme to get me painting again.'

'No, she *was* cleaning up. Anyway, I'll put them in the spare room. If you don't want them, maybe there'll be someone around here who might like them?'

'Yeah, sure.' She waves me away.

I don't care about these things anymore; I toss them onto the bed in the spare room. I want to ask her what she was doing out in the orchard, but I don't want the answer.

'How is Rhonda, anyway?' calls Destiny.

I stride back into the room, summoning the courage to confront her. 'She's great. Doing such a fantastic job with the gallery. And guess what?'

Destiny waits, always ready for gossip.

'She signed up someone amazing.'

'Really? Who?'

'You'll never guess.'

'So tell me!'

'Jeanne Jeanne.'

Destiny's eyes widen. 'Really! For when?'

'End of the year. Just managed to sign him up in time to include him in this year's calendar.'

'Wow! That's a real coup. That'll put the gallery on the map.' Destiny stares out the window, eyes glazed.

'That's not all,' I say, following her gaze out to the orchard.

'Hmm.'

'Destiny?'

'Yeah?' Her voice is distant.

'Hey, babe.' I sit beside her on the couch. 'You alright?' My stomach churns.

Her head jerks towards me. 'Oh, yeah. Bit queasy but that's nothing ...'

'I've got more news.'

She leans in a little to concentrate. 'Yeah?'

'Rhonda's met someone. I've never seen her so happy.'

Destiny smiles. 'That's great. She deserves it after that last fuckwit!'

I laugh, buoyed by her change in mood. 'Yeah, sounds like John is a good bloke. I suggested we have them out sometime soon. That okay?'

'Sure. You'll have to cook though, cos foo—' She's on her feet and rushing out the back door before I realise that she's heaving out her lunch.

'You okay?' I ask as she washes her hands in the kitchen sink, wiping her mouth with the back of her hand.

She nods but is pale.

'So ... what you been doing?' I hold my breath, anticipating the answer, *Fucking your brother.*

Destiny glances out at the orchard. 'Not much. Bit of gardening. Mostly been mooching on the couch; got a good book going at the moment. And Nugget doesn't really leave me alone!' She picks up the puppy who is chewing on her toes.

'Seen Sam today at all?'

Destiny starts. 'Mmm yeah, he came up to the house sometime. Wasn't taking much notice. Was engrossed in my book ...'

I watch her closely, trying to get into her brain, to hear her secrets. Nothing but a wall. Nugget squirms in her arms, licking her face. She giggles.

There's nothing like a dog to bring you back into the moment. I sigh. If something's going on, she isn't going to tell me. Who would? It's not like you go to your husband, *Hey, guess what? I just fucked your brother.*

'I might go down and give him his ciggies ...' I say.

'Okay. I'm a bit hot. Pretty icky after the heave, too. I'm going for a swim.'

I watch her small body retreat down to the river with the dog at her heels.

'Cooee!' I call as I approach the tent.

'Hey,' says Sam as my head appears inside the tent flap.

'Geezus, it's hot in here!'

Sam chuckles. 'That's summer in a tent, big brother.'

'It's steaming in here ...' *Have you been fucking my wife?*

'It's not so bad. Better than the below-zero that's going on in New York now.'

I scan the tent for signs. The bed is made, and Sam sits on a foldout chair besides a small table. 'What you been up to?'

The seconds tick by. 'Not much. Been exploring the farm a bit. Trying to remember it from when we were kids. Remember when Popa would let us light the fire?'

The memory floods back and I smile involuntarily.

'It's weird, though. There isn't a lot that I remember. I checked out the bunker. I think it needs a bit of work if it's to be any use for anything. Needs to go underground more,' says Sam.

Tell me! My curled fingers squeeze the packet of cigarettes.

'Hey! Ash, I can't smoke crushed cigarettes.'

'Shit! Sorry, I was zoning out.' I toss my brother the dented packet.

'I'm not that boring, am I?'

'No. Hey! When were you going to tell me about Jeanne Jeanne signing up with us?'

'Wasn't sure it was going to happen. When will it launch?'

'November. How'd you pull that off?'

'I told you I've been doing some serious schmoozing over there. The Americans think we're *exotic*. Maybe exotic's the wrong word. *Fascinating* might be a better fit.'

'It's a real coup for us, Sam. Well done!'

'Praise from my big brother! Maybe there are some things I can do right.'

'What's that supposed to mean?'

'Nothing. Forget it. It's good for me, too. Helps me to name drop when I go back.'

'When you going?' A mix of relief and sadness floods me at the thought of him leaving.

Sam shrugs. 'Haven't got plane tickets yet, but I have to be back there next month.'

'It's been good having you here.'

Sam smiles.

You gonna tell me something? I edge forward.

'Hey. Did you visit Moma?'

I'm not expecting the question. 'Yeah. She seems happy enough. Pretty lonely, though. We saw so much of her when we lived in the city.'

'So why not bring her out here? Destiny and her are pretty tight. You've got a spare room.'

Even though I have already thought about this, I'm impressed by his thoughtfulness. 'That's a great idea!'

'Wow! Two lots of praise in one day. I better stop while I'm ahead.'

You're such a joker, brother. Trying to deflect the truth …

'Yeah, you better.' I study the book Sam has been writing in. 'What you doing there?'

'Trying to write my artist statement for this exhibition in New York. You know how much I *love* writing.'

'Need help?'

'Nah, think I got it. Destiny helped me a bit.'

I cringe. *Destiny?* 'Sam?'

My brother waits.

'Are you over Destiny?'

Sam sighs. 'I'll always love her, Ash. But not the way you think. Besides, she doesn't love me.'

'Doesn't answer my question.'

'Look, Destiny and me, we were all wrong. We're too much alike. Two storm clouds. I really stuffed it up. I was too caught up in myself the whole time we were together. And that was only a few months anyway.'

Liar! 'I guess. Well, I might leave you to your artist statement. I'm going to talk to Destiny about having Moma out here.'

'Cool. Thanks for the broken ciggies!' He grins, holding the crushed packet aloft.

I head straight for the river, my brain full of thoughts and images that I can't keep out. But my own brother wouldn't do that to me, would he? It would be the lowest of low acts.

Destiny sits naked on a chequered blanket; Nugget is nearby nudging his nose at everything.

'Can that dog swim yet?' I ask, watching a rivulet of water trail down her back from her hair.

Destiny turns her head. 'He's a bit little still, but I took him in to cool him off and get him used to it.'

I sit on a river stone next to the blanket. 'Water good?'

Destiny closes her eyes. 'Hurry up and get in. It washes everything away ...'

'Sounds good.' I strip off my clothes. 'Cold?'

'Just dive in, you big baby!'

I duck dive into the clear water. It does wash everything away. I tread water, taking in the river with the trees above.

I watch Destiny sitting cross-legged on her blanket. Her eyes are closed, face up to the sun. I envy her ease with the world. Something brushes my leg and I yelp.

'What? Ash!'

I thrash through the water and scramble from the river. 'Something brushed my leg!' The terror is real.

'There's nothing in the river that can hurt you. Might've been a leaf or an eel.' Her eyes glitter.

'An eel!'

'You're such a city boy, Ash.'

Her face is soft, joyful. My love for her surges. 'It's pretty beautiful down here, isn't it, babe?'

'Hmmm …' Her eyes are closed again, her face inclined to the sun. Ripples of light bounce off the river, to the wall of rock on the other side, then back onto our faces.

Nugget barks as he pounces on something, his little paws holding it against the ground.

'Nugget! No!' Destiny rescues a small skink from him, but he continues his hunt, unperturbed.

I watch her walk back to the blanket, her small body lean and muscular. There's no sign of the baby yet, but I remember how beautiful she was when pregnant with Tomas. *Tomas …*

'What is it, Ash?' says Destiny as she sits down.

Stop reading my mind. 'I dropped in on Moma today. She seems lonely now that we can't visit as much.'

'We should visit her more. It isn't that far to the city. Or, better yet, get her to come out here again and stay whenever she wants. She can live here even.'

My God, I love you! 'I was going to suggest that she comes out here. Wasn't sure how you'd feel about it.'

'She's your grandmother! I never knew mine, so I've adopted her. Besides, this is *her* place.'

I move from my rock to sit next to Destiny. 'Thanks, babe. You don't know how much this means to me.' I brush my fingers across the top of her shoulders.

Destiny shivers. 'Let's call her!' Her eyes gleam.

I nod, the spell broken, and reach for my clothes. Destiny ties a bright pink sarong around her waist.

'Come! Nugget!'

Still busy hunting small lizards, Nugget lifts his snout, and takes one more sniff before sauntering after us.

I dial Moma's phone number. I allow it to ring longer than normal because she's slower these days. 'Hello?' Her voice is small.

'Hi, Moma. It's Ash.'

'Oh, hello, my darling. I only see you today. Is something wrong?' Her breath labours from walking to the phone.

'No, Moma. I wanted to ask you something.'

'Yes. So ask.'

'Destiny and I would love you to come and live with us out here.' *Please say yes.*

'Ah, Asher, my love. You not want old woman to hang around. I am happy here in my apartment.'

'No. Really. We want you to be here. Maybe you can come and stay again, but longer, and test it out?' I'm hoping this is a compromise she'll buy.

'I think about it, Asher. Maybe I will come for another weekend.'

'That would be great! I'll call you in a few days to give you time to think about it?'

'Okay.' She puts down the receiver, leaving me to a dial tone.

'What did she say?' Destiny asks.

'Maybe.'

'Maybe? What's that mean?'

'She says she's fine. But she might come for a weekend.' I scratch my head.

'Is it Sam?'

'Maybe.'

'Well, he has to go back to the States soon, so maybe she'll change her mind?'

I shrug. 'I guess.'

I jolt awake, Nugget barking at the door. 'Nugget! Would you shut the fuck up?!' I squint at the clock. Only just after midnight.

I smell smoke.

'Destiny! Can you smell that?'

'Huh? Wha ... let me sleep ...'

'I can smell smoke!'

Destiny moans and pushes herself up into a sitting position. 'Nugget!' She leaps out of bed and runs from the room.

I pull on my shorts and run out to the front veranda. The darkness is hard to penetrate, there being no moon. But the smell is unmistakable.

'Sam!' I drag on my boots, bolt to the orchard. The tent stands there, ominous in the shadows with flames dancing behind it. 'Shit! Sam! Sam!'

I run to the tent, screaming for my brother. The crackling of the flames is like laughter taunting me. It comes from a space close to the tent, but not in it.

'Sam! Wake up!' I throw open the flap of the tent.

'Geezus, Ash! What's all the commotion about? I just got to sleep.' He sits groggily in his army cot.

'Fire!' I yell, arms flapping.

Sam frowns. 'Where? You sleepwalking, Ash?'

I grab Sam by the shoulders.

'Alright, alright, I'm getting up.'

Flames now lap at the base of the tent, licking at the old, brittle canvas. 'Shit, where'd that come from?' says Sam, scratching his head.

His slowness irritates me. I don't answer, already on my way back to the house to get a bucket of water. I run back, dump it over the flames, retreat to the house. I know there's a hessian bag somewhere. Aren't you meant to beat at the flames with a wet hessian bag? Yes! There's a potato sack near the back door. I run to it, grab it, race to the tank, drenching the bag with water from the tap. By the time I get back, the flames are hungry, licking their way up the canvas. I beat at them with the wet bag to smother the flames. A thick cloud of smoke billows around my head. I cough, eyes watering, and slump to the ground. Sam stands nearby, his face crumpled.

'You been smoking out there?' I ask, pointing to the right of the tent.

'Uh, yeah. It was too hot in the tent to smoke. Thought it'd be better out there.' Sam hangs his head. 'I did stub it out though … thought I did, anyway.'

'Shit, Sam! You could've been killed. And the rest of us. Bruce warned me about this. Gotta get ready for this kinda thing.' I'm talking to myself more than him.

'Ash!' Destiny calls from the house.

'Over here, babe.'

Destiny sprints through the orchard, Nugget cradled in her arms.

I laugh.

'What?'

'That dog is getting too big to be carried.'

'No, he isn't ...' She holds him closer. 'What's going on here?'

'Sam's just trying to burn down the place.'

'What! Sa—'

'I'm okay,' says Sam, holding up his hands. 'Just being a dickhead. I'm really sorry, guys. Won't happen again.' He stands awkwardly in his shorts.

'I need a stiff drink!' I say, standing up. 'Sam?'

Sam nods at Destiny.

'At least you're okay,' says Destiny. 'Tent okay?'

'It's singed a bit,' I say. 'Nice big hole in that corner. Another five minutes and it would've been gone. Shit, Sam, you gave me a heart attack!'

Sam smiles weakly. 'Just keeping you on your toes, big brother.' He punches me on the shoulder.

I roll my eyes. We laugh.

I stride towards the house, legs trembling. Why didn't I listen to Bruce? We were so lucky that Nugget warned us.

'This boy earned his keep tonight,' I say, scratching at Nugget's ears.

'Yes, he did,' says Destiny, rubbing her face into the dog's neck.

Nugget wriggles free, bounding ahead of us to the house.

'I hope you've got something strong. Reality is sinking in,' says Sam. His hands shake as he rakes his hair from his face.

'Some damn fine whiskey coming up!' I say, bounding up the steps into the house.

'Uhh! That hits the spot!' says Sam, downing a shot of whisky.

I nod, grimacing as the liquid burns my throat. I remember that day … at home.

Sam pats his thighs. 'Could do with a ciggie now …'

I shake my head. 'My God, Sam. Really?'

'I'm okay, though. Just need calming down after that.' He refills his shot glass, toasts the dog, and downs it in one shot. Nugget looks at him quizzically from his bed, then goes back to his dreams.

Destiny yawns. 'I'm going back to bed. Too much excitement for one night.'

I nod and we watch her retreat to the bedroom.

'Me, too. Feel ten years older. You going to bed?' asks Sam.

'Won't it be smoky out there? You can take the couch if you like. I might sit up for a bit. Too wired now …'

Sam stands in front of me. 'Should be okay. Thanks for saving my arse, Ashie.' He holds his hand out to me.

I pull Sam into a bear hug. 'You scared the shit outta me, Sam. I'm not going to lose you, too.'

We walk down the short hallway out to the front veranda. I fall into the old armchair as my brother is swallowed by the darkness of the orchard.

The old apple tree at the front of the house sways.

'Hello, Popa. Yes, that was close.' I inhale deeply; the oxygen rushes down to my belly. 'I couldn't bear to lose him.'

The tree bows.

'What do you think of this baby? It's gonna be okay, isn't it?'

A moth flitters past my face and I swat at it automatically. The tree sways.

New oxygen in my body has calmed me. I descend the three steps of the veranda and walk over to the tree. I stroke the gnarled trunk with the palm of my hand.

'I've got to make sure I have my shit together, Popa. I need to protect my family. I've failed them once. And Destiny is coming back. Almost.'

The tree creaks.

I rest my cheek on the trunk. The bark is rough but cool against my skin. 'How do I do that? How did you get through all that crap that happened to you?'

Silence.

'I know. It's unspeakable. But you survived much worse than us. We can survive.'

A breeze skips through the orchard, rustling the leaves.

'I just need to be the strong one … I miss Tomas so much.' I pat the tree trunk and turn away. 'Thanks, Popa.'

As I walk back to the house, I know my grandfather is watching me.

I wake to a cacophony of birds. I turn onto my back, my shoulders stiff. I stare at the ceiling, reliving last night's events. It could've been so much worse. *Time to get Bruce in to help get fire-ready …*

In my mind, I wander around the property, surveying the land, the river, the house, the orchard. And the bunker. Would the bunker protect us? It's not as if a war would end up on the ground here, too far from anything, but a bushfire? At least having the river so close is useful to douse fire. But how?

Responsibility tugs at me. I'm not sure that I'm up for this. *I'll visit Bruce today.* I turn towards Destiny to find her and Nugget staring at me.

'What's he doing in here?' I ask, trying not to smile. Nugget leaps up and licks my face.

'Heavy night, huh?' says Destiny.

I lift the dog so that I can see Destiny's face. 'Yeah. You sleep okay?'

Destiny nods. 'What's this doofus planning?' She taps me softly on my crown.

I laugh. *You know me.* 'Might go talk to Bruce today. See what needs done around here. He did already warn me about fire.'

Destiny turns onto her back. Nugget takes that as an invitation to play. 'Can't do much if a fire comes through here. Just have to be ready to leave. Can't be prepared for everything, Ash.'

Nugget pounces on her foot as it moves.

'I guess. Gotta pee. You want tea?' I ask as I pull on a t-shirt.

Destiny smiles. 'Earl Grey?'

Yes. She's back. And still so beautiful. I grin as I mimic drinking with my little pinkie in the air.

'Come on Nugget, let's go take a piss and make the queen a cup of Earl Grey.' My English accent needs work.

Destiny twitters and snuggles under the bedcovers.

Bruce is very happy to hear that I'm taking action. 'Gotta finish my chores, but how about I rouse up some of the locals and we get a working bee happening tomorrow?'

'It's Sunday tomorrow. I can't ask people to do that.'

'You can't? Well, I can. You don't know country folk. They'll be here.'

'Why?'

'Look. It's about preservation of all the farms 'round here. If your place goes up, then we're all stuffed.'

'That makes sense.'

'Too right!'

I leave Bruce's house, happy to have a plan. The land around here is very dry. I'm not even sure cleaning up the place will make that much difference, so I'll need to have some kind of contingency for what we do if fire arrives. I have no idea how this works. But this is a start.

As soon as I get back to the house, I walk straight to the bunker. I haven't been near it since the day I found it. I stand at the open door and flick the light switch. It barely lights the room but I can see that it goes a fair way back. It could be somewhere that we can shelter if need be. But I've heard that fire gets destructively hot. Would we survive a fire, or would we just fry?

'Ash?' Destiny stands on the veranda, hands on hips.

'Hey, D, just over here in the bunker.'

'What did Bruce say?' She's tiny up there on the steps.

I walk back to the house, the debris brittle underfoot. It truly is a Christmas feast for a bushfire.

'He and his cronies are coming over tomorrow to help us clean up the place.'

'On a Sunday? That's embarrassing, Ash. We can't ask them to do that. We haven't even met them.'

'I'm starting to think that this is how country people are. They help each other. And like Bruce said to me, this affects the whole community if a fire starts here.'

'He has a point there. When we lived on the commune, that's how we did things. We'd have working parties. It's just hard to ask for help after living in the city for so long.' Destiny scans the gardens in front of the house and frowns.

'Don't expect your Earl Grey tea tomorrow morning. We'll be farmers!' I try to sound like a farmer, but it sounds like gibberish.

Destiny rolls her eyes. 'Such a comedian! I'd better go into town and get some food. Being a farmer is hungry work.' She scurries inside.

Bruce was right. It's eight on a Sunday. I barely have the crust out of my eyes. Here comes the mob. Old Ford pick-up trucks, utes, and makeshift things on wheels kick up dust as they park in a row along the road leading to the house.

'Right. Jonno, you take care of the north end …' Bruce waves out past the orchard while passing the man a hand-drawn map of the layout of the property. 'Take Sam, Tom, and Mick with you.'

'Want us to go along the river?' asks a stooped man of about sixty.

'G'day, Stan! Yeah, that'd be good. Take Luke and …' He scans the crowd. 'Henry.' He gives Stan a copy of the map.

Stan nods, leading his group towards the river.

'So, that just leaves us,' says Bruce, smiling at the remaining eager faces. 'Good on ya, Sue. Brought your whole crew, hey?'

Sue nods and gathers her four children around her.

'Righto, here's the plan. Sue, you and your mob start at the entrance and move along the road. Create a fire break by getting rid of as much dead stuff as you can. Too late in the season to burn off. Fire restrictions. But we can at least give a fire less to lick at.'

Sue heads down the road with her children.

'What about me, Bruce?' Destiny stands behind him, cradling Nugget.

Bruce turns and smiles at her with the dog. 'Geez, what you feeding that mutt? He's getting huge!'

'Yeah, he's getting a bit big to carry now.'

'I reckon!'

'What's my job then?

Bruce scratches his head. 'I reckon you should sit this out.'

'What?' Destiny frowns at him, letting go of a squirming Nugget.

'Ummm …'

Mary intervenes. 'We've got work to do, Destiny. We need to cook up a storm to feed this lot. They'll be starving when they finish.' She walks towards the house.

Destiny pouts, then follows Mary.

Bruce lets out a long breath. 'Right. Who's left? We're taking the south end … Now, here's what's gonna happen …'

Four hours later, the mob is back at the house inhaling the lunch that Mary and Destiny have prepared: cucumber sandwiches, sausage rolls, lamingtons.

'You were right about them being hungry,' says Destiny.

Mary nods.

'Hey, Bruce,' I say, wiping flakes of coconut from my chest.

'Yeah, mate?'

'What do you think about the bunker as a place to retreat to in case of fire?'

Bruce pauses. 'Top part would go up in a flash, but the underground bit would be okay.'

'Underground?'

'Yeah. Haven't you been down there? Your grandfather dug the biggest hole. Let me help …' Bruce trails off, no doubt remembering his teenage self.

'Wow? What's down there?'

'Don't rightly remember. There's a trapdoor somewhere. Huge room underneath. All concrete. I reckon you could fit about twenty people in there.'

I rub my chin.

'Wanna go see?'

The old door groans in protest once again. I flick the light switch. The ghosts stand in greeting.

'Hmm, now let me think …' Bruce scans the dim room. 'Over there, behind the bookshelf.'

Sure enough there's a trapdoor behind the bookshelf. We both grab the shelf, heave it aside. I'm impressed by my grandfather, discovering a whole new side to him. He'd been preparing to be hidden very well.

I pull the handle to the door. It doesn't budge. 'How many years do you reckon?' I ask.

'Geez. It's been a long time since they lived here. Maybe fifteen, twenty? Old Zeke worked on it for years. Maybe ten years before they left? I think it sent him a bit bonkers.'

Moma's words come back to me; the pieces are starting to fit together.

'I'm gonna get the crowbar from the car. Back's giving in,' says Bruce, rubbing his lower back.

We work at the door for the next fifteen minutes.

'I would never have found this,' I say, overwhelmed by the enormity of what Popa has – *had* – created.

'That's the idea.' Bruce sweeps his hand towards the opening. 'You wanna go first?'

'I guess,' I say, peering into the darkness.

'Here.' Bruce hands me a heavy-duty torch. These farmers are prepared for everything.

I stand at the top. I can't see any steps, so I expect the darkness will swallow me up. A mass of ghostly arms draws me into it. I get a flash of the ghetto as Moma has described it to me.

'Hey, looky here, there's a light switch!' Bruce points at the trapdoor opening.

Good one, Popa. I flick the switch. A dull light comes on in the stairwell. 'Wow! I can't believe that works after so long.'

'Probably needs a new globe – just about ready to die,' says Bruce.

I move my feet, ready to dive from this landing, clutching the torch for security. The wood groans.

'Don't worry, mate, your grandfather was a top builder. Just think how good that house is back there.' He bobs his head towards the house.

'He built it?'

Bruce chuckles. 'Didn't you know? Long time ago. I was a little tacka. Musta been the '70s. I remember him letting me paint the weatherboards.'

I sigh. *So much I don't know.* 'Okay, let's do this.'

It's hard to see in the room, but Bruce is right. Twenty people could easily fit in the space. Along one wall is shelving groaning with tinned and bottled food and other non-perishables. At one end are neat piles of folded bedding, army blankets, pillows, sheets. Another shelf is stacked with playing cards, Scrabble, Monopoly, pick-up sticks.

I am in awe. He built this with his bare hands. My throat constricts with gratitude and sorrow. The place is dim and very musty, but it won't take much to make habitable.

'How'd he do this – with concrete?'

'Dunno, Ash. Can't remember. They lived in that old army tent for years while they built the house but I dunno if he built this thing before or after that. I remember it caused a few rifts with Rebecca. And I do remember my old man marvelling at the engineering feat of it.'

Regret floods me. How little I know about Popa – how much I'd love to sit with him now and ask him so many questions. He was a very quiet, private man, so it was always hard to get much out of him.

'Well, that's that then. Let's get back to this clean up so everyone can go home,' I say.

We retreat from the room.

The ancestors withdraw back into the walls.

Ten hours it took to get this place sorted. But I'm happy now; we have enough wood to last two winters, stacked neatly at the back of the house. My bad leg throbs but I'm used to it now. More like a dull ache.

My dreams are filled with the bunker. I think I've seen too many war movies, but I saw a group of people down there, huddled together, woollen blankets wrapped around their shoulders. The scene doesn't fit with our reality, though, as no war will come here in my lifetime. Or will it?

My body is adjusting to living here. I'm awake at daybreak, the birds my alarm clock. My first thought is of the bunker. I leave Destiny snuggled in bed to go out to assess it.

Spiders have made a kingdom in the dry, dark corners of the room. I shudder. Of all creatures, they are my least favourite. Those big, fat squishy bodies …

I replace the light globe with a stronger one first. It brightens the room a little more, but not enough to really see it. I don't have Popa's skills to know how to light the place better. Maybe Sam's camping light would be good? I'll go ask him if I can borrow it.

I head towards the orchard where the old army tent sags.

'Hey, Sam,' I say, poking my head into the tent.

'Good morning, big brother,' says Sam, bookmarking his book. 'What's happening?'

'Can I use your gas light? I want to clean up in the bunker but it's pretty dim.'

'Sure. Want help?'

'That'd be good.'

Before long, the bedding is hanging out over branches in the old orchard. Spiders scurry from their hiding places. We cringe, shrug on old gardening gloves just in case. Redback spiders are rife in the area, or so Bruce tells me.

We check the food. Some of it is okay, but many of the jars and bottles are well past usable. We box these, stacking the cans on the floor. *How do you tell if canned stuff is okay?* I change my mind and stack the cans in boxes. I do the same with packets of spaghetti and rice, many of which have little nibbles in them. A small mouse has tried to get to the contents then given up. *I'll start from scratch with the food.*

By the end of the day, the trailer is loaded with rubbish. I don't want to be throwing it out, but the last thing I want is for us to take refuge there, only to be poisoned.

'Let's go to the tip.'

Sam nods, jumping into the car. This is what I love about my brother. We have always made a good team. It's also great to be doing something productive, making a start with this project. What exactly this project is, I'm not sure.

We drive to the tip, about three clicks away. I love these country places. The tip has the usual real tip stuff that isn't usable but there's a section that is full of reusable items like old chairs, windows, bikes and such that they sell.

'Hey, check this out!' says Sam, lifting a rocking chair from a pile of furniture.

'Wow! The stuff people throw away,' I say, stroking the armrests.

'This could be useful for D. When the baby comes?' says Sam.

'Yeah. Do you think it's strong? If it's here it might be broken.'

'Nope. It's in perfect nick.' Sam puts it on the ground and sits on it, rocking vigorously.

'Great. Let's try it. Put it in the trailer.' We trundle back to the car with our ten-dollar-treasure.

'What've you two been up to all day?' asks Destiny from the couch. She's pale, her mouth downturned.

'Hey, babe, you okay?'

She shrugs. 'Queasy. It'll pass in a couple weeks.'

'We've been cleaning out the bunker.'

Destiny raises her eyebrows. 'Didn't you already do that? It's a tiny room.'

I sit across from her; she rubs her stomach in slow circular movements. 'Bruce showed me something. You wouldn't believe what's in there.'

Destiny frowns.

'I mean, there's a trapdoor that opens into this huge room. Twenty people can fit in there.'

Destiny sighs. 'When would we need to go in there, Ash?'

'You never know. Could come in useful. Maybe you could use it as a studio?'

'You're kidding me, aren't you? Are there windows?'

She's so much fun to tease. 'Maybe we could use it for a naughty corner when this kid arrives.' I point at her stomach.

She sighs again. 'Very funny, genius. The place is weird to me.'

'So, you hungry?' I ask.

'Nup,' says Destiny, leaning her head back on the couch and closing her eyes. 'Food is the last thing I need. Can you make me a ginger tea?'

I kiss her as I pass, heading for the kitchen. 'Sure, babe. You want something, Sam?'

'Beer?' says my brother.

'Yeah, I could do with one, too.'

I hesitate. Do I leave them alone together? I shake the thought from my head. *Don't be an idiot, Ash.* I come back to reality when I nearly trip over Nugget as he bounds in through the back door.

'Hey, D. I forgot. Sam found something great at the tip. Might be useful for you when the baby comes?' I hand Sam his beer.

'Oh, yeah?'

'Yeah, come outside.'

The three of us, and Nugget, go out to the car. Sam lifts the rocker from the trailer.

'You found that at the tip?' asks Destiny.

'I thought it might be good when you're trying to get the baby to sleep,' says Sam. There's a hint of apology in his voice that I don't understand.

'It's a great idea. Thank you. I can't believe the things that people get rid of.' She sits in it – rocking gently – holding her belly either side.

She pushes herself out of the chair. 'Well, don't stand there like mullets. Can one of you put it up on the veranda?'

Sam lifts it above his head and carries it towards the house.

'Y ou sure you gotta go?' I ask.

'I've been here six weeks, Ash. You must be sick of me by now,' says Sam, stuffing clothes into a duffle bag.

'You're my brother. It's been really good to see you. How long you think you'll be gone?'

'I really wanted to miss the worst of their winter. They can keep those below-freezing temperatures. Exhibition isn't until April but I gotta start spruiking it.'

'Maybe you could come back for the Jeanne Jeanne opening? Baby's due around then, too.'

Sam pauses. 'Yeah, I think that's possible. My exhibition will be moving to San Fran, but I think it opens before that ...'

'Keep in touch, okay, Sam?'

'Of course. Why you say that?'

'Not sure why you even question it.' I hold up my hands, first and second fingers twisted together. 'I needed you over the past year.'

Sam's eyes water. 'Shit! I'm sorry, Ash. I didn't know what to do. That first month after the accident ... and the funeral ...

it was horrendous. I felt useless. There were times when I sat by Destiny's bed and willed it all to go away.'

'You sat by Destiny's bed?'

'Every night for two weeks. I wanted her to have someone there twenty-four-seven.'

'Really? No one ever said anything. I never saw you.'

Sam laughs. 'You know what it's like in there. The nurses are always busy. They probably just thought I was you.'

'I guess.' *You do still love her …*

'Look. Destiny and I … I know I blew it with her … I'm happy that you two are together, but it doesn't mean that I don't still care about her.'

Stop reading my mind!

'And I kinda knew that you could deal with losing Tomas much easier than she could.'

I start. 'What do you mean? I'm shattered.'

'No, I don't mean it like that. I mean … that you have the strength to work through it. Accept it. Much quicker than her.' He crosses his arms over his chest, tucking his hands in his armpits.

'I'll never accept it!'

'Yes, you already have. It's normal, Ash. You've gone through the motions and you're ready to start living again. Wanting this baby is a good sign. Accepting it doesn't mean you don't care about Tomas or you are okay about it.'

'Since when did you get so wise?'

'I have a lot of time on my own, too much time to think. I could see the change in you when I got back. You had hope in your eyes.'

'Bullshit! Don't get all mature on me.'

'It's true. But for what it's worth, I'm sorry I pissed off. I was a chicken, and I should've stayed.'

I have to embrace him now; any suspicions I've had are paranoia. 'It's okay. You're not the only one who found it hard to be around us.'

'Mum?'

I nod.

'She has trouble dealing with any kind of trauma. You'd think she was a Holocaust survivor, not Moma,' says Sam.

'Moma is incredible. I don't think we could've gotten through all of this without her.'

Sam nods. 'Shit! The time. I've got to get to the airport.' He holds his wrist up to prove the time.

'Don't worry. I know a back way. Let's go.'

Sam stuffs the last of his clothes into his bag and picks up his wallet and passport. 'I think that's it. Might go say bye to Destiny.'

We find Destiny in the spare room, rummaging through the paints that I dumped on the bed. Nugget has his snout to the floor.

'Hey, D, Sam's gotta go. What you doing?'

'Nothing much. Just cleaning up in here …'

Sam stands awkwardly in front of her. 'Bye, Destiny.'

She turns to him and smiles. 'It's been good to see you, Sam. Good luck with the exhibition.'

She's happy to see him go? I pick up Sam's duffle bag.

'I'll go start the car.' Nugget lifts his head at the word *car*. 'No, boy, you stay.'

I go sit in the car. Check my watch. We've got to leave. I honk the horn.

Sam rushes out, checking his pockets. 'Sorry.'

'Everything good?'

'All good. Let's get outta here! It's still going to be damn cold over there.' He zips his jacket, flipping up his collar.

I'm going to miss Sam. But we've got a lot to do around the place before this baby arrives. And it's good to have things to do.

Back home, I park the car under the tree, mount the front steps in two strides.

'Destiny, you here?' The house is quiet, so I'm guessing she's having a swim.

I think about checking the bunker. It's a gorgeous autumn day. The air lies on you like a soft blanket. Sounds funny, but it really is calming. I stand on the front veranda soaking it up. And there's Destiny, down the back of the orchard. Is she painting? Yes! I have the urge to run up to her, say, *Well done,* but I hold back. She's facing away from me, bent over her easel. I spot Nugget pouncing on something nearby.

A small breeze skips around the trees, whispering. *She's coming back … Thank you for your patience …* Walking over to the oldest tree I smile, 'Hey, Popa, how're you doing?'

The tree sways.

'I know. We're going to be okay.'

Nugget's ears are pricked up.

Afraid of breaking the spell, I retreat into the house.

'Nugget, no!' says Destiny, bustling down the hallway.

Destiny appears in the doorway, laden with her easel and paints. She has bright blue paint on one cheek. I rest both hands on the kitchen bench and smile. *Yes, this is it …*

'Hey, babe, what you been up to? Dinner's almost ready.'

'Nugget!' Destiny wrestles a paintbrush from the dog's mouth.

Nugget twirls and pounces, inviting her to play.

'Not now, Nugget! It's time to eat. I'm starved. What's for dinner?'

'Salad.'

'Salad! Is that all?'

'We've got so many tomatoes; need to eat them.'

Destiny frowns, dumping her equipment on the couch.

'What you been doing out there, anyway?'

Destiny turns her head, facing the orchard. 'Just … thought I'd try the paints … Rhonda gave me some hints about watercolours. I've hardly done much watercolour.'

'And?'

Destiny shrugs.

'Can I see?'

'If you want. Not sure about my technique. I don't seem to have the same control in my arm since—' She hands me her sketchpad, shrinking from it.

Of course the painting is exquisite. She's painted the old army tent that I haven't packed up yet. Surrounding it is the orchard, the trees bereft of leaves. The sun is setting, so the light is soft, muted.

It isn't finished, but I can see that it will be beautiful. I can already see it hanging on the wall.

'It's great, D. Can we frame it for the wall when it's finished?' I point to the mantelpiece behind her.

Destiny scoffs. 'Don't kid me, Ash. It's my first watercolour painting ever. I have a lot of work to do on my technique before anything goes up on the wall.'

'It's perfect to me.'

'Seriously, what's for dinner? I'm starved.'

'Salad. I already told you.'

Destiny groans. 'Aww, Ash, I'm starved. Don't forget I'm eating for two.'

'Oh, so now that it suits you, you like being pregnant?'

'Excuse me?'

I hold up my hand, deflecting her anger. 'Only joking, babe. I picked up some flathead tails on the way home. How does that sound with scalloped potatoes and salad?'

Destiny nods, pokes her tongue out at me and proceeds to pack away the paints into the spare room.

I exhale slowly.

Autumn heads into winter and we've settled into our own obsessions. Destiny paints daily now, and I potter around in the bunker.

Destiny's watercolour techniques are now under control. So she says. As she's improved, a strange evolution has occurred. Her colours have returned. I don't quite know how to explain it, but the black and white of our lives is returning to technicolour. It's not as it was before, but it's definitely heading that way.

Everything is running so smoothly at the gallery that I don't need to be there much. I've organised for Rhonda to have time off in June – her and John are going to Bali. I'll need to be there on and off to give Max a break. That'll be strange but a good chance for me to get a good idea of how things are going in there.

'Hey, Ash, tell me what you think of this.' Destiny is at the door of the bunker. I know she won't come in because the place gives her the creeps. I'm used to hanging out with Popa and his ghosts now.

I wipe my hands on a rag and take the painting from her. I'm transported back to the day I came out here last year. There's the waterhole. It's as inviting as I remember it. She's put in all the tiniest of details, like a leaf on the surface of the water.

'It's beautiful, D.'

'Really? You're not just indulging me?'

'No. I want to frame and put it up over the fireplace.'

She purses her lips. 'I was thinking of giving it to Bruce and Mary.'

I imagine Bruce's face when he sees it. He'll put it somewhere, pride of place. 'Good idea; he'll love it. But can you do another for our house?'

'I guess.'

'You know, this new style would make a great exhibition.' I'm hopeful.

'Maybe. It'll take me a while to build up enough pieces. I guess I've got a few months before this bub comes.' She rubs her stomach.

'What week are we up to now, babe?'

'What's the date today? The weeks roll into one here – I'm guessing about eighteen.'

'You could easily churn out twenty before it's born. One a week.'

Destiny is scornful. 'I'm not a machine. I'm an artist.'

I wobble my head, pursing my lips. 'Oh, excuse me, Your Highness.'

Her lip quivers but she manages to hold herself together. 'You can be such a prick sometimes, Ash.'

I bend down, kiss her in the hollow of her neck. 'Sorry, but you're so good to tease. What do you think we should call our new girl child?' I ask.

'Girl child? You know, you aren't that funny, don't you?'

I shrug, grinning stupidly at her. 'What about Madison?'

I can almost hear her brain ticking away.

'Not bad, but it's too American.'

'Shelly?'

'Too Aussie.'

'Kylie, Annie, Samantha?'

'Nothing jumping out at me.' She rubs her belly. 'Oh!'

'What?'

'It moved!'

I jump. 'What moved?'

'The baby, you doofus!'

'You mean there really is a baby in there? You're not just getting really fat?'

Destiny glares at me. *Yes, yes, yes. She is* so *back.*

'Can I feel?' My hand hovers over her belly. *As if I need to ask.*

'This girl is gonna be a little terror, I can tell already.'

'You think it's a girl, too?'

'I know.'

I'm not going to argue with her. I don't really care. I'm just so happy that I could burst. I gently place the palm of my hand on her tight belly. It's small and round. Not an inch of fat on her tiny frame.

'I don't feel anything.' I pull my hand away, disappointed.

'She was probably throwing a tantrum cos you were being an arse. It's still early. I don't remember any movement till about twenty weeks with—'

A heaviness descends as that weight comes down on us.

Destiny holds out the painting in front of her as if to study it but I know she is holding back tears.

My heart quickens. I try to think of something to say to get back to where we were. I have nothing.

'Wanna come see what I've been doing in the bunker?'

She's gathering tears, looking past me into the darkness of the bunker.

'No, thanks. Even Nugget doesn't like it.'

'How do you know?'

'He told me.'

I study her. Is she playing with me? But her face is serious, so I know she isn't. My skin prickles.

'Where is that little rascal anyway?' I stretch my neck out to look for him in the orchard.

'He's having a little nap in the last bit of sunshine on the veranda.'

We both turn towards the house and sure enough, there he is. But of course he's on the couch where he shouldn't be.

I'm ready to admonish Destiny for her lack of discipline but she just shrugs.

I tap away at my laptop; the little black and white television flickers in my peripheral vision, begging me to take notice.

The late news theme music catches my attention; the newsreader is especially animated. I stop typing. A bizarre scene is playing out on the screen. A plane flying into a tall building, igniting on impact. Smoke billowing from the site of impact.

Must be some sort of Hollywood blockbuster. I flick the TV off.

In the bedroom, I peel off the layers of winter clothing. Destiny stirs as I slide between the covers and gently sidle up to her. She mumbles something, so I wrap myself around her warm body and nuzzle into her hair, breathing in her warm scent. My hands find her large belly.

Hello, little girl. I can't wait to meet you. Not long to go now …

It's morning.

I lie in bed listening to the banter of the radio jocks, waiting for the seven a.m. news. Destiny hates this habit, saying it's depressing to listen to the news at the start of the day.

Destiny is already up. I grin, remembering the morning in the garden. I can hear her clunking around. She isn't usually up so early, but then she is unpredictable, so nothing surprises me anymore. I'm guessing the baby won't keep still and she's restless.

A black bird warbles a morning call outside the window, gawking sideways from the branch of the azalea bush. The news finally comes on. The breakfast crew is anything but their normal chirpy selves. Tragedy. Terrorists. People dead.

I sit upright, balancing on my elbows. I throw back the bedcovers and swing my feet over the edge. Searching around for some pants, something warm for my feet.

'Destiny!' My throat is hoarse.

I scramble around in the dark. *Put the light on, idiot. Damn it's cold.*

'Destiny, where the hell are you?' I call, peering into the brightly lit kitchen, disorientated.

There she is, out the back. She must be cold. She's hugging herself, wrapped in a big, chequered blanket.

'D, what are you doing out here? It's freezing?' I'm ready to berate her but her face is stricken. I stop, then move closer to her, wrapping my arms around her, her large belly getting in the way. 'What's wrong, D? Is it the baby? Is it time?'

'Nightmares ... last night.' She's shivering violently.

I imagine her dreaming about the accident, seeing our beautiful boy – lying in the road – lifeless. I've been there night after night myself.

'There was so much smoke, people screaming. Loud noises ... people wailing ... so much heat ... so hot. That's why I came outside, I was suffocating.' She pulls the blanket closer around herself for protection.

People wailing? I hold her tightly. She doesn't stop shaking; her face is streaked with tears. I stroke her hair, shushing and rocking her gently.

'It's still happening,' she says quietly.

'What's still happening?'

'It's not going to stop for a long time. This is going to hurt for a long time.'

We sway together in the morning light outside the kitchen window. I wish I'd put on more clothes. 'Come on, bub, let's go inside. I'm freezing my balls off.'

I gently push her towards the back door. She's exhausted but moves reluctantly towards it.

'Don't worry about it. It was just a bad dream. No one's screaming here. You'll be better once you get warm.' I steer her through the back door, letting the screen door clunk behind us, make her sit down at the kitchen table.

'No, this is very real. Somewhere in the world, something very big is happening or will happen soon, I can feel it.' Destiny pulls the blanket closer.

My patience is fraying, aware of the time passing and me being late for my meeting. I put the kettle on and get out all the stuff for tea, including her favourite cup with the butterflies on it. I will the kettle to hurry up. When it boils and snaps off, I jump. The birds are frantic outside now that the sun is coming up over the valley. We both sit with our steaming mugs in silence.

I check the clock; there's no way that I'm going to make the meeting now. I reach for the phone.

'Hi, Rhonda, this is Ash. Can you postpone my meeting with Colin today? A few things at home have held me up.'

'Ash, haven't you seen the news? It's ... it's horrible.' Rhonda is sobbing.

'What is?'

'New York, so many people dead.' Her voice becomes muffled.

'Rhonda, Rhonda, are you okay?' I can still hear her muffled sniffles at the other end, but she doesn't answer. I hang up and slowly put the phone on the table. My brain is making connections now. I can be damn slow sometimes.

'Destiny?'

Her eyes are woeful, red rimmed.

I walk towards the television. Destiny is shaking her head, but she stays at the kitchen table, cradling her mug of tea.

It's not hard to find a news report. Every station has one. The first image is of a person falling from a tall building. It doesn't take much to piece together the picture of what is happening thousands of kilometres away. The Twin Towers being attacked by terrorists. There is a lot of smoke, people crying in the street. I turn down the sound, but the pictures are still there. I sit on the arm of the couch, still wondering what to say to Destiny, then she's behind me with one hand on my shoulder.

'It's okay, Ash, I need to see it to make sense of my dreams.' She waddles to the couch to sit down, the blanket falling from her shoulders. The clock in the kitchen is audible in the silence as the moving images flicker on the screen.

Destiny sits bolt upright. 'Ash!'

I rush to her. 'What?'

'Where in New York does Sam live?'

My stomach cramps. 'Shit! I don't know. I've got his address but wouldn't have a clue where it is in the city.'

'Go get it.'

I rummage through the kitchen drawer for the envelope with Sam's address on it. My anxiety makes the search twice as bad as it needs to be. Desperation tugs me. What if I don't have it?

'Huh! Here it is.' I clutch the crumpled envelope with my brother's scrawled handwriting on the back. I read the address, but it has no meaning, no point of reference.

'I don't know where this is. You've been to New York, D. Do you recognise this?' I hold out the envelope to her.

Destiny scans the paper, shaking her head. 'I only went there once, and it was only for a few days. I wouldn't have a clue.'

'Shit!' I pace the room. 'He doesn't have a mobile phone. How can we reach him?'

'I don't know.'

I hold both hands at my head, tugging at my hair, willing something to come out of it. I stare at the TV, the ghastly scene of a city in chaos. 'Look! There's a number on the screen to call for international people, to see if their loved ones are safe.'

Destiny leans over to the coffee table, picks up a pen, and scribbles the number on a blank space of the envelope. She thrusts it at me.

I snatch it from her. Grab the phone, heart pounding. *What if it's bad news? My brother ... I couldn't bear it ...* I dial the phone, only to get an engaged signal. 'Shit!' I pace the small space around the kitchen table, then dial again, punching the numbers in furiously.

Engaged.

I slam down the phone. Destiny's face is white, eyes wide. I realise that she's thinking the same thing. *Calm down, Ash.* I stop, trying to centre myself.

I pace the floor again, trying to work out the best strategy for waiting. I shiver. The temperature must only be about five degrees. 'Hey, D, shall I light the fire?'

Destiny stares at the silent TV.

I need something to do. I pull on my gumboots to go outside. Nugget follows closely.

The sun is pushing its way over the ridge, tendrils of light and colour wrapping around the landscape. It's going to be a glorious spring day. But what of Sam? I imagine him buried in a pile of rubble, still alive, calling out for someone to save him but no one hearing. Hundreds of feet stamping past him, unaware of his presence.

Get a grip. He's okay. You know he's okay.

I pick up an armful of kindling from the woodpile and drag myself back inside, the warmth of the rising sun at my back.

Destiny is trying the number again. She puts the phone in her lap, waits thirty seconds, dials again. She repeats this while I set and light the fire. It helps to keep busy.

On the thirteenth call, Destiny makes a connection. 'Hello? Yes, can we find out about someone in New York?'

I can hear a muffled response.

'No, he doesn't live in the area but he works close by… yes, I'm a relative … No, not blood.' She holds the phone up to me. 'She wants to speak to you.'

I put the phone to my ear. The handset is warm. 'Hello? Yes … my name is Asher Anderson … I need to find out if my brother is okay.'

'Yes, sir, I cannot tell you if he's okay right now. I can only take your name and his and put you on the register. When we know something, you will be called back.'

I hold my breath, nodding at the phone. 'Samuel Anderson … yes, from Australia …' I read out his address from the envelope and repeat ours. I say, 'Thank you.' But I think she's already gone. I see her in a room full of telephones, buzzing frantically through the air.

I wrap my arms around Destiny. 'He's okay, D, I know it.'

'I think he's okay, too, but I won't be able to relax until we know for sure.'

'How about more tea?' I head for the kitchen. Anything to keep busy. While I know that my brother is safe, I don't know if he's okay. They're two different things.

With a hot cup of tea in our hands, and Nugget between us on the couch, we sit and wait, staring into the flames of the potbelly, surrounded by the dawning day.

The wait is excruciating. Several times, I pick up the phone to check the dial tone. I try the emergency number again, only to be told that I'd have to wait as there is no news yet. I must be wearing a groove into the floorboards of the kitchen as I pace up and down, staring at the clock, its ticking ten times louder than I've ever noticed. I can't remember a time when I'd had to wait for something with so much anticipation.

The phone rings. It's 11.34pm. I jump out of my ragged skin. Destiny, who had fallen asleep on the couch, bolts upright.

'Hello?' I shout down the receiver.

'Ash?' The voice is distant.

'Sam? Is that you?'

'Yes.'

'Thank fucking God. You're alive. I knew you were alive. Where are you? Where were you when it happened?'

'It's horrible, Ash. You can't imagine …'

'Sam?'

Destiny is leaning into me, frowning, holding out her hand for the phone. I ignore her.

'I'm okay, Ash. I wasn't there. But so many friends are gone. It's … It's like we've been thrown into some dark underworld as punishment … It's the start of some hellish war …'

'Where are you now?'

'Kelly's parents.'

'Kelly?'

'She's go—'

'Sam? You sure you're okay?' I want to jump down the phone line and grab my brother in an embrace.

'Sam?'

'Hello?' Someone else is on the phone.

'Hey! Who's this? Where's Sam?'

'This is Kelly's brother, Grant. Sam just needs a minute … we just got the news about Kelly. We've been waiting all night to find out if she's alive. She's … gone.' He struggles to get the sentence out.

'Grant. I'm so sorry to hear this. We've been watching it all unfold on TV. It must be distressing.'

'I can't even begin to describe it. This is world war, I'm sure of it … Here's Sam.'

'Ash?'

'I'm here.' I nod stupidly at the phone.

'I should go. The phone lines are seriously jammed up here. I'll call you tomorrow …'

'Ash!' Destiny snatches the phone from me. 'Sam, it's Destiny. You okay?' She nods, listening. 'We're here if you need to talk. Come back to Oz if you need to. You can stay here …'

She hangs up the phone. 'This is bad, Ash.'

'What do you mean? He's alive.'

'He's not right … Sounds funny … I wish he wasn't so far away. Could he be any further away?'

'He did sound funny, but he's had a horrific day. And Kelly's dead.'

'That's terrible! I think he was more into her than he let on.' She sits heavily onto the couch, holding her round belly.

'We should go to bed. It's been a long day.'

I open the back door to let Nugget out. Destiny's predictions are usually right, but what could be wrong? My brother is alive. *Thank you, God.* Sure, he may have been into Kelly, but they'd broken up. He'll get over it. Oh God, that sounds horribly crass. I do not actually know what Sam really thought of Kelly, or if there are other things that have happened to him since we saw him. He might just be in shock. Watching the TV from so far away is bad enough. I cannot imagine what it must be like in America.

I need to visit Moma. I've phoned her and Mum to update them on news from New York. What little I know at least. I haven't seen Moma for a week and I'm missing her.

I switch on the radio in the car for company to the city. Every station is running stories from the US. Awful stories. People jumping from the buildings from a great height to their death, firemen losing their lives trying to save others. I'm becoming morose so I turn the radio off. I can't listen to another sad, horrific tale of how someone has been burned to death or been trapped in a stairwell.

Arriving at Moma's, I steady myself. I take the steps to her apartment two at a time. She'll have the teapot ready, and cookies, maybe cake.

But she's sitting rigid in her chair at the kitchen table, listening to the radio, tears falling down her cheeks.

'It's happening again, Asher,' she says, her voice soft.

'What is, Moma?' I kneel on the floor in front of her, hold her hands.

'The war, it comes again …' she says distantly.

'No, the war ended a long time ago. You're safe now.'

'Ah, you young people has no idea. These people want to take everything over. They will not stop until they do. They don't care if they have to die to get it. They think that their way of life is the right one. If anyone disagrees, they must die.' She's trembling and crosses her arms, hugging herself.

Her mind is going. My stomach lurches. *Not you, Moma, please, not you.* I swallow the sudden lump in my throat. 'You don't need to worry, darling, we're safe. Australia is a long way from Europe.'

She looks at me as if I've just appeared from nowhere. The pause is seconds long. 'Europe?'

'Yes, where the war was. You're not in Poland now.'

She throws back her head and scoffs. 'You silly boy, I not lose brain. I not so old and simple yet. I know that my war is long time ago. I now worry about new war. This nasty thing that happens in New York. Who can be so evil that they begin to kill innocent people?' She laughs. 'Actually, I do know evil but this is new one.' She mutters to herself in Polish. 'Sam is in New York, no?'

I nod. She must forget that I talked to her a few days ago.

'He is dead, is he not?'

'He's okay. We spoke to him a few days ago ... but Kelly ...'

She waves me away, muttering again in Polish.

I stand – knees creaking – and turn off the radio. 'You need to stop listening to that; it's upsetting. There's nothing we can do to help because we're a long way from New York.'

I open the fridge to make something for lunch but it's bare except for a carton of milk past its use-by date, and some butter.

'Moma, have you been shopping this week?' There's no sign of her having eaten today.

'No, I not want to leave house. If I leave house, I come back to nothing.'

I sigh. 'Well, maybe you should come and stay with us at the farmhouse for a while?'

'There is no room for me there. You have new baby soon. I will get in way.' She stares out the window.

'We have the other bedroom. The baby won't need that for months.' I think quickly to try to guess what excuses she will come up with. 'Why don't you come with me now, anyway. You can see Destiny before the baby is born?'

Her eyes light up. 'Well, maybe for few days. Then I come back when baby is born? I can make some food so Destiny not need to worry.'

I'm surprised at how easily she agrees. She's forgotten about the danger of looters. I hope that Destiny will be okay with it.

'Let's go and pack you a bag.' I hold my hand out to her.

I go into Moma's bedroom to get a suitcase. When I get there and open the door, I fall over a suitcase that stands waiting on the floor. I lift it.

'Why have you got this packed already?'

'Ah, you grandmother is ready for this war. You forget that she already left her home once. Now she always ready for emergency.'

She pushes past me into the bedroom with new purpose, heading straight for the closet. She takes a coat from its hanger, puts it on and rifles in a drawer. She produces two large wads of cash.

I gawk at her. 'Where did that come from?'

'You grandfather not so crazy after the farm. He still make everything ready for the next war. He save ten dollar every week from his work at the factory and put it in the pile. This is to be ready when we must leave.'

I pick up the old suitcase, trying not to show too much concern. 'Okay, let's get going then.'

Moma has snapped out of her mood. She has been knitting clothes for the new baby and she'll look after Destiny. Relief. Our drive home becomes a planning session of cooking and more cooking.

Destiny leans on the doorframe at the farmhouse, waiting for me to come home. I'm not sure how she knows I'm on my way, but I don't question these things anymore. I smile when we round the bend in the road. Seeing her there with her large belly makes me so happy. She waddles towards the car, smiling when she sees Moma.

'Hi, Moma, you've come to visit us finally. How are you?'

Moma embraces her as closely as possible around her belly. 'Ah, yes, I come to see you before this baby is born. I make sure the house is ready and cook you some good food.'

'Thank God for that,' says Destiny. I try to mime a message to her, but she just frowns at me.

We unpack Moma's suitcase, hanging her dresses in the old wardrobe and make up the bed in the second bedroom. 'I not stay long, Destiny, my darling. This room is for new baby girl.'

Destiny smiles. 'It'll be a while till she needs her own space, Moma. You can stay for as long as you like. This girl is due any day now.' She rubs her tight belly in a circular motion.

'Hey, D, what do you think we should do with this?' I hold up the wads of money that Moma gave me.

Destiny raises her eyebrows and whistles. 'Where'd you get that?'

I point to Moma.

'Hey, Moma, where shall we hide this money then?' says Destiny.

'We could put it in the bunker?' I say.

'No way, too many ghosts, they'll spend it all.' Destiny dismisses me with the back of her hand. 'We'll put it in the outhouse. Nobody will think to look there.' She giggles at her own joke. 'Just make sure you don't use it as toilet paper, okay, Ash.'

She giggles again. Moma also smiles.

Destiny rummages in a kitchen cupboard and produces an empty Milo tin. She stuffs the money in it and waddles off to the outhouse.

'She seem happy,' says Moma. 'You are very lucky man that she is getting better and she love you. Soon you have new baby. You be a family again.'

'I know, Moma, I can't believe how much she loves living here. She's even happier now that you've come.'

'It is good to have another woman around when you are going to have a baby. It make you feel safe. You men are not so useful with a new baby.' She smiles at me cheekily and I'm glad that I've brought her here.

'Oh, come on, I'm very useful, aren't I, D?' I implore her as she comes through the back door.

'Only for some things. Like making us food.' Destiny plops onto the couch, her weighted body sinking into the cushions. 'I'm not going to be able to get up now.'

As I rinse out the cups, I wonder about the bunker. Would it keep us all safe if a war started? The idea of a war here, so far from anywhere, seems remote.

Rummaging in a drawer for a pair of scissors to open a packet of sugar, I spot the bright orange notebook. I'd looked at it briefly when I plucked it from the bunker but had since forgotten about it. I was interested in the information on the first page about the building of the bunker, but found it too hard to read because Popa's voice is so strong in the writing. I haven't told Moma about it either, I don't know why. I'll have to ask her about it later.

Moma and Destiny are deep in conversation. I pass them cups of tea and my heart swells with pride to see them so happy in each other's company, the two women I love the most in my life. What will it be like with the new baby now that Tomas is gone? I'm going to be surrounded by females. I scratch Nugget behind his ear.

'It'll just be you and me, mate, against all these women.'

Nugget closes his eyes, leans into me.

I watch Destiny talk. Her stomach is tight as a drum. I try my X-ray vision to get a glimpse of this new person waiting to join the world. I pray that it is a girl and that she's like Destiny. We don't need any reminders of Tomas.

T he small house is full of the smell of Moma's goulash;
Nugget lies curled in front of the fire, sighing, belly full.
The baby is days overdue.

'Ash?' says Destiny, sitting up.

'Yeah?' I'm fighting sleep, lulled by the food and the cosy
room.

'It's time.'

'What time?' I stretch towards the ceiling, roll my shoulders
forward, and check the clock above the fireplace. Nine-fifty.

'Time to go.'

I turn to her, stupefied.

'What're you on about, babe?'

'Exactly! The baby!'

'Shit! Really! How do you know?' I jump off the couch.

'I just know. Don't forget that the doctor said I'd need to
get in as quickly as possible because the last time wasn't a
long labour. This baby will be born soon.'

Moma stirs from her snooze. 'What is all this noise, my
children?'

'It's the baby, Moma. It's coming!' I say.

'Okay, my darling, calm down. You go get bag. I help Destiny.'

I pace the room. *The bag. Where's the bag?*

Destiny and Moma giggle. 'It in my bedroom, Asher.' Moma points behind me.

I run to the room and within minutes we're speeding down the highway to the hospital. We've practised this. We arrive in twenty-five minutes.

The hospital is a basic country hospital. I'm happy not to have to go all the way into the city because of the warnings about time. Destiny now has five-minute contractions and I wish that Moma came with us to keep me calm, but she stayed to keep an eye on Nugget.

'Mr Anderson, how are you? This baby finally coming?' A young midwife leans towards me to catch my attention.

'Yeah, eight days late, huh?' I feel faint.

She pats me on the shoulder. 'Don't worry about a thing. Your wife is very capable.'

Destiny is small in the hospital wheelchair. I try to remember the day that Tomas was born but it's hazy. This makes me angry. *Tomas!*

I remember something. Holding my tiny son in my arms while Destiny was in the shower. So small. A shock of black hair. *I'm sorry, Tomas …* I swallow, pushing back the hard lump that threatens to jam up my throat.

'Ash?' Destiny squeezes my arm. 'Are you scared, too?' Fear and pain contort her face.

I shake my head vigorously. 'No, D, not scared at all. I'm excited to see this little lady.'

Destiny smiles weakly, then grimaces; her hand squeezes my arm in a vice grip. I bite my lip.

'I'm scared. What if I don't love her?'

'It's going to be okay, D. We'll work it out together.' I massage her shoulder as another contraction takes hold.

'Well, let's go,' says a small nurse, beckoning us along the corridor.

I steer the wheelchair after her into the birthing suite on the east side of the hospital.

We sit on the double bed, waiting for the midwife. Our life is about to change, the fear overriding every other emotion.

'This is it!' says Destiny, standing suddenly, liquid gushing from between her legs.

I jump up. 'What do I do?' I run circles around her, the liquid lapping my shoes.

'Okay, Dad. How about you start by taking off your shoes?' says the midwife as she enters the room. She shakes her head as if to say, *Men are useless.* 'Now, Mrs Anderson, it says here on your file that you lost a baby?'

Destiny's head snaps up, her eyes wild. Her voice is squeezed as she says, 'He ... he ... Tomas was nearly four ...'

'No, I mean before it was born.' She's scanning the file to make sense of it.

Destiny kneels on the floor and drapes herself over the bed. A contraction rocks her and she cries out. I watch from my standing position at a loss. The midwife catches my eye and nods her head to the bed. I take this to mean I should sit down by Destiny. I do what I'm told.

I lean into her. 'You're doing well, babe.'

'What's she talking about, Ash?' Destiny's face is crumbling.

I scramble for an answer, but I can't think straight. Then another wave hits her, and she goes back into herself. You'd think I'd know what I was doing having done this before, but I don't. No instinct kicks in. I envy Destiny's natural affinity with it all. I squeeze her hand. Another contraction sweeps over her, and a guttural sound comes deep from her body. It scares me.

I hear a familiar voice out in the hallway: Mai. I groan. What? How'd she know? She can't be *that* physic. She's making a fuss out there. I try to concentrate on Destiny. She's between contractions so I relax. I stroke her back.

The midwife stands. 'I'll be back in a minute – just need the monitor. Must watch these babies who want to be born quickly.'

I watch her go. *You're leaving me alone?*

She's literally back in less than a minute. 'Destiny?'

'Mmm?' Destiny seems to be in a trance.

'Your mother is outside. Wants to come in. It's up to you.'

Another wave hits her. She grits her teeth, unable to answer.

I watch her body shimmer under the fluorescent lights. A sheen of sweat covers her back and her muscles flex under each contraction. I marvel at the strength of the human body.

'Ma'am, you can't just barge in. We need to ask your daughter if she wa—'

'She my daughter. Of course she want me. I need to help her with this baby.' Mai squeezes through the door and stands there beaming at us.

The nurse peers into the room. 'Destiny, are you okay with this?'

'Yes, it's fine.' She waves her away as another contraction comes.

'Lucky I make it in time. Rebecca good lady to ring me.'

Mai dumps her coat and bag on a chair near the door. I realise that Mai and Moma had a plan of action.

'So, what happening here? Baby close?'

The midwife nods. She's frowning at the monitor. My stomach twists. It never occurred to me that anything could happen before this baby is even born. Mai is unperturbed, patting Destiny on the arm.

'Good girl, you do well. Baby nearly here.'

I figure of all people, she'd know if something was going to happen. I unclench my jaw.

'Ah, yes! There the head. Destiny, the head is there. Look at all that hair!' Mai grins at me.

The midwife squats behind Destiny, ready to receive this baby. It's a little like someone waiting to be passed a ball in a game.

Destiny cries out and I hear a swishing sound. The midwife grabs the child by the shoulders as it slides out. A girl. So much dark hair.

Mai claps like an excited child.

I check the clock. It's 12.45 am, 20th September. Destiny regards her daughter with mild curiosity, then turns her head away to sleep.

Mai pats me on the head. With a toothy grin she says, 'Good job, Ash. I told you baby girl, no?'

I nod dumbly.

She pats me again, smiles at Destiny's back and leaves the room.

I sit beside the delivery bed holding my daughter, soaking up every detail of this perfect angel with her shock of blue-black hair. I pull back the muslin wrap that she's cocooned in and look at her feet. I count. Ten toes. I'm disappointed. But they always want ten toes – the doctors and nurses – so this compounds her perfection.

I tell her about her new family, and about those who have departed, like Zeke and Tomas. She sleeps peacefully, her lips pursed into a small smile.

I doze.

Just before sunrise, I'm startled awake to find Destiny sitting awkwardly in the bed, feeding the baby. They are framed by the large bare window, overlooking the park. I prop myself up on my bent elbow, watching them quietly. The baby snuffles and squirms. It isn't easy for Destiny, I can tell, the milk not come down yet. That's something I do remember about Tomas, the feeding battle in the first few days. The red-raw nipples. I wince at the thought. I rub Destiny's arm. Her face is in shadow as the rising sun starts to make a faint outline around her bent form.

'How you doing, babe?' I whisper.

'Tired.'

'Want me to take her for a bit?'

Destiny removes the sleeping child from her nipple.

'You go back to sleep. I'll sort her out for a while.'

Destiny sighs and slides down into the covers.

I bundle up the little parcel and tuck it into the crook of my arm, wander out into the corridor. The midwife is there, checking items on a trolley.

'Hullo, Mr Anderson. How is that baby girl going?'

'She's perfect. Hey, can I ask you …?'

She waits.

'You mentioned another pregnancy. You see, Destiny doesn't know about the baby. She didn't know she was pregnant. We were in the middle of dealing with losing our other son, so I didn't tell her. I was worried it might send her over the edge.'

The midwife, Nurse Meadows, purses her lips. 'I'm sorry for your loss. I can understand you not telling her. I won't mention it again. It doesn't affect her now, medically at least. But it is in her file, so she may find out one day.'

'Thank you. I want to wait until she's mentally stronger.'

'Fair enough. I'll leave you to enjoy your perfect daughter.' She pushes the trolley to the next room.

My daughter. *So tiny.* Her face is prune-like, still covered in a milky film. I wonder when we can bathe her. I study her features and laugh inwardly. She is so new and yet so ancient, her skin creased into lines and a soft covering of downy hair around the edges of her face. Her face contorts, as if about to cry, then settles again, the lips forming into that perfect bow.

How could you not love her? We made this perfect creature.

Thank God visiting hours aren't till after lunch. We're both exhausted.

I can hear chatter and laughter in the corridors. A tentative knock on our door. Destiny is sleeping soundly.

A head peeps around the door. Moma. 'Hello?'

I hold my finger to my lips and creep to the door. 'Hi, Moma. How'd you get here?'

'I brought her, of course.' Mum pushes in behind her.

'Hi, Mum. Let's just keep our voices down. Destiny's sleeping.'

They nod in unison, craning their necks over me.

I usher them to the two armchairs against the wall. I turn and scoop up the baby from the bed, placing her gently in Moma's arms. Mum's shoulders droop and she drops her head. I should've given her the baby first.

My disregard is immediately forgotten. They both bend over the bundle, making a fuss and coo in loud whispers. The baby is still unwashed, her hair sticking out at angles.

'What's her name, Ash?' asks Mum.

I shrug. We haven't talked about that yet. We threw names around during the pregnancy but never really settled on anything.

'Rebecca,' Destiny says from behind me.

'Oh, you awake, darling,' says Moma.

'You lot are the worst at whispering,' replies Destiny. I'm not sure if she's joking or sarcastic.

'Sorry, Destiny. But she's so beautiful. It's impossible not to be excited about her,' says Mum.

'We're naming her Rebecca?' I turn to her with raised eyebrows.

Destiny nods. 'She'll probably get called Re or Becca.'

It does suit her. *Hello, Re.* 'So, Moma, you hear that? We're calling her Rebecca.'

Moma frowns. I now see that Mum is slighted again, but she bends over Moma and squeezes her shoulder. 'They're naming the baby after you, Mum,' she says.

Moma's face lights up. 'Rebecca is her name?'

We nod in unison.

'But you know what Aussies are like, Moma, they'll call her everything but Rebecca – like Re, Bec, Becca, Becky.'

Moma's eyes are glistening with tears. I mouth, *Thank you* to Destiny.

'Rebecca Rose Anderson,' says Destiny with finality.

I repeat the name in my head. It seems the decision has been made, but I'll let her have this one.

I open the kitchen drawer to look for the diary. I hesitate before slowly grasping it and pulling it out from amongst the unpaid bills. I've never seen a notebook like this one. I think that maybe the bright orange is significant because of the '70s. That means that Zeke would have been writing in this book when I was a little boy visiting the farm. I caress the cloth cover.

Moma approaches the back door with some freshly laid eggs in her hands. 'Good morning, Moma.'

'Yes, it is, Asher, my darling.' She beams at me, holding up two eggs, one a creamy hue, the other brilliant white. 'I have already washed them under the tap. They will be good for some baking today. We must feed up Destiny now.'

'I'm sure she won't mind you doing that.' I kiss her lightly on the forehead.

'You look like you waiting to ask me question.'

'Yes, actually, I was thinking about this book.' I hold up the notebook.

'Yes, that is Zeke's book. What of it?' *Is she bristling?*

'I was hoping that you can read some of it for me? Most of it's not written in English. Do you think that Popa would be annoyed with me if we read his book?'

She reaches out to hold it, fingers the covers and cocks her head to one side. Sighing, she says, 'No, I think that Zeke would be okay with it. You know, I can remember buying this for him. It was for our anniversary. He did say that he wanted to write me some poems. But he never did that I ever saw. I got this for him from the Sunday market in the town. So many years ago …'

She shuffles towards the kitchen table, sits down.

'Let us have a small read. Zeke will let me know if it is not a good idea to read.'

She opens the covers. It crackles under her fingers.

Today I have planted many fruit trees. I have followed the idea of my father from when we did live in Poland. I am old now but I know that when I am gone, that my children, they will have much food because of these fruit trees. They will not know hunger like me and my brother and my sister did know hunger. How that hunger can eat at your body.

That is funny, to use the word 'eat' when talking of hunger, isn't it? But I remember when we were building our first house, my father, he insisted that we must grow fruit trees. We not even have a big piece of land, so it seems to be a funny thing to grow so many. But my father, he was smart man. How could he know that one day, there would be such a need for food? But anyway, the fruit was not ready when we really needed it because the trees were still too young. I am sure that those Germans who lived in the house afterwards, and who stole my father's house, they must have enjoyed those apples and peaches that us dirty Jews did plant. Did it poison them? I think that they would have forgot that a dirty Jew did plant them because their stomachs would have made them forget. But I would not forget the day that I did go back to my father's house after I was free again, to live in it. The people who was living there held a big gun to me and said that it was their house. What could I do? I had no paper to prove that I was my father's son or any proof that he did really own the house. I only had that piece of paper that they had given me, which was really very valuable at the time. I was given that paper at the end of the war but all it said was my name and it would be like a ticket to be given food. How much that paper meant to me because it said my name. This meant that the SS had not managed to take it away from me and now I had my freedom and food in my belly.

They had not won!

So, now I plant more fruit trees as my father did so long ago. I do hope that there will not be need for these fruits for survival but for my children, I will make sure that they will not go hungry. Anyway, if there is no need, my Rebecca can make her apple cake and I will feel happy. Her plum jam is also very good. I will let her make many jars of her plum jam and I will hide it in the bunker just in case.

I watch Moma's face as she slowly reads the pages. It's hard for her to read her native tongue. It is slow and stilted. Even more so when her throat constricts with the voice of her beloved Zeke. Many times she stops and pauses to regain her composure.

Young Asher was here with me to plant the trees. And his brother Samuel. Asher did help me with the water can but Samuel did not want to help. I cannot understand what it is that boy does want. He always must be first and he pushes his brother. So when I give it first to Asher, Samuel will go away with a pouting mouth. Why must he always be first? I wish he was kind to his brother. One day they will need each other. I would be happy to have my brother here even if he did always tease me and look down to me. It was because I was an annoying little brother but Asher is a good brother to Samuel. Always there is the jealousy.

I make the bunker better every day. Rebecca does frown at me about it. She does not think that we will ever need to use such a thing. In Australia are we not long way from those horrible things? This is what she say to me. I know that her thinking is good but I will be ready if it does happen.

The bunker is a good place for me to be quiet. I like to write in my book. It is good to be by myself even with my love of my Rebecca. Sometimes she nags me, so I will come here to be with myself and to think about all my plans. It is also good for me to come in here and feel the safety of this room. It is sometimes hard to feel this safety out in the open where many peoples can see you if they want to. They are things that make me be useful for a small time and also help me to forget my feeling bad that I have survived when my father and mother and brother and sister and all my other family did not have the pleasure of seeing the war ending and the freedom of the ghetto. I do hope that little Samuel, Asher, Arnold will not have to experience such things. If such a thing as war will happen, this will be where they can hide. I have make the plans so strongly that there is nothing that I will forget to include in the safety of this bunker. They will be able to live in here for many, many months without anyone even knowing that they are here. I know Rebecca, she does get tired of me talking in this way but she also knows what it is to be hungry. She will forgive me and my constant talkings of the bunker.

Moma stops.

I try to imagine Popa as a young man in Poland, but I have only ever known him with a shock of snowy white hair. There are no photographs of him as a young man. No photographs at all of him before they came to Australia.

Moma is silent. Her hands shake a little as she holds the book. Her beautiful blue eyes are pale and watery, and her pain is palpable.

'Moma, are you okay?'

'Yes, Asher, it is okay. I am remembering so many things. It is good that you grandfather has written this down. Some things are hard to hear, but it must be heard. The children need to know what really has happened, but they also need to know that we have survived it in some way. We have survived it and this means that they did not beat us. There is a comfort in knowing this. Even this mark does not control me.' She turns her hand to show me the tattoo number on her forearm.

'Are you not angry that your life was stolen from you? And what about your lost family?'

'Oh yah, of course, there is sometimes anger. When I am missing my family. But after the war is when I met you grandfather. This would not have happened. Zeke was the best thing that could happen to me in my life. So I had some blessing. And, my dear boy, without this, I would not have you, my beautiful grandson.' She smiles shyly at me.

I fight back tears. I don't understand how she can be so forgiving. I try to focus on the gum tree that sways in the small breeze outside the window but my vision blurs.

'I read some more,' says Moma quietly.

Today I am in sad mood. I have nightmares yesterday night. Bad dreams about my big brother Moshe. How I miss that simple boy. He was so strong and proud. Sometimes not so proud about his little brother Zeke because he could not always keep up with him. But there was many times when he did stick up for me. And this is what I have the bad dreams about. Because it was my big brother that did save me from the cattle trucks.

Moma stops again. She closes the book and sets it down on the kitchen table. What would I have done with this thing if I did not have her here to translate it for me? All these memories from the past that would have remained locked away.

'I read some more another day,' says Moma, voice quivering. She shuffles past me towards the bedroom. She makes motions to check on Re and Destiny. Both are sleeping soundly. Moma closes the door softly and goes straight to the kitchen. There, she smooths down her dress before putting on a floral apron that Destiny bought her for her last birthday. She retrieves a battered recipe book from a high shelf and begins earnestly rifling through the pages for a recipe. I often wonder why she even uses this book since I'm sure she knows every recipe by heart.

I know immediately what she is going to cook by the ingredients that she gathers from various corners of the kitchen. Plain flour, baking powder, eggs, butter, cinnamon, and a jar of her own stewed apples. She is making comfort food – my favourite: apple cake.

I pick up the notebook, turn it around in my hands. I flick the pages, wishing I could read it myself. Moma is fully absorbed in her task, and I know that the smell of it cooking will soon permeate the whole house, most likely enticing Destiny from her bed.

I need to clear my head. From the front veranda, I look at the fruit trees. Some would now be close to thirty-years-old. Some are withered and dead and probably don't have fruit anymore, but the apple tree at the very front is still vibrant and healthy despite its trunk being twisted and gnarly. There are some younger trees scattered around the property. I wonder when they were planted. Do trees drop fruit and grow new ones wherever they land? I doubt this, as there would be hundreds and hundreds of them scattered everywhere.

I walk over to the main apple tree, run my palm down its trunk. There is a dry mossy growth covering the whole trunk. Its whiteness reminds me of Popa. I caress its bark as if it were.

A gust of wind picks up and the branches sway in greeting. An old man and a young man stand in the sunshine talking to each other.

I forgot that babies don't sleep. Destiny is up again. Two fifteen. It's damn cold, too. I'm awake now, as is Nugget. The cat has prime position – as always – in front of the potbelly.

I throw another log into the potbelly and put the kettle on. May as well make a ceremony of it. Re is so tiny. Not robust like Tomas ... was. He guzzled milk like he hadn't had a meal for a week, but Re just fusses and squirms. I have brought the rocking chair inside to sit in front of the fire. Destiny and Re are snuggled in it with a crocheted blanket that Moma made for them.

Despite the fussiness, I can't take my eyes off this child. How is it that she is made so perfectly? There's nothing about her that is ill-made. Except the sleeplessness. Destiny is exhausted. I wish I could feed the kid so that Destiny could go back to bed.

It's pitch-black outside; can't see anything out the windows, just a dark square. It's safe in here, inside our little bubble. I have my most precious cargo packed in here. Except Sam.

Sam. I've tried to get in touch with him but it's hard. So many miles away. When was his exhibition? Will they still go ahead with it?

The house creaks on its stumps. How safe is this place, really? It would go up in a flash if it were bombed. The bunker would be a better option. We can't live in there, though. Destiny doesn't even like going in it. I can make it an option, set it up as our refuge. There's no way I'm losing any more bodies.

'Ash?'

'Hmm …'

'Wake up, Dada, I need a break. Can you take her for a bit? I need a wee.'

'Sure.' I receive the bundle and tuck it into the crook of my arm. She's sleeping! I inhale her warm baby smell. Someone should bottle that stuff; they'd make a fortune.

The kettle clicks. I pour boiling water into mugs. The butterfly for Destiny, the 'World's Best Dad' for me. Re is so light that it's easy to do this one-handed.

Nugget bounds through the door with Destiny as she returns from outside. He likes this night prowling.

'There's a cuppa there,' I whisper.

Destiny cradles the butterfly mug close to her and huddles up to the potbelly.

It's eerily quiet. I sit on the couch with Re nestled into me. The potbelly is roaring now. I imagine the flames to be the mane of a lion that is trying to escape the heat.

Destiny sits forward on her chair. Awake. Alert. On guard. 'Ash, what did Nurse Meadows mean about another baby?'

I was hoping she'd forgotten about it. 'Don't know, babe. Probably mixed up charts or something. She seemed a bit confused.'

'It was weird. Maybe she was talking about Tomas …'

'D, why don't you go back to bed? I can sort her.' I'm hoping for a distraction.

Destiny swivels her head to me. 'Now that I've gotten her to sleep you mean?'

I recoil. *Where'd that come from?* 'It's not as if I can do much, D. I don't have tits.'

She rolls her eyes.

'Go to bed, babe. You need sleep.'

Destiny swirls her cup, drains the contents.

I cringe when she slams the door, worried that Re will wake. But she snuffles quietly in my arms. I dip my head to inhale her again and whisper, 'Don't worry about your mama, Re, she's just tired.' I'm relieved that the conversation didn't continue about the baby, though. I'm not sure how I'll tackle that subject if she finds out I knew but didn't tell her.

This baby's hair shoots out in all directions, black against the white wrap. She's bundled tightly. I can't put her down. I don't want her to wake but I also like holding her. I can protect her here. Now. I'm overcome by a wave of love. It's so strong, a physical surge in my heart.

My mind flashes into the future. I see Re as a young girl. I already make her in Destiny's image. I know that she will be a lot like her. Physically at least. How will I keep her safe when she's running around, falling over things, swimming in the river, exploring without me?

I shake my head. *Don't get ahead of yourself, Ash. Let's get her out of this sleepless stage first.*

Nugget sits at my feet, snout on my knee. I pat him, scratch behind his ear. He closes his eyes in ecstasy. *Life can be this simple.* Nugget jumps up onto the couch, sniffs the baby's head and regards me with ease and trust. I forget that he shouldn't be on the couch.

'D! Check this out!' I wave at her from the veranda. She must not hear me because she doesn't move.

I walk through the orchard to where she sits painting. She's still. Wind churns through the trees. I can understand why she wouldn't have heard me. 'Destiny?'

She turns to me, eyes blank.

I hold Re out to her like a doll. 'Look, babe, she smiled at me.'

'It's normal for them to start smiling at this age. Or it could be wind.'

I put Re over my shoulder, and she belches. I know she smiled at me. She's going to be a smiley kid, this one.

'How's the painting going?'

Destiny shrugs. 'Can't get going today.'

'You tired?

'I guess.'

'Why don't you go take a nap? Or we could bring out a rug and sit in the sun. It's gorgeous out here. Or a swim? It'll be cold but refreshing.'

'Swim.' Destiny starts to pack her gear away.

Swim it is, then.

It's not quite summer but the sun has enough in it to warrant a swim. We set up on the beach, Re propped up in her bouncer. I smile and pull faces at her and she breaks out into a huge grin. Gurgles. *Yep, this is it.*

Destiny strips down. The baby body is almost gone, just a bit of softness around the middle. How does she do that? Her breasts are still large, swollen with milk. My dick stirs. *No, Ash, don't ruin this moment.* Re gurgles again. I turn back to her as she kicks out her little legs.

'Ah!'

My head snaps up. I smile. Water must be cold. Destiny has dived down. All I can see is her rippled body. She breaks the surface.

'Fuck, it's cold!'

'I bet that woke you up.'

She rushes from the water, grabs a towel, and rubs herself vigorously. She has goosebumps the size of grapes. Her teeth clatter.

'Cooee!' a male voice comes from up at the house.

'Expecting anyone?' says Destiny.

'No.' I peer up the track knowing that I won't be able to see the house. 'Think I should go see who it is?'

'Moma can entertain them.'

'Yeah, probably Bruce with some bread.'

'You going in?' asks Destiny.

'You kidding? Too damn cold.' I grin at her.

'Wimp.' Destiny pulls on her jumper, rubs her arms.

'No. Smart. It's like a bullet to the heart, that water.'

'Yeah. But in a good way. A heart starter.'

I note the twinkle in her eye, thanking the universe for this river.

'There you two are.'

My heart misses a beat to hear my brother's voice. 'Sam!'

'Who else?' He spreads his arms. He's full of bravado but it's forced. I hold my tongue. I hold him close. He's thin.

'What're you doing here?' Destiny steps forward to hug him.

'I heard there's a new girl in town and I thought I should introduce her to the famous New York photographer.' He cranes his neck to look at Re.

I pick up Re and hold her out to my brother. She gurgles and kicks her legs. Sam takes her from me, holds her aloft, grins at her. She smiles back.

'Wow! She's a stunner, just like her mother.'

Destiny twists her hands inside the hem of her jumper and scoffs. Sam frowns. He raises his eyebrows.

'But she is, isn't she, Ash?'

'One hundred percent.'

'Cold in?' says Sam to Destiny.

She fingers her wet hair and nods.

'How cold?'

'Ice.'

'How about you, big brother?'

'No way. Freeze my balls off.'

Sam laughs loudly, forced. Re starts crying.

'Shit, sorry,' he says, handing the baby to Destiny.

Destiny shakes her head, laughing, and jiggles Re, cooing to her. 'Shhhh, bubba ... it's just your silly Uncle Sam ...'

Sam rubs his arms. 'Need some practice at this uncle business … Swim might be good. Jetlag.'

I'm not sure if he's talking to anyone. He's closed off.

'That river will cure jetlag,' says Destiny.

Sam doesn't wait for reassurance, stripping his layers of clothes and discarding them as he approaches the river.

'He's lost a lot of weight,' whispers Destiny.

I study my brother. He's easily lost ten kilos. My stomach knots. For all his bravado, he's hiding something.

'Fuck!' Sam resurfaces in a flurry of water. 'Lucky I don't need my balls anymore. I think they just snapped off!'

Destiny and I laugh. It's good to have him home.

'So how was the exhibition?' I ask Sam as we walk back to the house.

My brother grins. 'Sold out.'

'Great! I hope you got pictures so we can see what you had.'

Sam shrugs. 'I can show you the website.'

'I thought no one has money at the moment.'

'People felt sorry for me.'

'They did?'

'Yeah. Australian man in a foreign city. Loses his girlfriend to the Twin Towers tragedy. Idiots totally inhaled it. Especially the couple of images with Kelly in them. They doubled in price when we decided to auction them.'

I look sideways at Destiny, and she raises her eyebrows. We all bustle into the kitchen.

'Moma!' Sam bends to hug her. Everything is forced.

'How's Kelly's family doing?' I ask.

Sam crosses his arms over his chest.

'Sam?'

'Hey! Enough about me. Tell me all about you guys. What've I been missing here? What about this little princess?' He picks up Re and she wriggles.

'What's to tell?' says Destiny. 'She sleeps during the day. Cries at night.' She takes the baby from Sam as she heads into the bedroom.

'What?' says Sam.

'She just fussy baby; she settle in a few weeks,' says Moma.

'So, Sam. You back here for good?' I ask.

'Yeah, I think so. The exhibition was going to Amsterdam, but there's no pieces left. Unless we just duplicate it. Waiting for my agent to tell me what's next.'

'You staying with Mum?'

'Yeah, but I was hoping I could hang out here. Go out in the tent again?' He's sheepish.

'Sure, so long as you don't burn the place down.'

We both laugh. Moma is confused.

I wake with the birds and turn towards Destiny. She isn't there. Geezus, I sleep through everything. I listen to the house. Nothing. Only birds going crazy for the new day.

Stumbling into the lounge as I pull on a windcheater, I see Destiny curled up on the couch with Tuxedo, Re sleeping soundly in her cot. My heart stutters. My girls.

The potbelly is glowing, so Destiny must have stoked it recently. Nugget is curled up in front of it. I need a piss urgently, so I tiptoe towards the back door. The floorboards creak. I hold my breath. Nobody stirs.

Nugget is all over me as soon as I open the back door. I give him a rub behind the ears. So easily pleased. I piss onto the lemon tree, check the garden. The sun is edging its way over the crest to remind me of *that* day last year. It must be just about a year, Destiny eating tomatoes straight from the bush. The tomatoes aren't nearly as advanced this year.

Something moves in my periphery, out in the orchard. Is Sam up? I squint at the tent but there's no sign of life. There it is again, a blur of blue. I pull up my track pants, rearrange myself, and turn towards the orchard. Can't imagine that Sam would be up so early, but maybe he's taking a piss, too.

'Nugget, here,' I whisper to the dog. I need to have a companion. One with better instinct than me.

I wander towards the tent. I'm not sure why. Sam probably was just taking a leak and will be back in bed now. But I can see a definite patch of blue between the trees, and I can't help but be curious.

'Sam?'

I approach slowly. I don't want to scare the shit out of him. He's standing between two apple trees, oblivious to me.

He doesn't answer, and I think that maybe he didn't hear me. I move closer.

'Sam?'

Nothing.

The hairs are up on the back of my neck. Nugget is busy sniffing at a rotten apple. I relax. Nugget would know if something was wrong.

I detour around the trees so that I'll arrive in front of Sam. If he's meditating or something, I don't want to disturb him.

His eyes are closed and he's swaying from foot to foot. He must be meditating. Never figured he'd be into meditation. I turn to go back to the house.

'Arrgh!' Sam grabs at his hair with both hands. *Shit, what's he doing?* His face is screwed up and turning red.

'Sam!' I rush to him and grab him in a bear hug.

'What the fuck?' says Sam, pushing me away.

I land on my arse with a thud. 'Sam! You okay?'

He frowns at me. 'Whaddya mean?'

I stand and brush myself off. There's no recognition in his eyes.

'Were you sleepwalking?' I ask.

He shakes his head.

'What were you doing then?'

He thinks about my question. Scratches his head. He looks back at the tent, then at his feet.

'Haven't got a fucking clue.'

'You feeling alright?'

'Never better!' He grabs me in a hug, squeezing every bit of breath out of me.

'Geezus, you scared the shit out of me.' I hold him at arm's length so I can look him in the eye.

'Sorry, Ash. Probably was sleepwalking. Seem to be doing that a bit lately … I'm starved. How 'bout I cook us a big egg breakfast?'

I'm hungry, too, but I'm worried about waking Destiny. 'Let's see who's up first. Don't want to anger the gods.'

Sam laughs more than warranted.

I open the back door slowly, wincing at every creak. This house is not good for sneaky business. Instead of quiet snoring, there is Destiny, Re, and Moma giggling on the couch.

'What's this? Having fun without us!' says Sam, strolling into the room. He pecks Moma on the cheek and reaches out for Re. She snuggles into his neck. I can't quite figure out their bond but it's undoubtedly there.

'Good sleep?' I say as I bend to kiss Destiny.

She beams up at me. 'She slept all night!'

'Really? Why were you out here then?'

'I was anticipating her waking up. She was so peaceful I had to check she was breathing …'

I know that feeling. Re's gurgling at Sam as he makes faces at her.

'So where's this big breakfast you promised me, Sam?'

'Yes! I'm starved. Who wants French toast?'

'I will help you, Samuel,' says Moma, pushing herself out of the couch.

Sam hands me my wriggly baby and follows our grandmother. I push all anxiety about him out of my mind. It was probably just a dream. Sleepwalking.

'Hey, babe, need to go to the gallery today to make sure everything is good for the opening next week. Want to come?'

'Jeanne Jeanne?'

'Yeah. The opening is going to be huge. Rhonda is just about wetting her pants with excitement.'

'I haven't been down there for months … okay. Let's take Re to the beach afterwards?'

'Great idea! Want to ask Sam?'

'Go for it, but I doubt he'll come.'

'Why you say that?'

Destiny shrugs and I watch Sam. He's fine. He's kissing Moma on the cheek, making her laugh. They're making a huge mess already. Now I can't remember if he can even cook

…

'Sam didn't want to come?' asks Destiny as we clip the baby seat into the back of the car.

'Said he had stuff to do.'

'Like what?'

'Don't know.'

'And Moma?'

'She's coming. Just putting on her hat.'

'What about Nugget?'

'Geez, we should just ask the whole neighbourhood!'

Destiny gives me her best puppy dog eyes and I sigh.

'Okay, Nugget, in you get.'

I open the back of the wagon to let him in. This might be a big enterprise just to go to the gallery, but I like it.

I've never seen the gallery so amazing. Rhonda has excelled. New pot plants at the entrance, organic scented soap in the toilets, vast floral arrangements that probably cost me a fortune. And the added touch – little pig figurines in unexpected places.

'Oh. My. God,' says Rhonda dramatically.

'What?' I ask, expecting some new crisis on the eve of the biggest exhibition we've ever had.

'Besides this upcoming exhibition, this child would have to be *the* most spectacular creature on the planet!'

We all laugh as Destiny hands over Re for closer inspection.

'How old is she now?'

'Two months,' says Destiny.

'Wow, you have changed so much since the hospital, young lady. We're going to have to keep an eye on you.' Rhonda holds the baby aloft. 'Getting any sleep, you guys?' She deftly puts the baby over her shoulder. Behind her, the walls are an explosion of colour.

'Slept through for the first time last n—' Destiny cranes her neck.

'Spectacular?' says Rhonda, turning into the room.

'Ash!' Destiny grabs my arm.

'Is beautiful,' says Moma quietly.

'It's going to sell out for sure,' says Rhonda proudly.

We line up in front of the walls and nod.

'*The Age* is dying to see it. They won't stop hounding me, wanting exclusive pictures.'

'Fantastic!' I say. People do still get excited by art. There's something about Jeanne's story. Pig farmer made big by his paintings. Of pigs. If I were to write it in a book, people would say that I was making it up. Pure eccentric, this guy.

'I love this story,' says Rhonda. 'I love a story about a pig farmer. The media are lapping it up, too. And he's so good at hamming it up.'

She stops to think about her last words. Even Moma gets it. I love her tinkling laughter.

'What's left to do, Rhonda? Need me to do something?' I walk along the hung frames, checking the placards for each image. Of course, everything is in complete order.

'All set. Wanna meet Jeanne?'

'He's here?'

Rhonda bites her lip and nods. I'm sure she'll burst at the seams any moment now.

As we enter the staffroom out back, a large-bellied man rises to greet us. 'Good morning!' he says, hand outstretched. He grins widely, showing perfect white teeth with a large gap between the two middle ones. I'm thrown off guard. He should be wiry and more artistic. The art world is going to eat him alive.

I shake his hand, surprised by the strength of his grip. I can't take my eyes off him. He's pure hillbilly. Check shirt, denim overalls, bushy beard, and tanned arms covered in tattoos.

She winks at me. I stifle a laugh.

'Fantastic paintings, Jeanne,' I say, feeling awkward.

He strokes his beard. 'Thank you. I have good inspiration.'

'Hey, Jeanne, how'd you get your name?' asks Destiny.

I silently shush her but am glad to have the atmosphere livened up a bit.

Jeanne Jeanne starts laughing – billowing laughter that fills the room and infects everyone in it.

'You won't believe it!' he says slyly.

'Try me!' replies Destiny.

'My daughter and me, we was sitting in the kitchen at the farm … she was reading out a story about me in the local paper. They were talking about my work and how beautiful it was but how unartistic I am. Nothing about me says painter. Not my name or appearance. We joked about it, thinking of a new name for me. Then my daughter says, "Jeanne Jeanne". I was confused. She pointed at my overalls, made from denim, like jeans …we laughed so much and walked around the house saying the name over and over again with a French accent.'

Jeanne wipes his eyes with the back of his hand, takes a deep breath. 'We even tried a French style with the clothes but I just looked ridiculous.'

'I love that story!' says Destiny, wiping her eyes.

'Me, too,' says Rhonda. 'I can't wait for the journos to turn up, expecting some aristocratic French guy.'

'What do you mean?' says Jeanne, affronted.

The laughter stops. I can almost hear everyone's heart pause.

'I'll have you know that I am descended from a very long line of aristocracy!'

'Oh! Jeanne, I didn't mean to offend you.' Rhonda's eyes widen in horror.

'Yes! A very long line of pig farmers to the aristocracy.'

Rhonda processes what he has just said. Jeanne winks at me, then explodes with laughter.

Relief relaxes Rhonda's face as she falls into her chair. 'Jeanne! You got me. You bugger!'

Jeanne's face is now crimson. 'I need a drink. Rhonda, you got anything?'

'You bet I have. Boss, is it okay to open a bottle? I think we need to celebrate.'

We all need a drink after that. I nod. Destiny squeezes my arm and takes Re for a wander around the gallery.

Jeanne leans into me. 'It never goes away, but you learn to live with it.' He watches Destiny retreat.

I frown at him.

'Happened to me, too. On the farm. Boy was caught under the tractor wheel. Worst part was that he lived and was a reminder every day for the next fifteen years.'

I gasp. *Was?*

'Yeah. Shitty, huh? Like I say, you learn to live with it. Laughter is just about the only thing that helps. And maybe art. And my beautiful daughter. Wife died of a broken heart …'

Destiny is out of earshot, thank God. I'm lost for words. I realise that Moma has been sitting quietly at the other end of the table. I smile. She ducks her head.

'Rhonda, maybe we should open something stronger than champagne?'

She is aghast. 'It's not even midday, Ash.'

Jeanne snorts. 'Brandy?'

'Yes! There's a bottle of brandy in my office. Client gave it to me last year.'

'Now we're talking,' says Jeanne, straightening up.

Rhonda shakes her head.

Destiny returns with Re, who's squirming. She needs a feed. 'Going out to your office,' she says to me in passing.

'She's still suffering,' says Jeanne matter-of-factly.

'What do you mean?' I ask.

'I can see it in her eyes. She relives it every day. She's a startled rabbit.'

I don't like what he's saying. Destiny is fine. She has to be.

'Has she been painting?'

'Yeah. She's into watercolours at the moment.'

She's painting, so she must be okay.

'That's good. Painting much?'

I'm uneasy talking about her when she's in the other room. 'She's always out in the orchard with her paints.'

'Finished many paintings?'

'Not really. She says she isn't inspired. But she's out there for hours.'

'Give her time. It hasn't been that long?'

I flinch. 'Getting close to two years.' Feels like ten to me.

Jeanne nods.

Destiny enters the room.

'What are you lot talking about? You look like big sad sacks!'

I throw back my shot of brandy.

'Bit early for drinking, isn't it?' says Destiny, eyeing each of us.

'We're celebrating, luv,' says Jeanne, standing up slowly, his big frame looming over her.

Destiny doesn't respond. Re fidgets in her arms.

'Might be time to go down the beach?' I say to her.

'Righto, I'm off to my hotel,' says Jeanne.

'Hey, Jeanne.' Destiny is bouncing Re in her arms.

'Yes, love?'

'What's your real name?'

'Ha! It's James Smith. Nuthin' more common than that!' Jeanne chuckles.

We all laugh and walk together through the gallery, the watchful eyes of pigs upon us.

I can't get Jeanne's words out of my head. Destiny *is* better. She's painting, got a new baby, plays with Nugget. Happy to have sex with me.

I dissect each of these things. She does have each of them, but is she engaged? Fucked if I know. And if she isn't, what the hell do I do about it? I know that being here by the river helps, but is she just in no-man's land? Shit, I'm useless. I don't even have the clarity to see what's going on with my own wife.

Is she even happy to have sex with me? It's not like we used to be, but we've been together a long time and there's another baby. Re. My God, she's beautiful. How does Destiny feel about her? She's very attentive to her needs. Feeds her, attends to her when she cries. But maybe Destiny's just going about the motions.

'Asher?' It's Moma.

'Hmm?' I gaze at her withered hands.

'You like some apple pie?'

'Need you ask? Where's Destiny?'

'She out in the trees, with her painting.'

'Re?'

'Sleeping like an angel.' She beams at me.

'She's beautiful, isn't she?'

Moma nods.

'What do you think, Moma, about what Jeanne said?'

Moma frowns.

'Destiny being a startled rabbit.'

'Ah, yes. He is a little bit right. But she just need more time.'

'Will it ever be the same?'

'No, my darling. It will never be the same, but time will make it easier.'

My stomach drops. *Fuck.*

Moma passes me an enormous slice of pie. It sticks in my throat.

I haven't been in the bunker for a few days. I stand in the centre of the lower room and survey everything. I've been building up the non-perishables for months now. Piece by piece. I didn't want Destiny to know what I was doing.

I walk along the wall of shelves, ticking off my list. Yes, I have a list. Matches. Tick. Candles. Tick. Salt and pepper. Yes. Is there anything I've missed? How do you calculate for five people? How many days or weeks might we need to be down here? I figure there's enough here for about three or four weeks. Not long enough. People were in the ghetto for years. I can't store enough stuff for years.

I panic. This is useless. There's no way that I can prepare for any decent amount of time. We have Destiny's veggie-patch. I guess if we needed to we could come out to it and get supplies. But what if someone has taken over the house?

I can't do it. I can't prepare for the worst. At best I can keep us safe for a month. I just have to hope that's long enough. Wait! Maybe I can set up some hydroponics? How do they work? Do they need light? If they need light, then I need power. Most likely electricity will be out.

Who would know about this stuff? Sam? No, he was never any good at anything but art and chatting up women. Bruce? I doubt it. I'll have to research. Maybe there's something that can work without electricity. But then I'll probably need more room down here.

I rest my palm on the end wall. Can I excavate more down here? Would the place collapse? Popa, talk to me. You were the engineer. Can I make this room bigger without the whole place coming down?

Calm down, Ash. Do some research. It's good enough now, but you can probably make it better. I wonder if I could make a tunnel that comes out near the veggie-patch? I mentally measure the distance to the other side of the house. Too far. It would take me months and I wouldn't even know how to navigate it to end up at the right spot. And there's no way any of that could happen without Destiny knowing about it.

'Woof!' Nugget is at the top of the stairs. He shares Destiny's opinion about the place.

'Hey, boy, whatcha doing?'

He whines.

'Is it time for food?' My watch says too early.

I climb the stairs and scratch him behind the ears. He trots off; I get the impression I should follow him.

I trail Nugget to the back of the house. He keeps turning back to me to make sure that I'm keeping up. He must want some food and is just stooging me, but then I see Moma at the foot of the back steps.

I run.

'Moma!'

She lifts her head awkwardly and waves feebly at me. 'I am okay, Asher. These silly slippers ...'

But she isn't okay. Her left foot is stuck between the two steps. Shit! I should've known that they weren't safe.

'Can you get up?'

Moma pushes both hands against the steps but doesn't budge. It's not like she has a lot of weight to move, frail little bird that she is. More frail now, scattered down the back steps.

I manoeuvre myself behind her and hook my arms under her armpits. She's easy to lift. I put one of her arms around my neck and my right arm under both her knees. She's like a child. She twitters.

'What's so funny, troublemaker?' I ask.

'One day it was me carrying you in my arms like this. You were a cuddly boy.' She beams up at me and it is infectious.

I carry her into the lounge room and sit her gently into the couch. 'You think anything is broken?' I say, checking her legs.

'No, just an old lady's pride. I think my ankle is a little twisted.' She grimaces as she lifts her leg.

I drag over the ottoman to wedge it under her ankle. 'Don't move, I'll get some ice.' I rush over to the fridge, scramble around in the freezer for ice. There's no ice. Shit!

'What's all the excitement in here?' asks Destiny as she comes in through the front door.

'Moma fell down the back steps. There's no fucking ice!' I stand there stupidly with one hand in the freezer.

She laughs.

'What?'

'Just use a packet of peas, Ash. Didn't you ever get a black eye as a kid?' She reaches past me, breathing hot breath in my face as she hauls out a packet of minted baby peas. 'And don't swear in front of your grandmother!'

I follow her over to the couch.

'Let's see the damage, shall we?' She gently strokes Moma's leg, adjusts it and wraps the peas in a tea towel. 'Looks fine, Moma. You can just sit there quietly while Ash makes us a cup of tea. What you think about that?'

Moma nods, shifts in her seat.

Squeals come from the bedroom. 'Aha, someone wants in on the action.' Destiny disappears into the room, closes the door.

We listen to her talking to Re. There's no way anyone can tell me that she isn't doing okay. She reacts perfectly to every situation. Maybe it's me who isn't doing okay. I can't even look after a twisted ankle.

Nugget sits quietly at the back door, wagging his tail.

'And you, boy, are the best rescuer there is,' I say. 'Did you see him come get me when you fell?'

'No, my darling. I am being too sorry for myself.'

'This dog here came over to the bunker and told me to come back to the house.' I ruffle the back of his head, and give him a bit of leftover beef from last night's dinner.

'He is good boy,' says Moma.

'Have I been missing a party?' says Sam, at the back door.

'Moma twisted her ankle and Nugget came to tell me.'

'Yeah, right. Hanging out in that bunker too much, big brother.'

'No, fair dinkum. I was down in the main room of the bunker. There's no way I would've even heard her yell if she did. This boy deserves a bravery award or something.'

'I'm sure a belly rub is all he needs,' says Sam, squatting down and giving Nugget the best rubdown any dog could ask for.

'You seen Sam today, D?'

She purses her lips. 'Nup.'

'Think I should check on him?'

Destiny shrugs. I raise my eyebrows at her nonchalance.

'Jeanne Jeanne opens tonight. You still want to go?'

'Of course!' says Destiny. Her reaction is over-exuberant.

'Sam was planning to go, wasn't he?'

'Why don't you go talk to him instead of asking me a trillion questions?'

'Cooee!' I call as I approach the tent. I lift the flap and stick my head in. 'Anyone home?'

Sam peers over the top of a book.

'Haven't seen you all day. You okay?'

'Fine. Just reading.'

'Good book?' I try to decipher the cover but I'm not close enough.

'It's okay. Anything I can do for you?'

'Just checking about tonight.'

'What's tonight?'

'Jeanne Jeanne opens.'

'Already? Not really up to crowds at the moment.'

'You don't have to go. It'll be fun though. You'll appreciate the humour in his work.'

'Maybe. If not, I'll go during the week. When it's quiet.'

'Okay. You sure you're okay?'

'I'm fine. Just don't feel like talking to people.'

'You! The life of the party?'

Sam bristles. I think I've overstepped, but into what I don't know.

'Can't you just take my word for it? I don't want to fucking go!'

I raise my hands. 'Geez, sorry. Didn't know it was such a touchy subject. You were always the first to party it up at these things.'

'Well, that was then. This is now. There's more to life than stupid parties with poncy artists swanning around licking people's buttholes.'

'Fine. Point taken. I'll shut up.'

'Good.' Sam goes back to his book.

I back out of the tent, replaying the conversation in my head. Where did it go wrong? Was I out of line?

'He coming?' asks Destiny as I enter the kitchen.

'No.'

'Really?'

'He's quite adamant about it, too.'

'Wow. He okay?'

'Says he is, but he was really over the top.'

'Just leave him. Maybe he needs some time out.'

'I guess. So, it's just you and me tonight. Date night, huh?'

Destiny snorts. 'Some date. Mingling with poncy arty people.'

'What's with you and Sam and poncy-ness suddenly?'

'What?'

'Sam said he didn't feel like hanging out with poncy people.'

'You do have to be in the mood for it.'

'But you and he are both arty people! I bet he did major schmoozing in New York.'

'Probably did. But you feel like you're prostituting yourself.'

'That's a bit extreme.'

'No. We make art for art's sake. We shouldn't have to talk to people to convince them to buy or make them like us.'

'So all these years, with us owning a gallery, you've felt like this?'

'When I was younger it was different. I loved the attention.'

'And now?'

'It's all kind of meaningless.'

'Since when?'

'Let's just get ready. Don't we have to leave soon?'

'No! Tell me what you're on about.'

Destiny exhales.

I hear the ticking of the clock.

'There's before and after.'

'What the fuck?'

Destiny twists the hem of her top, avoiding my face. 'Tomas ...' Her voice is so low I'm not actually sure if I've heard correctly.

'What about Tomas?'

'Nothing is the same.'

What?

'What're you talking about?'

'There's before and after. Everything after is meaningless.'

My brain scrambles to understand. Meaningless? How can she say that? What about me? And Re? And this place? She's happy here. I open my mouth to protest but she's turned her back on me and is walking towards the bedroom.

'Destiny?'

'I'm going to get ready for tonight.'

The opening is full of poncy people. The most down to earth are Rhonda and Jeanne Jeanne. He's just himself. Big, brazen. A grizzly bear full of sugar. For someone who doesn't like prostituting herself, Destiny is like a five-dollar hooker down on Acland Street in the '70s. I've never seen her like this, even back when I first met her. Now I realise it's all an act. But no one will have a clue.

I scan the walls. It's one hour into the opening. We haven't even done the speeches yet and at least sixty percent of the pieces have sold stickers on them. The place might be full of poncy people, but they're putting food on our table for the next six months.

'Happy, boss?' Rhonda has sidled up beside me.

I squeeze her shoulder. 'You've done an amazing job. Thank you.'

'You aren't happy?'

'What?'

'Your mood doesn't seem to match the wife.' She inclines her head towards Destiny, who is waving her arms about in the telling of some wild story.

'Looks can be deceiving.'

Rhonda grabs my arm and pulls me towards the back office. She pushes me in and shuts the door behind her.

'Okay, what's going on?'

'It doesn't matter. Nothing you or I do will change things.'

'Stop talking in damn riddles.' She crosses her arms and reminds me of my mother whenever I got in trouble.

'Destiny told me this afternoon that there was our life before and after Tomas. Nothing has meaning anymore.'

'Wow! You wouldn't think that tonight.'

'Tell me about it.'

'You know what's going on, don't you?'

'Any clues would be most welcome.'

'She's scared.'

I snort. 'Who isn't?'

'Stop that and listen. Destiny is shit-scared that if she says yes to life and moves on that she is saying that Tomas didn't matter.'

'It's nearly two years, Rhonda.'

'Geez, you can't put a timer on this!'

'And what am I meant to do if she never gets past this?'

'I don't have all the answers. It might take years. You just gotta stick by her and that beautiful daughter. Eventually your zest for life may rub off on her.'

'How'd you get so cluey about this?'

'I'm a woman, for a start, but I've got a little experience of my own.'

'What?' My stomach cramps.

'I haven't lost a child, but I had three miscarriages.'

'Shit! You never told me.'

'Not exactly a topic of convo. I also decided a long time ago to not let it define me.'

'I'm so sorry, Rhonda.'

She shrugs. 'Life happens. I know how hard it was to lose children that I never even knew. I can't imagine what it must be like for you two. Don't take this the wrong way, but I think for women it's worse. There's that whole umbilical thing with a child. It's never really severed.'

I hug myself. I don't want to hear this. I want everything to be on the mend. Normal.

'At least she can pretend to be okay,' says Rhonda, nodding towards the gallery.

'Not like Sam.'

Rhonda straightens up. 'What's wrong with Sam?'

'I don't know. He's very moody. Pretty much broods in his tent all day. He's either like a sloth or really snappy.'

'Is that why he's not here?'

'He has the same opinion as Destiny about these things. Told me as we were leaving that it'll be full of poncy people.'

Rhonda splutters. 'Sam said that?'

I smile involuntarily. 'I know. It's a joke.'

'What do you think his problem is? Something happen in New York? It's not like he was actually caught up in that whole Twin Towers thing.'

'He won't talk about it. Changes the subject any time we get near it.'

'Maybe Kelly meant more to him than he lets on?'

'I've thought that, too. And I guess we weren't there. We don't know what the place was like after 9/11.'

'So, Ash, you're living with lots of fun people at the moment.'

'It's not that bad. D puts on a good act most of the time. And I have Moma baking me pies. And then there's Re.' I smile at the thought of my daughter.

'You're smitten with that girl, aren't you?'

'Is it that obvious? You saw her. Perfection. That's why I have trouble with D's take on things.'

'Give it time. Re's still a baby. You're all getting used to a different life.'

I sigh. 'I guess. Thanks, Rhonda.'

'No problem. Feel free to unload anytime. Now, let's go open this exhibition!'

'Don't see the point really. Most of it has sold.'

'Ha! We must keep those poncy people happy.' She waves her right hand in the air in a queenly salute.

'Did I ever tell you how great you are?'

'Not enough.'

'Well, you are and I really appreciate everything you do.'

'Thanks. I get pretty good commissions, so I'm happy.'

'But you're more to me, us, than just a gallery manager.'

'I'd like to think I'm part of the family.'

I wrap my arms around her in a bear hug. 'You're the big sister I never had.'

'Wait. Make that little sister. Makes me feel younger.'

I laugh and we walk out onto the gallery floor.

indigo

'You seen Sam?' I ask Destiny.

She shakes her head, mouth full of bobby pins.

I laugh. 'Is her hair long enough to put in pins?'

'It gets in her face and then ends up full of food.'

Re gurgles, extending a grubby hand to me. 'No thanks, bubba,' I say. The mushed-up bread is not appetising.

'What you want Sam for?'

'Just haven't seen him for a few days. Thought he might like to take a trip into town.'

'Feel like I haven't seen him for months.' She strokes Re's hair.

'He's been holed up out there for months. Hey, you painting today?'

'No. Thought I might go into town and see if there are any mums and bubs groups.'

I'm impressed. 'Good idea. She's around us too much.'

'What were you going in for?'

'Just need some supplies for the bunker.'

Destiny grunts. 'It's been six months. No war started yet.'

'I know. It's pretty well set now. Just a couple things left.'

'I agree you should see if Sam wants to go.'

'Okay.'

I go out to the orchard and approach the tent, listening for a sign of life.

'Cooee!'

'Heard you coming a mile off,' says Sam when I push my head through the flaps.

'Wanna come to town for a drive?'

'Yeah, why not? They got a travel agent in there?' He puts his book face down on the table.

'You going somewhere?'

'Maybe.'

'I think there's one – part of the post office.'

'Cool. Let's go.' Sam pushes his feet into his runners.

'Where you going?'

'Amsterdam!'

'Amsterdam?!'

'Is there an echo in here?'

'What's in Amsterdam?'

'Next exhibition. Maybe.'

'That's great! You got new shots to show?'

'Just another retrospective.'

'I haven't been to Amsterdam. You?'

'Briefly. It's a cool city.'

'When you going?'

'Depends on flights. Prices.'

'I'll miss you.'

'Ha! You won't even know I'm gone. I've been a shit visitor. How long's it been – four, five months?'

I scratch my chin. 'Something like that. Time's kinda warped out here.'

'You can say that again.'

'Time's kinda warped out here.'

Sam laughs. 'I'll miss you, big brother. You got those dad jokes down pat.'

I punch him in the shoulder.

'Let's go to town.'

Sam holds the tent flap back for me and I see a glimmer of the old Sam. It lifts me. But as we walk back to the house, I see his diminished physicality. He seems about ten years older than he should.

'Next week?' I ask.

Sam is facing me, plane tickets in hand. 'That was the soonest they had. And it's just before the busy season, so price is pretty good.'

'Didn't know you were in that much of a hurry.'

'Taking the bull by the horns.' He mimics this but it's more like he's trying to hump something.

'Right. Well … wanna have a dinner with family before you go? Get Mum out here?'

'No. No fanfare. I'll spend the next week doing the rounds. I won't be gone that long. I'm just scouting things really.'

'Fair enough. Need me to do anything? You okay for cash?'

'Still got plenty from the New York show. Not like my expenses have been heavy here! Probably got enough for at least six months.'

'Yeah, but Europe's expensive.'

'Got people to stay with. I'll work it out.'

He sounds so sure, but he's a ghost of himself. Sallow eyes. Almost a crazed aura about him.

'How about you have a haircut before you go?' I ruffle his head.

'I'll get Destiny to give me a buzz.'

'A buzz! You're not going into the army, are you?'

'My god, Ash. Where do you come up with this stuff?' Sam laughs.

'What?'

'If I get it nice and short, I won't need to worry about it for months.'

'Yeah, but Sam with a buzzcut? I don't think I've ever seen it.'

'Don't you remember when we were in primary school? Nits?'

'Never got them.'

'Yeah, but I always got them. Must like me. Mum got so frustrated that she gave me a number two all over. I didn't talk to her till it grew back.'

'Sounds vaguely familiar.'

'There you go. Where's Destiny? I'll ask her.'

'She'll be back soon. Wanna wait in the coffee shop over there?'

'Sure. I'll buy you a coffee. They do good coffee in this town?'

'Yeah, they're not as backward as you think.'

'Well, well, well. Look what the cat dragged in,' says Bruce as he pulls his ute in to park beside us.

'Hey, Bruce. How's it hanging?'

'Bit to the left today, buddy.' He laughs at his own joke.

'We're about to grab a coffee. Wanna join us?'

His face lights up. 'Love to. Hate coffee, but. Tea will do.'

'How's Mary doing, mate?' I ask him.

His usual bright face drops. He is a tall, broad man and he instantly shrinks before me.

'Oh, she's okay. Now that we know what's wrong with her, we can work out how to deal with it.'

'It's tough, though, for you?'

'Too right. She hardly knows who I am any more. Sometimes she thinks I'm an intruder and screams at me to get out of the house!'

Sweet little Mary. It's hard to imagine what it must be like for your memory to go like that. I clasp Bruce's shoulder. 'Let me know if there is anything I can do, okay?'

I know he finds this very hard to open up about how tough it is so I don't push it. He nods at me.

'What's all this riffraff doing in the street?' Destiny has come from the chemist and stops the pram just short of us.

'Hello, Destiny,' says Bruce. He is so in love with my wife. But not in a creepy way. More like a fatherly thing.

Destiny unclips Re from the pusher and kisses Bruce on the cheek. He smiles.

'This a party or something?' Destiny balances Re on her hip.

'We were going to check out the coffee here while we waited.'

She nods. 'I'd love a coffee. Let's go. What's the occasion?'

'Sam's going to Amsterdam next week.'

Destiny's head snaps back. 'That's a quick decision.'

'Like I said to Ash. Grab the bull.'

Destiny frowns, shakes her head. 'Okay …'

'I went to Amsterdam once.'

We all turn to Bruce.

He blushes. 'They got good beer there.'

'Ah yes, but what about those red lights?' says Sam, putting one arm around his shoulder.

'Yeah, well, I was a young bugger. Just followed the crowd. Sure opened my eyes.'

Sam pats him on the shoulder. 'Nothing wrong with that, mate. Might be visiting them myself.'

Bruce pulls back.

'Joke!' says Sam, lifting his hands in defeat. 'Now I really need a coffee. Let's go. Enough standing around in the street.'

I am not sure how this happened but Re is a big girl now. Goes to playgroup. Miss three-and-a-half going on thirty-five. I can't get my head around how the time flies. Tomas would be, what? Nearly eight? Maybe nine? Shit, that's something I should know.

The post box is stuffed with letters today. I haven't come out to town for over a week. It's all boring stuff. Phone bill. Reminder from council about the upcoming elections. Vote for Bill Pearson. A letter to Destiny from Finn, who's moved to Byron Bay. That's not so boring, but I won't open it.

At the bottom of the stack, a postcard. It's from Sam. Haven't heard from him for about three months. He's been moving around a lot over the past three years.

I turn the card in my hand. The photo is of the main street of Berlin. It's magical under snow.

I can imagine him in Berlin with the Bohemians. I have no idea what he's been doing though. He never gives much detail. It'll just be a postcard every few months from a different city. I'm lucky if there's more than a paragraph.

I turn the card again and try to decipher my brother's scrawl. It's a poem, I think. And then he's tried a bit of German. I'm sure there's some message in the whole thing that I don't get. Either way, it gives me no clue as to how he is. At least he's still alive.

I stand in the main street of town. What a glorious autumn day. I'm like a local now, though the people always remind us, jokingly, that we're new around here. But it's been more than four years. Where does it go?

Nugget's tail goes off as I approach the wagon. He's a strong, burly dog now. Wouldn't hurt a fly but I'd put my life in his paws, that's for sure. Does four years make us country bumpkins? I don't mind if it does.

I sit in the car and wait for the girls. I scan the local paper for news but it's the usual stuff. A Country Women's club of some sort baking cakes, John Sullivan taking out the prize for best in show for a bull …

'Anyone in there?' It's Destiny tapping my skull. Must have dozed off in the warm car.

'Hey, babe. How was it?'

'Was okay.'

'Don't sound so sure.'

She shrugs and starts unhooking Re from her stroller. 'Not really my kind of thing. But Re needs it.'

'What's so bad about it?'

'Dunno. There's one woman who hounds me.'

'Hounds you?'

'Yeah. Wants to know more about me. Always asking questions. Like she's stalking me.'

'Maybe she's genuine. Wants to get to know you better.'

'Maybe. But I don't.'

'Why?'

Destiny stares out the window. Shrugs. She does a lot of that these days.

'Dadda.'

'Hello, bubba. You have fun at playgroup?'

Re nods and smiles at me, then claps.

'Who you play with today?'

'Tommie.'

Destiny and I both flinch.

'Really? What you play?' I ask.

'Dinosaurs!' She claps wildly.

I stretch for Destiny's hand, but I can't reach it. I try to catch her eye and I see she has tears welling. 'What, babe?'

'She's been talking about this Tommie for a couple of weeks now.'

'It's a common name. There's probably a few of them in her group. We can't avoid it forever.'

She brushes a tear from her cheek. 'That's just it. There aren't any Tommies in her group.'

'You sure?'

She nods, struggling to speak. 'She's been playing with Tommie at home, too.'

I sit up. 'She tells you?' I wrack my brain for an explanation. There'll be a simple one I'm sure. 'Probably an imaginary friend. Just a coincidence with the name. Maybe she's heard us talk about him?'

Destiny wraps her arms across her body.

'It's been a long time now, D. Four-and-a-half years. You can't get emotional hearing his name.'

Her head snaps around and her nostrils flare. I haven't seen that for a while.

'Don't give me that shit about time healing wounds. It'll always be like yesterday.'

'I didn't say that it would go away. It's just … isn't it time to move on?' I know immediately that I've chosen the wrong words.

Destiny's eyes bulge. 'Move on?'

'You know what I mean.'

'Do I?'

I sink lower in the seat. I catch Re in the rear-view mirror.

'Daddy, look, funny doggy.'

Across the road is a manicured poodle. It is ridiculous, but I freeze. I'm suddenly back in the car on the highway, Tomas pointing to the horse.

I turn to Destiny, but she's closed up, mouth tight.

'Let's go home. Moma might have cake for us.'

'Yummy.' Re claps.

'That'll fix everything,' says Destiny, clasping her seatbelt.

I lasso my anger for her. I don't want to fight in front of Re. There is so much I want to say. Four years is long enough.

There is cake. Of course. Destiny takes off to the river as soon as we get home.

'Hey, Moma,' I say as we dump gear onto the kitchen table. She smiles, so frail.

'Hello, my darling boy.'

'How's your morning been?'

'Good. Good. I have been busy. How was the playgroup?'

'Re, tell Moma about playgroup.'

Re scrambles up onto a kitchen chair. 'I play dinosaurs.'

'Ah, ya, dinosaurs is fun. Would you like a piece of Moma's cake, my darling?'

Re nods. 'Popa wants a big piece.'

Moma gasps.

'Hey, bubba, who wants a big piece?' I ask Re, squatting down beside her.

'Popa. He say you make his best cake.'

Moma shuffles over to a chair and sits down heavily.

'How do you know Popa?' I whisper, the name catching in my throat. Her face has no malice. I've never seen a more innocent child.

Re is serious, her mouth pursing in concentration. 'I always know him.'

I kiss her on her forehead. 'Where do you see him?'

She points to the chair next to me. I turn, almost expecting my grandfather to sit there grinning at me. But it's empty. Every hair on my body stands on end.

If it's possible, Moma looks whiter than usual.

'What do you think, Moma? You got enough of that cake for Popa?'

Her chest heaves.

'You stay there. I'll finish serving up.'

Moma bobs her head.

'What about Tomas. Does he want cake?' I turn to Re.

She shakes her head, mouth full of food.

'He's not hungry for Moma's cake?' I act surprised.

'He swimming with Mummy.'

Moma sits upright; her hands shake.

'It's okay, Moma, Re has met them both. She talks to them all the time, apparently.'

'I not hear her say this before.'

'Me either. But Destiny tells me it's been going on a little while. It's just more noticeable now because her speech is becoming clearer.'

Moma faces the empty chair suspiciously and places a hand over her heart.

'Popa say, "Hello, my darling",' says Re to Moma.

Moma covers her mouth to stifle a yelp.

'Why you sad, Moma?' Re slides off the chair and goes over to her. Pats her hand. This child is definitely going on thirty-five.

Moma strokes her head. 'Moma not sad. Just surprised to hear from Popa. It been long time.'

Re nods knowingly. 'Popa say the cake smells very good.'

Moma closes her eyes.

I stare at the empty seat again. Surely if I waited long enough something would appear? Nothing. Can she be making this up? There are photos of Popa and Tomas everywhere. And we talk about them often. Maybe she's just built a picture of them in her imagination. She'll probably grow out of it. It's unnerving, though.

Destiny and Nugget clatter in through the back door. Her hair is wet and smoothed back. I can tell the river has cleansed her. I'm starting to think that the river and the dog are the only thing keeping her together.

'Smells good in here. Any of that cake left?' She pulls the empty chair from the table, the uneaten cake on the table next to where she sits.

Moma half stands. 'Asher, my love, cut her another piece.'

Destiny frowns. 'This piece is fine.'

'Mummy, you sit there.' Re points to the chair at the far end of the table.

What's going on, Ash?' says Destiny.

'That's Popa's piece of cake. He's sitting in that chair.'

'Oh … Okay, you better cut me another piece. So … is Tomas having cake, too?'

Re nods vigorously. 'He hungry after big swim.'

Destiny gasps. 'He was with me?'

'He with you all the time, Mummy.'

'He is? Why?'

'Cos you sad.'

Destiny sits down, covers her mouth.

'No, Mummy, that Popa chair.'

Destiny bounces out of the chair and moves to the end of the table.

I put a mug of tea in front of Destiny and rub her back. She's quivering. I'm not sure if it's from the cold river or *this*. She wraps both hands around the mug and brings it under her nose. Inhales the steam, closes her eyes. Let's out a long breath.

'What wrong, Mummy?' says Re, scooping cake into her mouth.

Destiny opens her eyes. 'Nothing, bubba. I'm just happy that Tomas is here.'

'What about Popa?'

'Him, too.'

Re giggles.

'What's so funny?' asks Destiny.

'Popa is making a mess.'

We all look at the cake, but it is untouched.

Moma twitters.

'Why are you laughing?' asks Destiny.

'My Zeke was always a messy eater!'

I stand at the kitchen counter. Destiny and Moma become more fluid before me. I squint. I see no signs of Tomas or Popa, but I don't doubt they are here because I want them to be. In a way I've been talking to them for a while, anyway.

'Mummy?'

'Yeah?'

'Can Tommie and me get the eggs?'

'Um. Sure. Make sure you take a basket.'

Re slides off her chair and grabs the basket from the end of the bench as she passes. Nugget trots after her.

'Shit! We're all going mad!' says Destiny, grabbing Popa's piece of cake and slamming it on the kitchen bench.

'Why do you say that?' I ask.

'Do you see anyone sitting here?' She points at the chair, then sits in it.

'No. But that doesn't mean there's not something. You've had weird stuff like this happen before. When you were a kid. Don't you talk to Tommie?'

'Yeah. But that's just wishful thinking.'

'What's wrong with that?'

'We're all going to end up in the loony bin.'

'What about your dreams? Remember when you dreamt about the Twin Towers?'

Destiny waves me away. 'Coincidence.'

'What about that time you dreamt about Mandy's grandmother dying?'

Destiny shrugs.

'What about when you were a kid and you saw someone at the end of the bed and he was talking to you?'

'Just dreams ...' she says half-heartedly.

'She's only three. Couldn't possibly make this stuff up.'

'It's giving me the creeps!' Destiny jams her hands into her shorts' pockets.

'Look. She'll probably grow out of it. She'll make more friends with kids at playgroup and forget all about the invisible ones.'

'She does play with other kids. But Tomas is always there, too. They seem to play along with it.'

'What do you think, Moma?' I sit next to her and hold her hand.

Moma squeezes my hand. 'She is very special child. She might grow out of it, but now it is very real.'

'How do you know it isn't wishful thinking?'

'Ya, it could be. But what of it?' She raises her shoulders.

'If we end up in the loony bin it doesn't really matter,' says Destiny. 'Look! She's yakking away to someone. What are they talking about?'

I stand behind her to watch our daughter. She has her arms stretched high, indicating something large, then she bends down to pick up the egg basket. Nugget trots ahead of her towards the house.

'Quick, they're coming back.'

We all sit back at the table, resume our positions.

'Only one egg,' says Re to the room. She stands on tiptoe to reach up to the kitchen bench. Nugget scurries around the table collecting cake crumbs.

No one speaks. Re clambers back up onto her chair and scans the faces around the table. She blinks.

'Popa say he real.' She cups her hands and rests her chin in them.

Moma rises from her chair. 'I think Moma need a nap.'

'Okay, Moma. Popa have nap, too.'

Moma smiles feebly and shuffles to her room.

'Daddy?'

My heart croons at her voice. 'Yes, bubba.'

'Uncle Sam. He come home?'

I turn to her. 'What do you mean?'

'Popa. He say Uncle Sam in a big bird. Tommie say he flying on a tera …teractyl.'

'Pterodactyl?'

She nods gravely.

'I don't know where he is. I haven't heard from him for a couple of months.'

'He be here soon.'

My brother …

'It would be nice to see him,' I say.

She bobs her head. 'Is Uncle Sam your brother?'

'Yep.'

'When he come you play with him?'

'Probably.'

'You play dinosaurs?'

'Sure. We can all play dinosaurs.'

Re claps.

We stand amongst the apple trees, facing the house. I turn to my right and look down the dirt driveway. She said soon. When is soon? Is it today, tomorrow, next week?

There's no car coming, and I know I can't stand here waiting for something that might not even happen.

'Want to go for a swim?'

Re claps and jumps up and down. 'Nugget, too?'

As if I could stop Nugget from swimming in the river. 'Of course.'

'And Tommie?'

'You bet.'

'And Mummy?'

'Let's go ask her.'

'What about Moma and Popa?'

'You can ask, but Moma might be tired.' She gets frailer by the day.

'Can we take picanic?'

'Wow! This is like an expedition now.'

'Maybe we find dinosaurs.'

'Maybe I am a dinosaur. RRRaaahhh!'

I chase her into the house.

'What's all the racket, you two?' Destiny is cleaning paint off her forearms.

'We go swim with you and Tommie and Nugget and Moma and Popa and Daddy and a picanic!' She doesn't stop to breathe.

'A picanic!' says Destiny, drying herself with a towel.

'You been painting?' I ask her.

'Good detective work!' Her sarcasm is laced with love. I melt into it.

'What you working on?'

'Such nosiness. Let's just say that I've broken through a wall.'

Yes!

'Can I see?'

'Later. Let's get sorted for this picanic.'

The river welcomes us with autumnal charm. The water is placid. None of this dick-shrivelling nonsense. Diving into it is inviting grace to my body. Destiny sighs when she breaks the surface and I concur.

'Daddy! Daddy! Throw Re! Throw Re!'

This is our game of late. Pure water baby, this one. I throw her into the air and she plunges into the depths. I hold my breath momentarily, then she resurfaces and laughs.

'Again, Daddy.'

We repeat this countless times. My arms tire.

'Hey, bubba, want some juice?'

Re shakes her head.

'How about some of that picanic?'

'One more.'

'Okay. Last time, bubba.'

We collapse onto the picnic rug. A wet family, dog included.

Re squats on her haunches, munching on a carrot stick. I wish I had such stamina. She nods her head.

'Good picanic, bubba?'

She nods again as she fingers the sandwiches. 'He here, Daddy.'

'Who? Tommie?' I sit up. I wish I could see and talk to him.

'Tommie always here, Daddy.'

Of course he is.

'Popa?'

'No. He at house with Moma. He not like swimming.'

This is news to me. 'Why he not like swimming?'

She shrugs.

'I don't think he knew how,' says Destiny. She's lying on her back, her arms across her face to shield off the sun.

Makes sense.

'Cooee!' A familiar voice from up the hill.

Destiny sits up. 'Sam?'

'Re said he was coming.'

'Really?'

I cooee back.

'Now this is the place to be.' My brother emerges from the trees. I stifle a gasp. He's dangerously thin, his hair cropped short.

He stands before us, the sun behind him. He's in shadow so I can't see his face very well.

'So, what sort of greeting is this?' He extends his arms.

I embrace him, aware of every bone protruding through his skin.

Re is sitting on her feet, staring at her uncle.

'And this must be the beautiful Rebecca.'

Re is confused.

'We call her Re. You remember?'

He holds out his hand. 'Sure. Hello, Re.'

Re is suddenly shy.

Destiny laughs. 'Just give her five minutes and you won't be able to shut her up.'

'Destiny. You're looking very good.'

She smiles and wraps herself around him. 'Don't they have food in Europe?'

No beating around the bush with this woman.

Sam laughs. 'Came via India. Went on a bit of a detox.'

'Bit of a detox? Sam, you look like you've been in a concentration camp.'

He frowns at her. 'That's a bit harsh, D. Don't worry. I'm sure Moma will fatten me up.'

We all nod in agreement.

'So, where is she?' says Sam. We're in the kitchen.

'She's probably having a nap,' I talk over my shoulder, packing leftovers into the fridge.

Sam heads for the far bedroom. 'She's not in there anymore. That's Re's room. Bruce and I built Moma a granny flat.'

'You built a granny flat?'

'Yeah. Maybe some of Popa's genes rubbed off?'

'I doubt it. I still have the scar from the big billycart crash of '78.' He extends his left leg to reveal the jagged scar on his calf.

'Hey, I was a kid! Anyway, I was more an assistant. Bruce was the brains.'

Sam nods.

'Is kettle on?' It's Moma, shuffling through the back door.

'There's my beautiful girl!' Sam stoops down to embrace her.

Moma recoils. 'Is this my Samuel?'

'Yes! I'm sorry I was away so long.'

'Where has you been? You come from Auschwitz?'

'That's funny, Moma. I've just come from India. Been detoxing.'

'I not make joke. You are skeleton. It is bad to treat you body like this. What is this detoxing?'

Sam sits at the kitchen table. He's exhausted. 'I've been trying to cleanse my body. You're right, I've mistreated myself.'

Moma sits, too. They are both frail in different ways.

'Don't worry, my darling. We will fatten you up.'

Sam's eyes well. 'I love you, Moma.'

'I love you, Samuel. I am very happy that you finally home.'

'Me, too. I'm so tired.'

'Who's up for a cuppa, then?' says Destiny, putting the teapot in the middle of the table.

'Mummy, cake?' Re scrambles up onto the end chair.

'Yes, bubba. Moma made a yummy rhubarb slice.'

Re claps.

'It's a wonder you lot aren't all fat!' says Sam, pointing at each of us.

'Country living. Fresh air. All gets used up,' I say, patting my belly.

Sam leans back in his chair. 'You are all very healthy. And happy. Being here is good for you.'

Destiny smiles. I've just realised that she's been doing a lot of that lately. Smiling.

'Destiny is painting again.'

'Ah, the artist is back. What you working on?'

'Not sure yet. But this place is my inspiration. I'm working on something about the seasons.'

Sam nods. He's opening her up to a conversation that I'm not so good at. Why is that? I'm jealous.

'Can I see?'

I haven't even seen any of it yet.

'Not yet. I'm still developing the idea.'

'Tommie say your painting very pretty,' says Re, mouth full.

Sam sits upright and frowns at me.

'I bet it is,' I say, rubbing Nugget's head.

Sam looks back at Re, brow furrowed.

Re giggles.

'What's so funny, bubba?'

'Tommie say Uncle Sam is a tera, teradac …' She frowns at the word.

'Pterodactyl?' I prompt her.

She purses her lips, nods.

Sam is confused.

'You are a bit like a pterodactyl,' I say, patting my brother on the shoulder.

'We knew you were coming,' Destiny says to him.

Sam points at himself and Destiny nods.

'What do you mean?'

'Re told us you would be here soon. We just didn't know when soon was.'

He must think we're all mad. Maybe we are.

'How did you know I was coming, Re?'

Re tilts her head. 'Tommie told me you were in a big birrrddd.' She jumps off the chair and runs around the table, arms extended, flying past each of us.

Sam catches Moma's eye. She bobs her head, a twinkle in her eye.

'What's going on here?' he asks me.

'Don't worry, Sam. We're not going mad. We thought so at first. But ever since her speech has become clearer, she's been telling us stuff like this that we couldn't dispute.'

'Like what?'

'Things that only Tomas or Popa would know.'

Sam scratches his head. He's eyeing Re. Probably thinking that she's possessed.

'Give me an example.'

'Wasn't that one?' I say.

'It could be a coincidence.'

I can't think of anything on the spot even though it's now a daily occurrence. 'D?'

She's rubbing her shoulder. Thinking.

'Popa and the cake?' she asks.

'That could have been a coincidence, too,' I say.

'You guys have been putting ideas into her head.' Sam is agitated.

'No. We haven't.' I steady him with a hand on his shoulder.

'Is Popa here now?' Sam is talking to Re, his voice quivering. She nods.

'What's he doing?'

'He sitting next to you.'

Sam jumps up, wraps his arms around his torso.

Re giggles. 'Popa say, "Scaredy cat".'

Sam takes a step backward. I'm guessing that he's assessing each of us for a scale of madness.

'Popa say he sorry.' Re is facing her uncle.

'Whaddya mean?'

'He sorry for smacking you when you did drop the wase.'

Sam gasps.

'Wase?' I ask.

'She means "vase",' says Sam. His bottom lip is trembling.

'What's she talking about?'

'I smashed a vase. Popa had brought it from Poland. I think it was his mother's.'

'Gran muver,' says Re.

'Shit!' says Sam under his breath.

'I don't remember that,' I say.

'You were somewhere with Mum. Maybe air cadets or something? I think it was a weekend thing that you went to with the air cadets. Remember? You had to do some survival thing.'

The memory floods me. A handful of stupid city kids unable to fend for ourselves.

'So what happened with this vase?'

'Remember Macca? He came here during one of our school holidays. We were playing cricket. In the house. Right there in the lounge.' He points past us indicating the other room.

'All this land and you had to play cricket in the house?' I say.

'It had been raining all weekend. We were going stir crazy. Dumb. You should've seen how many pieces that thing shattered into. I couldn't believe it.'

'And Popa gave you a hiding?'

'The one and only hiding I ever got in my life. It's not like Mum ever took enough notice of us to give me a hiding.'

I get you.

Sam sits down. He's spent.

'So. We all mad?' I ask him.

'Probably. Me, too.' He takes a big gulp of his tea, his Adam's apple riding up and down his neck.

'How long you back for, Sam?' asks Destiny.

'For good. No more travelling for me. All I want to do is sleep.'

Destiny embraces him. 'It's good to have you back. It's been too long. You can stay here for as long as you like.'

'Yeah. We can build you a granny flat, too!' I say.

'The tent will be fine for now. I like being out there in the orchard.'

'Popa say, "Me, too",' says Re.

We all laugh.

W e buckled down for the winter, and Spring is already peeking through. It's good to have my family together. Sam insists on staying out in the tent despite the cold – says it invigorates him. It's cold enough to make your balls drop off, if you ask me.

He spends a lot of time out there reading. And sleeping. Moma has managed to fatten him up a little and his hair is becoming unruly. So he's more like Sam, but isn't Sam. I can't get in there, into his head, to find out what's going on. I figure living out here will smooth things out, like they have for Destiny.

I step out onto the veranda. Destiny has taken it over as her studio.

'Damn cold out here, D. Come inside.' I jam my hands into my pockets.

'Wimp,' she says.

'Bruce did a good job making this into a room, but it still isn't that warm.'

'It's good over here, next to my little potbelly,' she says, standing back to study her work.

I haven't seen this one. The detail is exquisite. The autumn light, the shades of brown and cream of the tree trunks. Wisps of mist. I whistle.

'It's getting there,' says Destiny, adding a highlight.

'I can almost feel the texture of the trunk.' I step closer.

'There's so much character in those trees. It's almost like they inhabit personality. I can sense the ghosts of the past are living there.'

'I don't think you should sell this one, D. It should go above the fireplace. Exhibit it, but don't sell.'

'Really?'

'Yeah. When we first came out here, I used to talk to that tree. It seems to be the oldest one in the orchard. I honestly felt like I was talking to Popa then. And he talked back.'

She turns to me, eyes glistening. 'It does have a wise feel about it.'

I pull her to me, stroke her arm. I rub her belly, nicely rounded at twenty-five weeks, grateful that she is less opposed this time.

'Do you think this is a boy or a girl?' I say into her hair.

'According to Mum, it's a boy.'

'Boy it is, then. She's never wrong. Any ideas for names?'

'Tomas crossed my mind, but it would be too weird.'

'Yeah. How 'bout Sean? Your dad would love that.'

'Maybe. Let's wait till we meet him and let him tell us.'

'Deal. Maybe Re will tell us?'

'Tell you what?' asks Sam, coming up the steps.

'What to call this baby.'

'Doomed,' he says, no trace of jokiness about him.

Destiny stiffens. 'Get serious, Sam.'

'Not much for the next generation to look forward to, is there?'

'I said enough!' Destiny rises on her toes. Just grew five centimetres.

'Okay, cut it, you two,' I say. 'Not much to be done about it now; it's half cooked.'

Destiny punches my arm. 'Nice way to talk about your son.'

'Yeah, well, at least I had the good sense to make sure no kids get made from this.' Sam indicates his groin in a foul way.

'Whaddya mean?' I ask.

'Got myself sterilised years ago. After Kelly.'

'You mean after New York?' I say pointedly.

'Same difference.' He scowls.

'What happens when you meet someone and want kids?'

'Not going to happen. I'll get myself a dog.' He brushes Nugget roughly.

'Can you get him away from me, Ash?' asks Destiny.

I nod and push my brother towards the front door.

'You know I'm right. All the next generation has to look forward to is terror and poverty.'

'Yeah, well, ask Moma her opinion on that.'

Sam shuts his mouth.

'Go on, ask Moma what she thinks this generation will get compared to hers.'

He waves me away. 'Forget about it.'

'No. Stop mouthing off!' I push him down the hall into the lounge. Moma sits on the couch reading a book with Re.

'What is so much fuss?' she says to Sam.

'Don't worry, Moma. Me and Ash were just having a *discussion.*'

'Some discussion. He thinks that the next generation are doomed. What do you think?'

'It make no difference. There are bad people in the world at any time in history. You just live the best you can.'

Sam scowls.

'Daddy, Daddy!' Re holds a drawing up to me.

'In a minute, bubba. Let me put the kettle on.'

'Let me see,' says Sam, grabbing the paper from her.

He sits at the kitchen table and flattens the crumpled sheet. From my angle there is lots of vibrant colour. Another artist in the family.

Sam snorts. 'Even Re knows. Hey, what is this?' He holds it up to Re, pointing at the centre of the page.

'That fire, Uncle Sam.'

'What fire? Over there in the potbelly?'

She frowns. 'That little fire. This is big fire.' She stands on tiptoe and stretches her arms into the air.

Sam arches his brow. 'So where is this fire?'

She jumps up and down on the spot. 'Here, here, here!'

'What? Here in this room?'

She's growing bored with the questions. 'Silly man. Not *in* the room. The whole house.'

Sam slaps the tabletop. 'I damn well knew it! We're all going to burn in hell. Seems pretty fitting in my books.'

'Stop!' I slam a cup onto the benchtop.

Re giggles. 'Silly Uncle Sam.'

'It's just a four-year-old's drawing,' I say, filling the teapot.

'Ha! This is Re we're talking about. The girl who talks to

dead people and predicts the future. Look at this!' He shoves the picture under my nose.

I take the paper, hold it away from me. It's dominated by red and orange scribble but is undoubtedly a house on fire.

'Is this going to happen here?' I ask Re.

She nods and purses her lips. 'Shhhh.' She waves her arms like flames.

Sam waves his arms in the air, too. 'Just like I said. Doomed.'

'That's enough. We know your opinion.' I turn to Moma to gauge her reaction.

'Yes. Enough, Samuel. If it happens, we will deal with it.'

'Looks like that damn bunker might come in useful, huh, Ash?'

I resist punching him in the face.

'Probably will.' I've had enough of him now. *Go back out to your tent.*

Destiny comes in, wiping her arms with a towel.

'Take a look at this!' Sam shoves the drawing under her nose.

'What is it?' says Destiny.

'Your daughter agrees with me. We're going to burn in hell!'

I think my brother might self-combust. He hops from one leg to another.

'There're no people in this. We aren't going to burn, are we, bubba?'

Re shakes her head. 'No, Mummy.'

Sam snatches the paper from Destiny 'Can I keep this picture, Re?'

Re is confused, then her face lights up. She nods.

He swoops down to her and kisses her on the forehead. 'Thank you, gorgeous. I'm going to hang it in the tent now.' He leaves the room. The air clears instantly.

'I don't think he should stay here much longer, Ash,' says Destiny, dropping onto a kitchen chair.

'Where can he go?'

'Your mother's house. They can swap horror stories.'

Moma chuckles. 'They probably kill each other!'

My heart solidifies. This isn't Sam. He needs help. A small hand brushes mine.

'Sam okay, Daddy. He be better soon.'

'What you mean?' I squat beside her.

'Sam go somewhere soon. Then he not be sad anymore.'

I wish I could decipher her riddles. It's exhausting. I stroke her head and smile; remember I'd made tea.

'Cuppa's ready,' I say, standing upright.

'About time!' says Destiny.

We sit with our steaming cups at the kitchen table. The chatter has left and we listen to the roar of the flames in the potbelly. I close my eyes and imagine that sound amplified if this house were on fire. Not this house. This house isn't going anywhere. Not if I have anything to do with it.

I'm standing in the doorway to the bunker. It seems just yesterday that I was here, pushing at the door to see what was inside. I don't know why Destiny hates it so much. To me it's homely. When I suggested that, she scoffed. I close my eyes, stand still. Maybe if I really concentrate, I might be able to tune into what Destiny is on about. Nothing. Nothing but the cool draught that weaves past my ankles when I open the door.

It's time to take an inventory of supplies in here. If something happens, we may need to be in here for a little while. Okay, so there are four adults and one child. Actually, one-and-a-half children. What happens if Destiny goes into labour when we're in here? Shit. That would be a disaster. Moma is too old to help. I have at least been to two births. I doubt that Sam would be any good. I shouldn't think of the worst. But I will make sure we have surgical scissors or something in here, some first aid stuff. If I have enough in here for two weeks, I'm guessing that will get us past the worst of anything.

The shelves are very well stocked. Just need water. No use storing that till the last minute. I ease open the second door.

It's nice and cool below. There are four beds down there. Didn't count Sam when I was doing this, as he was overseas. Better see if I can find another camp bed. There're candles, matches, some games, books, drawing stuff. I better make sure that Destiny brings down that painting of the tree.

I sit on the nearest camp bed. There's nothing malicious here. What is Destiny on about? Maybe it's just the closed space?

'Daddy!'

'I'm down here, Re. Careful of the stairs!'

Her little heads pops out of the darkness. 'What you do, Daddy?'

'Just making it nice and cosy in here, bubba.'

She nods her head with appreciation. 'It dark.'

I flash the torch in her direction. 'We've got lots of lamps down here for when we need them. What you doing here? Is Mummy having a nap?'

'No,' she says.

'Mummy not having a nap?'

'Mummy yelling at Uncle Sam.'

'Why?'

'He won't stop talking.'

'About what?'

'He say, "burn in hell, burn in hell" all day. Mummy not like it.'

Shit. 'Is Moma up at the house?'

Re doesn't answer.

'Re?'

Still no answer. I direct the torch at her again and her moon face beams back. She's nodding at me.

'I guess I better come back?'

She nods vigorously.

I make a mental note of what supplies are still needed and chase Re out of the bunker.

'Do you like it in the bunker?'

She shakes her head.

'Really? Why not?'

'It dark.'

'That the only reason?'

Re shrugs.

'Something else?'

'A man live there.'

'Really?'

'He got black hair. He very skinny and wrinkly. And his skin is like chocolate.'

'Is that right. Would you eat him?'

Re looks at me like I'm an idiot. I see a cloud of dust down the track.

'We've got a visitor.'

'It Bruce. Will he have more honey?'

'I don't know, bubba. Let's go say hello.'

Bruce parks at the end of the drive. He lurches out of his ute, followed by Browny. The dog immediately finds Nugget at the foot of the steps to the house. They run off, chasing each other.

'Bruce, Bruce! You got more honey?' says Re, rushing up to him and grabbing his hand. Bruce stoops down and ruffles her hair.

'Sure have, little lady. Last batch for a while, I reckon.'

'It so yummy with Moma's bread,' says Re, jumping on her toes.

'Best way to eat it. Reckon your Moma will make me a tea?'

Re stops jumping and bites her lip.

'What's going on? Rebecca okay?' asks Bruce.

'Yeah, she's fine. It's Sam. He's causing a bit of unrest in the household,' I say.

'Is he now?' Bruce places a fist on each hip. I'm guessing he's ready to box my brother.

I stifle a laugh. 'Don't worry. I'm sure that Destiny has sorted him out.'

'Too right.'

Re grabs his big square hand to lead him to the house. He stoops to reach her.

'I might have honey in my tea,' she says matter-of-factly.

'You should do that,' says Bruce, winking at her.

'Hey, Bruce. Do you know anything about the history of this place? Like way back before Popa had it?'

'Not much. Only what my dad told me. Huge settlement here for years and years. Squatters or something.'

'Were there Aborigines here?'

'There would've been – this is Taungurung country. Why?'

Bruce stops walking. Re tugs at his hand.

'Nothing. Don't worry about it. Just something that Re said.'

'Well, if ya really want the full story, go down the library. Grace there knows everything there is to know about the history of this place.'

I probably won't go. It doesn't matter what the story is. All I know is there might be a burial site there, under the bunker.

A crash comes from the house. 'Oh boy. Maybe Destiny's getting stuck in already?' says Bruce, smiling.

You can just about see the steam coming out of Destiny's ears. Sam sits triumphant on a kitchen chair, arms folded across his chest.

'What's going on here?' I say to Destiny.

'Don't worry about it,' she replies.

'What broke?'

'It's nothing to worry about, Ash. Your brother and I were just having a conversation.'

I turn to Sam. He stares straight ahead.

'How you going, Bruce?' asks Destiny, pecking him on the cheek.

'I'm good, love. That belly of yours is just about ready to pop. Not having twins are ya?'

She punches him playfully. 'Cheeky. Still got weeks to go. Want a cuppa?'

'Thought you'd never ask!' He hands her the tub of honey.

'I want honey in my tea, Mummy,' says Re.

'Magic word?'

'Please.'

Sam snorts and Destiny bristles.

'What's your problem?' I ask him.

'You lot make me sick, playing happy families, like nothing is wrong.'

'Nothing *is* wrong.'

'It's coming for us. We'll be overrun soon.'

'Sam! I've had enough of this. I think you should leave. Go stay at Mum's or something.'

He sits upright, fists on thighs. 'Ash! You need to get your things in order before it's too late.'

'Geezus, Sam. Can you just go? We're ready for anything that might happen. Nothing worse can happen to us than already has.'

Destiny nods in my periphery.

'Fine. I'll be in my tent!' He stomps out of the room, slamming the door behind him.

'Well. I see what you mean,' says Bruce, sitting at the kitchen table.

'Don't worry about Uncle Sam,' says Re.

'Why you say that, bubba?' I squat beside her.

'He go away soon. And then he be happy.'

'Really? Where's he going?'

She looks up at the ceiling.

'Re? Where's Uncle Sam going?'

She sighs. This time she points to the ceiling. 'Up.'

'What do you mean up?'

'He go up. Into the sky.'

'In a bird?'

'Nooo. Daddy!' She is exasperated.

'So long as he's happy,' I say, drained by riddles.

'Yes, Daddy. He not be sad anymore.'

'He's not sad, bubba. He's angry.'

'He very, very sad. He cry all the time.'

I haven't seen him cry for years. She's wrong.

'So, Bruce. Are we sorted here for bushfires?' I ask.

Bruce starts, mouth full of cake. 'Mmm … mate …' He swallows his food. 'I reckon you're pretty well set. Is the tank full of water?'

Destiny nods.

'Yep. Do you think that the bunker is good to hide out in?'

'You got ventilation?'

'I think so. Can you look things over?'

'Sure thing. You know, bushfire season is still a ways to go?'

'Yeah. Just want to make sure everything is ready. This baby's gonna be due in the middle of the summer.'

'No worries, Ash. But I reckon this summer will be pretty tame. Can feel it.'

'Yeah? Re reckons this house is gonna burn down.'

'Does she now? By a bushfire?'

'I'm assuming. Why else?'

'This is the country, mate. Bushfires aren't the only hazard.'

'All the more reason to make sure the bunker is good to go.'

'What? You think war's coming?'

I shrug. 'Who knows? Might be nothing at all.'

Bruce piles sugar into his tea.

'Don't you want honey?' asks Re, incredulous.

'You have it, love. I have honey on everything. Good to have something else.'

Re nods and drags the tub towards her.

'How's Mary going, Bruce?' I ask.

His body slumps. 'She's good. Fit as a fiddle.'

'You know what I mean.'

'Mostly she doesn't know who I am. Every now and then there's a little spark of recognition. She'll say something about the past and my heart pounds, thinking she's back. But then she'll get confused. Like she's never seen me before.' He adds another sugar to his tea.

'Sorry to hear that. Anything we can do?'

He shakes his head, chin to chest.

Destiny stands and wraps herself around his shoulders.

'You think you have your whole life mapped out. But life has other plans for ya,' says Bruce.

We sit at the table, contemplating this statement.

violet

I'm called from a dream. I sit up, check the clock. I've only been asleep for an hour or so. Destiny is snoring.

It's nothing.

I slide back under the covers. Listen for sounds outside. The noises of the bush are soothing. Frogs. The river. It's surprisingly noisy when I concentrate on it. I close my eyes and try to find my way back into the dream, but it's gone. I don't even remember what it was about. I think about Mary and her memory. She's gone downhill so quickly. It's surreal to have the physical person but not have them present. Despite her frailness, Moma is very much still present and sharp. And wise.

There must be a way that we can help Bruce and Mary. They've done so much for us. Taken us into their family. I don't know how. Life's a bitch.

I'm wide awake now. And I need to take a piss. I'll get up and do a round of the house, take a piss, check on everyone. It's getting milder; the spring frosts seem to have passed. I throw on a windcheater but don't worry about shoes. It's warm enough.

Nugget follows me out to the lemon tree, excited to be on an adventure in the middle of the night. Sorry to disappoint you, little guy. My piss hisses as it hits the ground and I watch the steam rise into the night air. Nugget growls.

'Shh, boy. It's nothing.' I strain to separate the usual night sounds.

Nugget whines.

The moon is high and bright, casting an eerie glow over everything. I walk around the back of the house, along the south side towards the orchard. I'm struck by how the moon is making the whole orchard glow. But then I realise it isn't glowing from the light of the moon. It's on fire!

Sam!

I sprint towards the tent, but the fire has cut off access. I skirt around the outside of the trees in order to get to the tent from the other end. There's something a bit déjà vu about this, and I wonder if I'm dreaming. I shake myself. Try to concentrate. Last time Nugget woke us; why not this time? I can't see the tent through the flames. Is it gone? Sam?

'Sam!'

I rush to where the tent should be in the far corner of the orchard but there's nothing. Only flames.

I'm paralysed. Is he in there? Maybe he's gotten out? If he is in there he's gone. My brother! No. Please. No.

I scan the orchard. The flames are licking at the trees with hunger and approaching the house. Shit! Where's Nugget? He's right at my heels.

'Come on, boy, let's get the girls out.'

I retrace my steps around the perimeter of the orchard. Maybe there's time to get the water pump started up to put out the fire. I'll get everyone out first, then see what I can do. I check to see that Nugget is close behind. He's at my heels. He understands. Good boy.

'Destiny! Moma! Everyone, wake up!'

I'm racing to the house, up the front steps. Lucky we don't bother with locked doors. I see a light go on in the granny flat. Moma is up. Good.

'Destiny!'

'Daddy?' Re is standing at her bedroom door, squinting into the bright light, hair wild about her head.

'Hello, bubba. Put some shoes on, quick. And put on a jumper too, okay?' I stoop down to her, to make sure she's heard me.

'It's too hot for a jumper.'

'It's colder outside. Just hurry!' I leave her scratching her little head. 'Destiny!' I slam through the door to our bedroom.

Destiny half-sits, eyes closed. 'Geezus, Ash. Is it the day of the dead or something?'

'Quick, get dressed. Shoes. Bag. Fire!'

She rubs her eyes. Can she be any slower?

'What's going on?' She pulls herself upright, her belly bulging.

'Don't talk, just get going. The orchard is on fire. Sam is gone!' I pull on my boots, a jumper. Stuff my wallet, our passports, car keys into a backpack.

'Sam gone?' Her eyes are wide open now and full of horror.

'I don't know where the fuck he is. Please. Get up. We gotta get into the car.'

'Can't we use the water pump?'

'We can. I will. I want you and Re and Moma in the car. The place has been on fire a while. I want you to go over to Bruce's.'

She lunges out of bed, the belly no longer holding her back. 'Re! Baby, you getting shoes on?' She pulls on a jumper, leggings, and bends down for her shoes.

'Mummy? It's too hot for a jumper,' whines Re.

'That's okay, put it in here.' She holds out a large bag and stuffs the jumper in. 'Quick, where are your shoes?'

Re looks down at her feet and back at Destiny.

Destiny laughs. 'Silly me. You already put them on! Good girl. Let's go get Moma.' They race from the room, adding things to the bag as they go.

Moma is ready to go. She's done this enough times, I'm guessing. She turns to the orchard, shaking her head, tears in her eyes.

'D, I want you to drive over to Bruce and stay there till I say it's okay.'

Destiny is mesmerised by the fire. 'Where's Sam?'

'I don't know. The tent is totally gone. If he was in there … Let's hope he went off somewhere.'

Re starts crying.

'What's wrong, bubba?'

'Uncle Sssam,' she blubbers.

'It's okay, I'll go find him.'

Re knuckles her eyes. 'He gone, Daddy. I miss him already!' The blubbering becomes high pitched.

Shit, Sam!

The fire is rapidly making its way towards the house. The old tree will be gone soon.

I snap out of it. 'Okay, D, get going. I'll try to put this thing out and then come over to Bruce's.'

Destiny nods and turns the ignition. Nothing. *You've got to be kidding me? Shit!*

'Try it again,' I say, head almost inside the car.

Nothing.

'Again!' I say.

There's not even a groan from the engine.

I pull at my hair. 'Okay, you'll have to walk over to Bruce's.'

I open the driver door and get ready to help her out. I look at her belly and realise there is no way she can walk that far at any pace.

I can't think straight. My ears are full of the crackle and whoosh of the fire and Re's blubbering.

'Right. You're all going into the bunker!'

'No way!' says Destiny, crossing her arms over her belly.

'Yes way. There's no choice. It'll only be for tonight. A few hours at best.' I pull her out of the car.

Moma and Re stand holding each other, both with tears in their eyes.

'Right, you two. Go to the bunker. Take Nugget. Re, you know how to turn on the lights?'

She bobs her head.

We walk single file to the bunker, which is only about fifteen metres away but closer to the fire. I don't know how much time we have before it reaches the edge of the orchard and then the house. I've never even seen a fire like this before.

The bunker is dark. And gloomy. Re turns on the lights, which are dull, barely lighting the way.

'Keep going!' I urge them forward, 'Go down to the bedroom. There's no way the fire is a threat down there.'

We shuffle slowly. 'D, you get them settled. I want to go get something. And to see if I can get the water pump to work.'

Destiny's face whitens. 'No, Ash, let it all go. We have everything we need here. Don't worry about it.'

I kiss her forehead. 'I won't stay up there if it's unsafe, babe. I promise.'

I try to leave but she clutches me, her slender fingers digging into my wrist.

Moma's voice cuts through. 'Come, Destiny. We get ourself sorted. Ash smart boy. He be back soon.'

Thank you.

'Daddy! Where's Tuxedo?' says Re.

Tuxedo!

I scramble to the door of the bunker. The fire is almost to the edge of the orchard, heading straight for the old tree.

The tree!

I won't be able to save it. But maybe I can find the damn cat.

The painting!

I must get the painting. It's just there, on the porch. I close the door to the bunker and measure the distance. There's plenty of time. I'm not even sure that the fire will get to the house because there is nothing on the ground between it and the orchard. But then I see flames in the air. Are they jumping? From treetop to treetop?

I watch a clump of fire sail through the air and land on the corner of the roof. Surely that won't take? But it does! The flames curl and lick at the gutters. There must be dry leaves in the gutters. I haven't cleared them out for weeks.

I measure the distance to the veranda steps. Ten. Fifteen? I can do this. I check behind me that the others are safely inside. There's no one there. I can't hear voices so I'm guessing they are down in the basement now. Do we have water? No. Shit. I run. Around the north side of the house to the water tank. I fill the two buckets with water and run back to the bunker. The fire is now taking over the corner of the house. I leave the buckets of water just inside the door of the bunker and run back to the tank.

There's the water pump. The enamel is gleaming. New. I haven't learnt how to use it yet. Bruce was going to come over next week. At least he's connected it. Problem is that the fire is on the other side of the house. Damn! *You're useless, Ash!*

I run around the north end of the house again, to the bottom of the veranda steps. The fire talks to me. *Yumyumyum. This house is gooood.* It's directly above Destiny's little studio. I mount the steps and turn into the built-in area. The painting sits on its easel. I grab it with two hands and retreat down the steps and over to the bunker. I'm sweating.

We now have a small amount of water, and the painting is safely in the bunker. No sign of the cat.

Now what? Can I put this fire out? Can I find the cat? I stand in front of the house, watching the flames like an idiot. Should I save anything else? More paintings? Yes. I bolt up the steps again but fall short. Parts of the ceiling fall in. Soot and flames swirl around me.

Still no sign of the cat. There are too many things that need saving. I imagine Sam in the tent, flames enveloping him. Please don't let that be what happened. *Sam, don't be gone.* I step backwards along the veranda.

I go back to the water tank. I'll have one more go at this pump and see what I can do. It sits before me smugly. I grab the hose. It's long but will it reach right around the south side of the house? Only one way to find out. I grab the end of it and take it in that direction. It does reach. I go back to the pump. It has a pull handle. I'm guessing it starts like a lawn mower.

I pull the handle and the machine groans. I hate these things. They only start if they want to. I pull again. Two groans and then a puttering. Damn. I see a lever down the side. Maybe that's a choke or something? I move it up and pull the handle again. Nothing. Shit!

'Ash!' Destiny is on the other side of the house.

Damn!

I run back around the north side of the house.

'I'm here! Get back in the bunker!'

'Just leave it, please!' She holds her belly as if in pain.

'I'm just going to see if I can get the pump working. Then I'll come down.'

'Don't worry about it. It's just a house. I want you to come back down.'

Her face is ashen. Sweat dribbles down the side of her face.

'Give me five minutes.' I turn to go back to the pump.

'No! Look at the fire. Even if you can get it going, it'll be hard to put out on your own.'

She's right. The fire has moved past the little studio and is making its way into the centre of the roof.

'But, babe, Popa built this house.'

'I know. But it's just a house.'

Just a house ... but Popa ... the diary. *I must get the diary!*

And I must find Tuxedo.

'D, please go back in. I'll be one minute. I promise.'

Destiny doubles over, clutches at her stomach. 'Please, Ash. Leave everything. I need to lie down now!'

I stop. The flames crackle above. The baby. It can't be born now. Not here. 'Okay, babe, let's go.' I wrap my arm around her waist and steer her back towards the bunker.

Our eyes water, the smoke now a thick mass above our heads. Something large falls into the house – I'm guessing a main beam.

Sorry, Popa.

We stop short of the door to the bunker and turn towards the house. Flames leap and dance across the front veranda, devouring the paintings, the cushions on the old armchair and Re's little wheelbarrow. The front window explodes, and the curtains are swallowed in flames. This fire is hungry. It races through everything with pure gluttony.

'It's beautiful,' says Destiny, barely a whisper.

'What?' I'm incredulous.

'There's so much beauty in the colours and the rage.'

She's right.

'Actually. It's not rage. It's glee. See how excited it is to devour everything, like a hunger pure and unadulterated.'

We watch silently for a few seconds, mesmerised by the spectacle.

'Popa's house,' I say.

Destiny leans into me. 'I know. But we put the memories there.'

Water lands on my left cheek. I wipe it away. 'Is it raining?' I ask.

Destiny turns her head to the sky. 'I can't feel anything. Wait. Yes, it's spitting.' She closes her eyes, face turned upwards.

It's very light and I wonder if it is wishful thinking. 'How's the pain?' I rub her belly.

'Seems to have gone,' she says, eyes closed. I wonder if it was to get me to come with her.

'Let's go down. Moma will be worried,' I say.

Destiny opens her eyes. 'There'll be nothing left when we come out again.'

'I know.'

We turn and enter the bunker.

M oma sits upright on the end of the army cot. Re lies in hers, cuddling Nugget.

'Here you are. Moma was worried,' says Moma.

I kiss her forehead. 'Sorry, Moma. I wanted to see if I could get the water pump working but the fire got too big.'

'The house. It gone?'

'Not yet. But it will be very soon. I'm so sorry. I couldn't save it.'

'It only a house, my darling. We are all safe, together. That is main thing. But Samuel?'

'I don't know. If he was in the tent … but he may have gone walking. He's been doing that a lot lately.'

'He happy now,' says Re from her dark corner.

'Are you still awake, young lady?' I try to sound stern.

'Nugget won't stop licking me!' she pipes up.

Nugget sits up at his name and looks at each of us for direction. Is it time for a game? Re shines her little torch on his face and we all laugh.

'What now?' asks Destiny, lowering herself slowly onto her cot.

'I guess we try to get some sleep. In the morning, I'll go over to Bruce's and see if he can put us up while we work out what to do.'

Destiny hugs herself, shivers.

'You okay, D? Baby settled?'

'This place gives me the creeps. I won't get any sleep with these ghosts talking to each other all night.' She peers suspiciously to the corner of the room as if it's plain to all that there are ghosts standing there.

I swivel my head, but there are only shadows. I turn to Re but she's talking to Nugget.

'Let's try to rest anyway. I think it'll be a big day tomorrow.'

Moma bobs her head and pulls the covers back on her cot. I help her climb into it and tuck her in.

'Good night, my darling Asher,' she says, stroking my cheek. Her fingers are cool and soft. I realise that this is all that matters but can't help feeling an overwhelming sadness at the loss of the house. The house where we were making new memories. Good memories.

I kiss Moma's palm and tuck her hand in under the blankets.

Destiny wriggles and shuffles to get comfortable, her belly making it hard to fit on the cot. I tuck my big jacket behind her so that she half sits in the bed.

'Hop in with me?' she asks.

I tilt my head but realise that she isn't joking. 'There's no room in there for three. I'll bring my cot closer.'

This satisfies her and she closes her eyes.

I go over to Re's bed to tuck her in. She's already asleep, Nugget snuggled along her side. They'll be warm at least. Nugget defends his sleeping position.

'Don't worry, boy. Tonight, you can sleep wherever you like.'

I drag my cot closer to Destiny and lie on top of it. I'm too tired to take off my boots. I listen for the fire but it's quiet down here; anything could happen out there, and we wouldn't know about it. I'm not sure whether to feel secure or worried about that.

I close my eyes. Listen. The candle sputters, casting dancing figures around the room. There are mostly dark shadows, and I am loath to turn out the light. I don't want it to use up too much of our oxygen, though, even though Bruce said ventilation is pretty good down here. Bruce. He's going to go off at me tomorrow for not using the water pump. I should've gotten a lesson from him when we set it up.

Nothing to be done about it now. It wouldn't have saved Sam anyway. Sam. What did you do? Are you out there?

I blow out the candle. The darkness is heavy. It presses down on me. I wonder how long we could manage to live down here. Even after a few minutes my eyes don't adjust to the light because it is pure darkness. Not even a tiny skerrick of light leaks into the place.

I feel for Destiny in the dark and find her arm. Our hands join and I squeeze. 'You okay?' I ask.

'I would be if they'd stop nattering,' she whispers.

I laugh under my breath. 'Just one night, babe, I promise.' I wonder how many promises I've made in my life, then broken. *Tomas, Sam, Popa, Tuxedo …* When will I get to a point where I won't have to make or break promises?

I sink back into the pillow and let the darkness swallow me whole.

I wake with a start. There's no more light with my eyes open compared to with them closed. Am I dead?

I remember the fire. The house.

I was dreaming. This is me trying to come out of the dream. I blink. It's still blackness all around me. I sit up and feel around the bed. I'm on the army cot, fully clothed and Destiny's cot is right next to me. *Fuck. Not a dream.*

I feel around for the torch. The light. I'll turn on the light. I crawl to where I think the stairs are. I have no sense of direction and can only scramble around, feeling things like a blind man. I'm a blind man with no extrasensory skills.

Something sharp jabs my knee. Shit. The pain shoots up and down my leg. I grunt.

'Ash?' It's Destiny.

'Can't find the light switch,' I double over in pain.

'Want my torch, Daddy?' Re's tiny torch sends a pencil beam of light around the room.

'Good girl! See if you can light up the light switch.'

She points the torch at all angles around the room as if it were a disco.

'There it is!'

She holds the torch beam on the light switch, and I hobble over to it, only about a metre from where I stand.

I flick the switch. Nothing. I flick it again.

'Power must be out from the fire.' I try to hide my anxiety.

'Maybe we should all go out and see what the damage is?' says Destiny.

'I don't even know what time it is,' I say, stalling.

I search my way along the wall to the shelves. I know there is a camping light somewhere. I find it immediately and turn it on. The dull light is bright to our eyes, so accustomed to the dark now.

I hold the light over my watch: 6.23. I can't remember what time it was when we came down, but it would've been around 1.00. I don't know if I'm ready to see it. All three faces, well four if you include Nugget, watch me, waiting for my direction.

'The house. It'll be gone by now.'

No one answers. Just blink at me. Waiting.

'Maybe I should go check it out on my own, then come back with a report?'

Three heads shake *no* in unison.

'Okay. I guess we can't put it off. Let's get our shoes on and go out.'

We slowly make our way up the stairs in the dim light, feeling our way as much as seeing. Nugget runs ahead and back again as if to hurry us along. I stop everyone at the top of the stairs. Moma is out of breath and Destiny struggles, too. Re just has little legs and she is still half asleep.

'Okay. Are we ready for this?'

No reply.

Only Re has little comprehension of what we are about to see. We can hear a bit more up here. Birds have started the day and I think there's a light drizzle. Maybe it has lessened the impact of the fire.

We stop at the door. I can smell smoke, but it's mixed with that damp smell you get after rain. I hold my breath, pull the door towards me.

Light streams in. Despite having the light inside, it's nothing compared to real light. That brilliant Australian light that can be brutal, even in the early morning. I squint to adjust to the glare, shielding my eyes from the rising sun.

I blink, then turn to where the house would be. I'm reluctant but I can't delay this forever. I open my eyes, anticipating a black pile of rubble.

There's half a pile of black rubble. Smoke rises from it in places, but it seems to be out. The rain must have been heavy and halted it. The front veranda, Destiny's studio, is gone. That means all the paintings. And the two bedrooms are gone, but it has stopped at the kitchen. The potbelly is covered in soot and debris. The table and chairs are still in one piece, also blackened from soot. Further back, the outhouse still stands, totally untouched. I remember the stash of money that Destiny hid in there.

None of us speak, taking it all in. Nugget trots forward, nose to ground, exploring this new phenomenon. I watch his tail follow him, rudder-like.

Re tugs at my shirt. 'Daddy. Is my bed gone?'

I squat down beside her. 'Yes, bubba. But Daddy will make you a new room with a new bed, okay?'

Her eyes widen. 'Can I have a fairy bed?'

'Sure. You can have whatever bed you want.'

'I want a fairy bed, too,' says Destiny, no trace of a smile.

'You can have whatever bed you want, too.' I squeeze her hand.

'The orchard. Some still stands!' Moma points to our left.

She's right. A handful of trees remain, including the oldest. I walk up to it and place my palm against the bark. Some of the tree's leaves and bark are singed but mostly it is untouched.

The tent. There's nothing but burnt debris.

Sam. My stomach falls into my boots. *Please, God, let him be out wandering in the bush. Please let him be down by the river.*

Each of us stays in our thoughts, unable to break the silence. Birds twitter around us as normal.

'Daddy ...' says Re, pointing towards the road.

Bruce's ute rambles towards us. There's no dust this morning. Everything's damp. I see his face thrust forward over the steering wheel – determined. He expects the worst.

The ute pulls up and Bruce is almost out of the car before he's switched off the engine.

'What the hell happened here? I saw smoke over the paddocks when I got up.' He takes off his hat, whistles in astonishment. 'Couldn't get the water pump to work?' He turns back to me, eyebrows raised.

I'm lost for words. Wait for the recrimination.

'You're all safe. That's the main thing. But where's Sam?' He scans the yard either side of the house.

I stare at my feet. My brother ... Sam, where are you?

'Ash?' Bruce steps forward.

'I don't know, Bruce. I think the fire started in the tent. If it did ...'

'Sweet Jesus ...' says Bruce.

Destiny chokes back a sob, wraps her arms around her torso. 'He might be wandering around, Ash. Go find him. He was always wandering around. He's probably down by the river.'

I don't wait for more instruction. I sprint towards the back of the house and follow the track down to the river. Nugget follows me, barking with excitement.

I check the tipi. Not there.

I arrive at the beach clearing and stop at the river. No Sam. The river beckons me. *He's here. He's here.* I frown, trying to see into the water but it's dark, vapid.

'Sam! Sam, where are you?'

I run along the edge of the river, scanning the bank for any signs of him. I trip on branches, tree roots. Half-slip into the river where the bank is soft. 'Sam! Sam!' My voice grows ragged and I realise that I'm crying.

Please. Not Sam, too.

Who am I pleading with? I don't know. I wipe my eyes, blinded by tears and hope that he materialises when I open them again. Nothing. Only the river whispering to me.

I run back to the main beach. There's nothing. No sign of him being down here. No clothes, no cigarette butts. Nothing. I sink to the ground. 'Be happy, little brother. Be happy,' I whisper to him.

I sit and wait. No amount of waiting will bring him back. Fuck it. I know that. There's nothing I can do. Another promise broken. But he was broken anyway, and I didn't do that.

I walk slowly – my injured leg aching with a dull pain – back up the track to the half-burnt house. Bruce is talking to Moma and Destiny, arms flying akimbo.

Moma's eyes bore into me. I shake my head. She hangs her head and sighs deeply.

'Ash?'

'Sorry, D. No sign of him.' I pull her towards me as she crumples.

'Righto,' says Bruce, forcing cheer into his voice. 'At least your flat is still good, Rebecca.' He points to the granny flat, which is untouched.

'That good,' says Moma. 'At least we have somewhere to sleep.'

'How about we get you lot sorted and start to clean up this place?' says Bruce. He turns and stands upright, as if saluting the house that Popa built. Each of us turns with him to watch the steam rise from the blackened ruins while a cockatoo screeches overhead on its way to the river.

And there she is! Tuxedo emerges from behind the granny flat, as if she has slept through the whole thing.

It is a gorgeous autumn day, Destiny's favourite time of year. The whole town is here, crammed into the little church on High Street. The sky is piercingly blue and clear, the sun warm and soft. Inside the church, Bruce is up front, battered hat in hand, talking to the celebrant about the music for the ceremony. Bruce is uncomfortable in his suit. It's probably one he hasn't worn for a long time.

Bruce is stooped. I'm sure he has aged ten years in the last year. It has been painful to watch Mary decline. It got to the point where he could no longer care for her, and he had to put her in the dementia ward at Sunnybrook. That was so hard for him. He persevered for so long, but she was getting dangerous. Setting fire to things. Wandering off when he was trying to keep the farm going.

He visited her every day at Sunnybrook. Someone asked him why he visited if she didn't know who he was, but he just said that he knew who she was, and he would never just leave her there. He fed her lunch every day, then he'd brush her hair and read to her.

Mary didn't last long once she went into care. Maybe three months. She was strong and healthy when she went in, which made it hard work for the staff, I think. She would lash out at other patients or steal their food, and so they started to give her drugs to slow her down. I visited her a few times with Bruce. She had no idea who I was. The change in her was dramatic and I could see how it affected Bruce. It is such a terrible disease. The person diminishes so long before the body goes.

'How you doing?' I rest my hand on Bruce's shoulder.

'Hi, mate. I'm okay. Would ya check out all these people!' He scans the crowded room. 'Packed to the bloody rafters.'

'Yeah, well everyone loves Mary,' I say.

'What wasn't to love?'

He clutches his hat in both hands. It gives him something to focus on. I wonder if he has had a good cry yet. Or maybe he is relieved that it is all over?

'What'll I do now?' He holds back tears.

'I don't know, Bruce. Gotta just take one day at a time. Let's concentrate on sending her off properly?'

My words are feeble and I remember my anger at these kinds of platitudes after Tomas died.

Tomas.

I turn to the crowd. There is Moma – now ninety-three – tiny next to Destiny, three rows from the front. Re and Foxx jiggle their legs further along the pew. Yeah, I know, we called him Foxx. And, boy, does he live up to his name. He is nothing like the other two, most like Destiny and Sam. Full of passion and motion. I swear he goes from zero to one hundred in two seconds flat. The tantrums. The highs and lows. And Re is forever trying to watch over him to keep him safe.

But Tomas. Where are you now, my boy? Have we recovered from losing you? How old would you be now? Almost a teenager? No, it can't be that long. I try to conjure an image of him. That thick, dark hair. I know he would be handsome and kind. He was a sweet-natured boy.

And Sam. Is he at peace? We found his remains in the orchard, but it was hard to work out how the fire started. What dark place did he go to? Did he start that fire or was it just another careless cigarette not butted out properly?

'Ash?'

I open my eyes. Destiny.

'What?' I say, trying to bring myself back to the moment.

'Where'd you go?' Her face is soft, concerned.

'Oh, just thinking about Tomas and Sam.' I hope this doesn't upset her.

'Me, too.' Her eyes well but she holds it back.

'How'd we survive that?' I ask her. Dumb question, I know.

I reach out for her hand, and she leans into me.

'Can you believe this turnout?' she asks.

'Actually, I can. Mary was well loved by everyone around here. She's gonna be missed.'

Bruce is surrounded by family.

'At least he has a lot of support,' says Destiny.

'That's how,' I say.

'What?'

'That's how we survived.' I gesture to the whole room. 'People like Bruce, and Moma. Our family. They all helped us get through it.'

'Yeah.'

I know that's all she can say and it's enough.

Acknowledgements

The seed of this story began after the tragic events of 9/11 in the US in 2001. As with many story ideas, it has evolved from the original idea and many people have been part of the development of it.

Essentially, it has been in my head for twenty years but would not have been completed without the encouragement and mentorship of Les Zigomanis. Writing is a lonely pursuit and I'm a lazy writer, so without Les to push me, it would still be at the 20,000-word mark that it was for so many years and possibly never finished. Thank you, Sir Les.

My writing group has workshopped many of the chapters and helped me to flesh out characters. Thank you to Lynne Siejka, Mandy Burton, Michele Finey, Carol Challis and Kim Challis for over fifteen years of friendship through our *Mud* writing group.

My book group has always been supportive of my writing and were keen to be my beta readers. Thank you to Heather Davis, Dana Hume, Louise Milligan, Claire Collier, Mandy Dunn, Kirstin Lyons, and Kathy Burgemeister for fifteen years of sharing books and friendship.

To classmates from the novel class in the Diploma of Professional Writing & Editing many years ago, and Edwina Preston, for early feedback.

Thank you to Laura McCluskey for that last proofread, picking up my laziness with commas and ironing out the little details.

To my son, Jack, who painted the perfect image I had in my head for the cover. Your talent in everything you do has always inspired me to be better at what I do. May your creative talent lead you to the life you deserve once you finally discover how to show the world the amazing artist I know you are.

To my family for always supporting me (there are too many to name) but especially Kev Howlett, my partner in life who supports me always, I love you.

About the Author

Born 17 February 1968, Blaise van Hecke spent much of her childhood on a commune on the south NSW coast and speaks with love and wonder about the magic of her childhood. She

went from being barefoot to wearing a uniform and enduring rigid routines at an all-girl boarding school in Melbourne where she learned to be a 'young lady'.

Books and storytelling have always been at the heart of everything she does. Through Busybird Publishing, she runs workshops teaching writers the art of storytelling, and has helped over seven hundred authors publish their books. She is a champion of helping people find their voice.

Her story, 'Eleventh Summer', came second place in the biennial short story competition with the Society of Women Writers (Vic) in 2007, which has since been published in the anthology, *Mud Puddles*, and the anthology, *Thirteen Stories*. She's had other stories that have been published in *Blue Crow Magazine*, *21D Magazine*, *Fellowship of Australian Writers*, and *[untitled]*.

Blaise is also the author of *The Book Book: 12 Steps to Successful Publishing* and co-author of *Self-Made: Real Australian Business Stories,* and a contributor to the health-conscious series *Healthy Body* and *Healthy Mind.*

In 2018, she published a collection of short stories as a memoir about her childhood, called *The Road to Tralfamadore is Bathed in River Water.* She then published her memoir, *50 Days for Fifty Years: Walking the Camino de Santiago,* about walking the Pilgrim's Trail.

She first began work on this novel, *The Colours of Ash,* in 2007, and would routinely revisit it around taking care of her family, running a household, and managing her business, Busybird Publishing (www.busybird.com.au).

It is her first novel.

Reader Questions

1. Destiny's father, Sean, suggests to Destiny that eating an apple a certain way is bad luck. What superstitions did you grow up with?

2. Mai shows everyone her love through food. Is this something you are familiar with?

3. Everyone deals with grief in different ways. What came to mind when Moma was telling Ash how hard it was for her?

4. Do you think men and women deal with grief the same way?

5. Who is your favourite character in the book and why?

6. Do you think that the country house helped Ash and Destiny in their recovery?

7. Can you ever fully recover from losing a child?

8. Is a miscarriage and death of a child the same?

9. Sam is obviously damaged when he returns to
   Australia for the last time. What do you think
   was happening with him?

10. Rebecca has lived through some harrowing
    times. Why do you think she has managed to
    survive them?

11. Does art, or creativity, help with mental health?

12. Do you believe in fate, or do you think that you
    can control the outcome of events in your life?

13. What influence does Bruce have on Ash and
    Destiny?

14. Re has strange gifts. Have you ever had
    experiences like hers?

15. How does community shape our life?

The road to Tralfamadore is bathed in river water

In the early 1970s, a single mother and her four children find themselves alone on the east coast of New South Wales. They join the 'Back to the Earth Movement' at the idyllic land known as 'Tralfamadore'.

The family choose a spot on a hill bound by a river and creek, building a home using river stones and found objects. They sustain themselves on homegrown produce and fresh air.

For Blaise and her siblings, as well as children from the other homes scattered in the bush amongst nine dwellings, life is unrestrained and full of adventure.

Eventually, many of the Tralfamadorians leave to become sannyassins as part of the Rajneesh Movement in India, wearing orange and changing their names, but not before they've brought a little Indian culture to the bush.

Told in a series of ethereal vignettes, *The road to Tralfamadore is bathed in river water* is a memoir that depicts a childhood full of both naïvety and wisdom during an era of radical social change.

'A beautifully rendered portrait of a place and time, a family and a community. Nostalgic, tender – and yet clear-eyed.'

– **Inga Simpson,** *Understory: a life with trees*

'I love this book. It is at once magical and real, both earthed and enchanting. It captures the innocence and spontaneity of a child's view of the world, tempered by the child's wry, sharp, affectionate observations on the antics of the wayward, loving, flawed, yet wise adults that weave in and out of her life. It was a joy to read.'

– **Arnold Zable,** *Writer, novelist and storyteller*

'A dreamy excursion into an amazing way of life that captivates and mesmerises, and will challenge everything you know.'

– **Lazaros Zigomanis,** *Pride*

50 Days for Fifty Years

Blaise sets off to celebrate her 50th birthday to give gratitude for her life – a walk of 50 days for fifty years, following the Way of St James in the north of Spain.

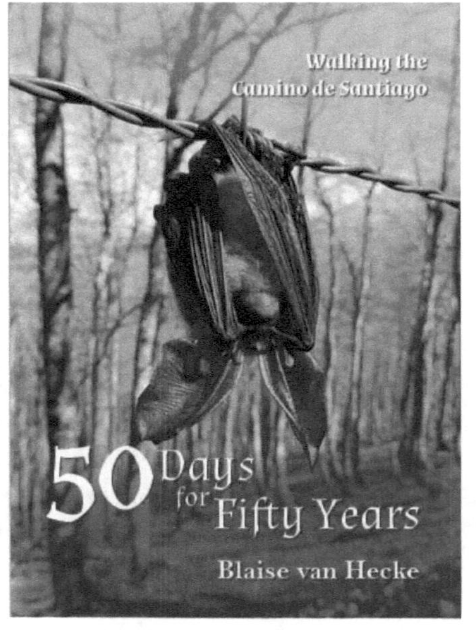

What Blaise learns on the Camino de Santiago is gradual, just like the step-by-step journey of over 800 kilometres by foot. With each passing day, the pilgrimage brings more knowledge and understanding into her heart. Beliefs she's always carried blossom into truths that remain with her well after she returns home to Australia.

50 Days for Fifty Years is a gorgeous full-colour memoir that celebrates a journey through life, and the realisations that come with a long, contemplative sabbatical.

The Book Book

12 Steps to Successful Publishing

Everyone has a book in them. We all have a story we want to share with the world. But where do we start?

The Book Book will help break the process into small, manageable steps, providing invaluable tips, insider knowledge into the publishing industry, as well as the inspiration to get started and to keep writing to the end.

Don't let this opportunity go to waste!

Trust in *The Book Book* to help you find the way.

The Book Book is the very first in our *Easy Publishing Series*. Each book is designed to provide the reader with an easy guide into some aspect of writing and/or publishing.